A Deeper Dive
By
Christopher B. Pelton

A Deeper Dive

©2022 by Christopher Pelton

Second Hardcover Printing

PsychoToxin Press

All Rights Reserved

www.psychotoxin.com

Dedication
To Neil, Stephen, Rod, Piers,
and all the others who showed me
the power that words have
and the magical worlds
that they can bring to life.

Introduction

When I published my first collection, I noted that all of the included stories were written during the first nine months of the Covid 19 pandemic. While most of the world was adjusting to their new "normal", I was right at home as I had been long before the outbreak. With a renewed focus and very little external distractions, I was able to create a plethora of stories and begin to lay the groundwork for my literary universe. I am very proud of the work that is in that book. The stories, and the way I created them, set very strict limits and I feel made me a better writer. I became more aware of language and the best way to get a point across without being verbose.

While far from being any kind of runaway hit, the book sold a few copies, (enough that I got to file my taxes as a professional writer) and gave me confidence to dig deeper. To push myself further as a creator and explore some of the stranger places that exist in my mind. What I didn't foresee was that two years later, the country would pretty much be in the exact same place. Despite being a cynic with a fascination for the idea of the utopian/dystopian future, even I couldn't foresee what has happened in the last two years. The events of the outside world always have some effect on artists and creators and I am no different.

Growing up as a fan of both comics and the old school Universal horror movies, the idea of a shared universe was nothing new to me. I was familiar with how such things are built and, more importantly, how to avoid the pitfalls that many others have fallen into. There are a couple of stories in the first book, and a few in this one that help to establish the groundwork for a much bigger story. Not to compare my work to his, but think Stephen King's Dark Tower Saga.

The continued madness that seeps into our society has grown past the point of absurd, while simultaneously becoming terrifying. When I look out my "window," I find myself inspired and disgusted.

Once again all the tales in this new collection were written during the period of 2019-2021. Some have undergone minor tweaks, while others had to be almost completely rewritten due to some disturbing similarities with real world events. There are some things that scare even me.

If you are new to my work, welcome. I hope that one or more of these stories brings a little light into your day. If you are returning after enjoying my first book, it's great to see you again. I'm glad I didn't scare you off. Hmm, maybe I'll have to try a little harder.

Christopher B. Pelton
Bridgeport, CT
2/16/20

Three O'clock

For the sixth time in five years, Michelle sat in the passenger seat of her father's Chevy pickup as he navigated unfamiliar roads using the Waze app on his phone. The two had only been in town for a couple of weeks, and they were still trying to familiarize themselves with their surroundings. Given his line of work, it was not at all surprising to find them moving from one town to another. At least, that was her understanding of the situation. Sometimes, though, she wondered how much of it was her fault.

"In a quarter mile, your destination will be on the left. 223 Cedar St. Walter Reck Elementary school." As the truck continued down Cedar, Arthur glanced over at his daughter, who looked more glum than usual.

"What's going on inside of that head of yours, kiddo?"

Several moments of silence were followed by a slow sigh.

The school's entrance was coming up, and there was already a substantial line of vehicles waiting for their turn to enter the driveway. Arthur eased the Chevy into his place in the standard zipper method used by almost all school drop off zones. Every once in a while, Arthur had seen such transactions escalate into verbal sparring, and on one occasion, physical violence.

From the back seat came the voice of his eleven-year-old daughter.

"This just seems to get harder every time I have to do it. New town, new school, new everything, and it's impossible for me to get comfortable in these new circumstances because at any moment something could change with your work, and we'll be off again to god knows where." Tears ran down her cheeks. It broke his heart to see her like this, but it was better than the alternative. At least for now.

"I know how you feel, little love. I'd love it if we're able to stay here for a while. My boss told me there are several open projects in town and the surrounding area. It should keep me pretty busy for a while. It sure would be nice to unpack our things instead of moving them into another storage space." He offered a sympathetic smile to the girl. He hated the deception, but he needed to keep her safe, so he did what he had to.

"That would be nice, Daddy. Maybe I'll even be able to make friends at this new school. Their website made it look quite nice." Michelle offered, wiping the tears from her cheeks. During their conversation, the Chevy was now at the front of the line. Arthur leaned over and kissed the girl on her forehead. She giggled and slid out the passenger side rear door.

"Have a great day, kiddo," Arthur waved out the window as he pulled away from the drop-off zone. Returning to the house, he hoped if they could both make it through this first day, there might be a chance for them here. Arthur sat down at what passed for a kitchen, powered up his laptop, and logged in to www.needajob.com. Let the day's job hunt begin.

The inside of the new school was vibrant. They covered the walls with student art and flyers for clubs and events. There was a trophy case filled with various successes in academic competitions. To her right was the Administration office. She turned on her heels and headed in.

Muriel Steiner had worked as the secretary of Walter Reck Elementary School when Walter Reck was still the principal. She was approaching her fortieth year as a member of the local teacher's union. They had sent generations of children to Muriel. In all of her years at the school, she had watched both fathers and sons pass by her desk. Whether they were awaiting a dreaded visit to the principal's office or dropping off the daily attendance sheets, Muriel was always there with a smile, whether in sympathy or appreciation. She liked to think that even a minor act of kindness improved the children's days. And for forty years, this proved to be the case. It was this smile that greeted Michelle as she entered the office.

"Well, hello, there, sweetie. You must be Michelle." Muriel said in a warm and welcoming tone, the result of years of practice.

"I am, and today is my first day here at Walter Reck."

"Excellent. Mrs. Tooney, the principal here, is out of town for a conference, but she left all the things we're going to need to get you going. Come on back and have a seat and let's see what we can do."

Aside from a few questions about insurance, the two had gone through all the paperwork, printed out her class schedule, and packed what they like to refer to as a starter kit for parents. It included schedules, calendars, phone numbers to call for various reasons, etc. If something was going on at the school, you had no excuse not to know about it.

"Well, all of your paperwork is in order, so why don't we take a walk down to Mr. Kehoe's Class. It's where you should be right now."

The sound of Muriel's modest heels echoed through the empty hallway. Mr. Kehoe's Class was straight down the central corridor from the office, a left before the exit doors, and three doors down on the left.

Through the window on the door, Michelle could see her new teacher. He was a tall man with a shock of red hair. The sign next to the door read…

Mr. Kehoe Room 110
Fifth Grade American History
Fourth Grade Social Studies

Muriel knocked on the window before turning the knob. Swinging the door open, the two walked into the classroom. Muriel handed a folder of papers to the history teacher. They passed a concerned look between them, and then Kehoe stood up.

"Class, we have a new student joining us today; this is Michelle Palmer. Please tell us a bit about yourself."

Of all the awkward moments Michelle had to go through every time she switched schools, and this was the third time in five years, introducing herself to a new class of strangers was one that didn't seem to get any less uncomfortable.

"Hi, everybody. My name is Michelle, but you can call me Chelle. My dad and I just moved into town a couple of weeks ago. Because of his job, we've had to move around a lot. We're kind of hoping that we can stick around for a while. This seems like a nice place to live."

From the back of the classroom, Billy Mitchell, not the brightest crayon in the box, a little uncouth, but otherwise nice enough, shot his arm up in the air. Kehoe looked towards the boy, shook his head, and called on him.

"What is it, Billy?" Kehoe asked.

"What happened to your mom?" Billy inquired of his new classmate.

Kehoe opened his mouth to chastise Billy, only to find himself interrupted by Michelle.

"It's okay, Mr. Kehoe. Mom passed away when I was five years old. I remember her a little. After that is when we started moving about. It was really hard on my dad to keep living in the same place where mom died."

A hush fell over the student body. The two adults in the room shared an uncomfortable look. The children just sat at their desks, staring at the unfamiliar girl with the dead mother. Kehoe broke the silence.

"All right, Michelle. There are a couple of empty desks towards the back there. Grab one and I'll put an order in to get you a new textbook. In the meantime, does anybody want to share their book, Michelle?"

A great deal of mumbling had started as eyes from all around the Class offered nothing but blank stares. None of this was surprising. She was used to being the new kid and always being shunned by her new classmates. Finally, a hand shot up to volunteer. It was good old Billy Mitchell. He slid his desk closer to Michelle's.

"Hi Michelle, I'm Billy." He offered his hand. Michelle shook it with enthusiasm.

"Very nice to meet you, Billy." taking the offered hand into her own.

At the front of the Class, Kehoe picked up where he had left off. As best as she could tell, it had something to do with the War of 1812. Michelle wasn't too concerned about it. As soon as she got her book, she could catch up pretty quickly.

Once the bell sounded, Michelle pulled out her class schedule to see what came next. Math. Mrs. Decker room 133. A glance at the sign outside Kehoe's Class read 110. The next Class couldn't be that far away. She walked through the door just before the bell rang. Inside was every classmate that had been in the Class before. There were two fifth-grade classes, and they followed a reverse of the schedule. The only time the two groups had any interaction was during lunch. This was a relief to Michelle as she wouldn't need to do the dog and pony show about her arrival to town in every Class. These kids had already heard it. She took an empty seat and prepared for class.

After Math class came English and then thankfully lunch. She had been in a hurry this morning and did not have time for breakfast. Now lunch was less than an hour away. In English Class, they handed her a paperback copy of a book called My Brother Sam is Dead. It was a historical fiction story that tells the story of two brothers separated by the Revolutionary War. Michelle had never heard of it, but she was a fan of history, so there was a better-than-average chance of her liking it.

Michelle sat in her seat at the back of Mrs. Coppola's English class, eyeing the clock like a hawk. She felt like her stomach was eating itself. She couldn't remember being so hungry all her life. The second hand crawled across the face of the clock. For a moment, she could have sworn she saw the minute hand go backward. And then, after what seemed like an eternity, the bell rang.

Being new to things, Michelle was still navigating the ins and outs of the school. When she came across a load of kids taking a right turn into an open door, she knew she had located the cafeteria. After her extensive travels, Michelle had become convinced there was only one company who designed public school cafeteria kitchens for every public school. There may be minor variations, a stove where a sink usually is, a refrigerator where the stove goes. Slight changes aside, they were all the same. She went through the line, picking or declining from the day's options. At the end of the line, she pulled a crumpled five-dollar bill from her pocket and handed it over to the cashier. Change in hand, she exited the lunch line and stared out into the jungle that was an elementary school cafeteria. Looking around, she spotted a sparsely occupied table in the far corner of the room. As she slipped her way through the busy aisle, she did her best to ignore the glares and whispers. Once again, this had become a part of her life. She made it to the rear of the room, to find the table's only other occupant, the affable Billy Mitchell.

"Hi Billy, is it okay if I sit here with you?"

A look of shock spread over the boy's face. No one had ever wanted to sit with him, let alone a girl. He nodded his head up and down.

Michelle slid into a seat across from her new friend.

After a moment or two of awkward silence, Billy spoke.

"Nobody ever wants to sit with me. They pick on me a lot. I know I'm a little slow, but I do my best to keep up. Of course, that doesn't stop them from calling me a dummy or the S word head."

They are all the same. No matter what school you go to, there's always a kid like Billy and a group of kids who feel the best way to inflate their egos is to pick on a kid who wants nothing more in life than somebody to talk to. It made her angry.

"You know what, Billy, someday you will do significant things while those kids will be the ones pumping your gas and bringing you your pizza."

Billy gazed upon his new friend with awe and maybe even a little crush. It was then that Jason Ayirs interrupted the two. When you try to visualize what a 10-year-old school bully looks like, you would see Jason Ayirs. An arrogant little asshole that didn't meet the usual criteria for bullies. He came from a wonderful home, a happy family, and was a mediocre student. He just decided one day to be a dick, and currently, his favorite target has been Billy.

"Well, well, well, what do you know about this? Looks like you found yourself a little girlfriend there shit head. You must be new here because anybody who's been here a while knows how pathetic it is to hang out with this pant load. Runaway before it's too late." Jason said. Stopping long enough to pick food off of Billy's tray.

A look of defeat fell over Billy's face. From what Michelle could gather, this was a regular one. If there was one thing she had learned over the years, it was that a bully will not be tolerated.

"Do you think being an ass makes you look cool?" she asked their uninvited guest.

Jason's eyes appeared as if they were going to come out of their sockets. It was clear nobody had ever spoken like that to him before.

"What did you say to me?" he scowled in her direction.

"I'm pretty sure you heard me," Michelle responded.

"You can't talk to me that way, you little bitch." A sneer crawled over Jason's face as he grabbed Michelle's jacket. What happened next was too fast for the human eye to pick up. Later, when viewed on the security tape, it was a blink, and you miss it type of moment.

The moment Jason laid his hand on Michelle's jacket, she was up, twisting one arm behind his back, and using the remaining hand to slam his head into the table. The whole thing took less than two seconds.

Once the yelling began, the entire cafeteria flocked to the far corner to see what all the buzz was. Much to the delight of the assembled student body, it was the school bully getting his comeuppance. The crowd cheered and clapped, overjoyed by this turn of events. Of course, this did nothing to improve the bully's mood, but right now, they didn't care.

"Hey you kids, break it up down there. Go back to your tables or outside if you've finished your lunch. Let's move it along now." ordered Mr. Crawford, third-grade science teacher, and current lunchroom monitor. Crawford parted the children as if they were the Red Sea and made his way to the epicenter of the problem.

"Ah, Mr. Ayiers. I should have known. Billy, has Jason been bothering you again?"

Billy glanced over at Michelle and then at Jason, whose face was red and twisted in rage. He looked up at Crawford and shook his head.

"Oh, come on, man, that's bullshit," Michelle interjected.

"Young lady, you watch your mouth." Crawford scolded.

"I will apologize for my words, but not for the sentiment behind them. Billy and I were just sitting here having lunch when this ass... guy walked over and started messing with Billy. I asked him nicely to depart, but as you can see, he failed to comply with that request."

Crawford looked over at Billy. He could see terror behind the dazed boy's eyes. He was also curious to hear the story of how Jason's forehead had become bruised. Based on his history of bullying, Crawford sent Jason down to the principal's office. On his way out the door, he bellowed.

"Oh, you're going to get yours, Mitchell. I may be on my way to the office now, but nothing will stop me from beating your ass at three o'clock."

Billy's glance shifted to Michelle. He didn't know how to fight. He hadn't even done anything wrong.

"Don't worry, Billy, we'll figure something out."

"How did you learn to move like that?" Billy inquired.

"What are you talking about? Move like what?" That was when the bell rang. Class was back in session. It was now 12:30.

Gym period was next, and throughout her academic career this was her worst subject. Not that she couldn't run and jump and all that; it was that there seemed to be no point to it. Michelle headed back to the gym teacher's office so she could introduce herself to Mx. Slade. There was no reason to bring up her poor athletic skills. Let that be a surprise. The suspense lasted all of five minutes.

"Good lord, in my fifteen years as a Phys Ed teacher, I have never seen a child less coordinated than you." This produced a burst of riotous laughter from her classmates. She was sweating a little.

"I'll tell you what I'll do. For the rest of the semester, why don't you just hang out on the bleachers, and once Class is over, you can pick up the equipment. How does that sound? Is that something you think you can handle?"

Bile rose in her throat and Michelle ran out of the gym to the nearest girls' room and lost what little lunch she had eaten. Michelle could hear the interrupted sound of laughter as the doors swung open and closed behind her.

The rest of the day, there was no doubt about what everyone was saying about her. Not that any of this was new, but she liked what she had seen of the town so far, and as with everything else in life, all she wanted was the familiar. Michelle wanted to walk up the same path to the front door every day. The girl wanted a room of her own, so she did not have to continue living out of boxes in various motels. Other than a couple of minor issues, it was a pretty good first day, and she knew that tomorrow would be better.

By 2:45, the buzz had traveled through the halls about the impending dust-up. Word going around was that neither was even going to show up. That the whole thing was a misunderstanding, and they had resolved it. Schoolyards have always functioned in the same way. The word changed like the wind. There was only ever one way to find out, and that was to be there. The bell rang at 3:00 P.M.

Within thirty seconds, half the school had emptied and made its way to the park across the street. Fighting on school grounds would have been a stupid move. All that would happen was teachers would separate them, and at least one of them would end up being suspended. Across the street, however, these concerns did not exist. Kirby Park was a public park. There could be trouble if a cop was around, but those odds were less than a run-in with a teacher on school grounds. A large circle, two or three kids deep, had formed to prepare for the scuffle. The crowd was ready.

Billy hadn't seen Michelle leave school after their last class. For the last five minutes, he had been frantically searching the hallways of the school. He had hoped she would be there with him for the fight. She was the only friend he had ever had, and it was his deepest wish that she would have his back. He had been kidding himself. No one wanted to be friends with a loser like him. Half the time, he couldn't tell if people were laughing with or at him. As time went on, he became unable to differentiate between the two. Taking a deep breath, he picked his backpack from the ground and headed out to Kirby Park.

In the boy's room on the second floor, they heard a loud cheer go up from outside.

"Sounds like Billy just got to the park. I'll bet he's as confused as the rest of them right now."

Michelle looked out the bathroom window and could just make out the circle of kids waiting to see a fight.

"See Jason, this is my first day at this school, but I've been to a few in my life. I've lived in six towns in the last five years and do you know what they all have in common?"

"A bitch like you," Jason responded, spitting in her direction.

"No, my dear boy, it's people like you. People who think that being an asshole will make them prom king someday. No matter where I've been, it's always the same routine. You and your kind are some of the worst examples of humanity. Now that I've taken away your strength, tell me, what does it feel like to be a victim."

"Fuck you! That's how it feels. Eventually, this tape will give, and I don't care if you're a girl or not, I am going to destroy you."

Michelle suddenly went dizzy. Her heart was racing, and her skin dried and flaked away. The floor burst into flames and engulfed her. Jason had tried to scream, but what came out was incoherent babble. His mind would not accept what his eyes were telling it. Michelle emerged from the flames, her skin a cracked black and red canvas. Two wings had sprung from her back as two horns broke through her skull. She stepped closer to the terrified boy duct-taped to the urinal.

"See Jason, I don't have a personal issue with you. The hate and bile your kind spews into the atmosphere is what we thrive on. Today, however, was our first day at this school. You probably won't be surprised to know that it can be difficult to make friends when you're always the new kid. Today, for the first time in a long time, Michelle made a friend. A boy that you bullied so badly that I was called upon to come out to deal with it. When I have to come out for things, nobody leaves happy," she sparked a single flame on her index finger and held it close to his face.

"Come on now, you don't want to do that." Jason offered, terrified. "I swear I'll leave Billy alone. I'll leave them all alone."

"Jason, you and I both know that's just not true. Right now, you're willing to tell me what you think I want to hear, so I don't take this finger here and jam it into your eye socket. Now isn't that closer to the truth?"

Furiously Jason shook his head to clarify that was not the truth,

"It's like this, Jason, Michelle, has been here for one day. In that time, you've threatened her, laughed her at and she has been made the butt of jokes. Now I know this wasn't all you, but it involved you on more of a one-on-one level. So do you see my problem here?"

And in a split second, the creature that may or may not be Michelle had Jason's right eyeball roasting on her flaming finger.

"Ha, I guess you can't." Under normal circumstances, the scream that came from the bathroom would be audible downstairs, but because of the significant amount of noise being generated from the gathering in the park, it was all but drowned out.

Michelle awoke to find herself wrapped in a black cotton blanket and in the passenger seat of her dad's Chevy.

"Daddy?"

Albert pulled the truck over onto the shoulder. He pulled his daughter close to him.

"It's okay, honey, I'm right here."

"Where am I? How did I get here."

After previous episodes, Albert had gotten creative when answering questions.

"Well, I picked you up after school, we came back to the house and started packing for a trip, and you fell asleep on the couch. I picked you up and brought you to the truck."

"Are we moving again, Daddy?" the tired child asked.

"I don't know yet, honey. Why don't you put your head down and go back to sleep? I'll wake you when we get to where we're going."

"That sounds like a good plan." the girl cuddled up against the corner of the back seat.

Albert took one last look at his daughter, set the GPS to the address the folks in the exorcism chat room had given him, and pulled back onto the highway.

Aviophobia

Patrick stood in front of his bedroom window, sipping what was sure to be the first of many cups of coffee of the day. On the horizon, the morning sun had begun to illuminate the sky before him. He watched as the last remnants of the previous evening's storm was pushed off to the east. For the first time all week he found himself able to take a deep breath. His anxiety had been on the rise over the upcoming business trip and had kicked into overdrive upon the announcement of a severe thunderstorm warning. With the clouds moving on, the day appeared to hold some promise after all.

When the alarm sounded, Patrick silenced the clock and started his morning routine. He had prepared his travel bag the night before, and it sat at the foot of his bed. At 7:15, he was out of the shower, and enjoying his second cup of coffee, while scrutinizing the day's events. The airline ticket displayed a departure time of 2:00 PM. He lived a little over an hour from the airport, assuming traffic was moving at a regular clip. According to various sources he had found on the internet, Patrick had built an additional two hours into his schedule, allowing plenty of time to arrive, park, and get through security. He had downloaded a map of the inside of Sikorsky International to his phone allowing himself the opportunity to familiarize himself with the airport's layout.

Despite having convinced himself that he would hit the morning commuter traffic, he was fastidious in his last check of the house. With the windows and doors locked and the sinks turned off, Patrick double checked to make sure there was no expired or close to expiring food in his refrigerator. From the looks of things, everything was in perfect order. If it wasn't, he would either spend the entirety of his trip monitoring the ins and outs of his home through the security system, or worst-case scenario, he would work himself into such a state of insecurity that he would refuse to leave the house. This morning that was not an option. He slung his carry-on bag over his shoulder, walked out to the parking lot and climbed into his 2014 Prius. His original plan was an Uber to the airport, but the timing and cost were not comparable. So he took his time, did the math, and concluded that it was cheaper to park the car in the short-term lot as his trip was at most going to be three days. The car's clock showed 8:25 as he pulled out of his driveway and headed towards Bradley International Airport.

Patrick couldn't say he hated to fly. Truth was, he had never been to an airport, let alone on a plane. Despite endless reassurances and unsolicited opinions that told him that flying was safer than driving, this did not provide him with any additional peace of mind. A three hundred and fifty-ton metal tube, moving through the air at seven hundred miles an hour, was just something Patrick couldn't wrap his head around. His therapist had suggested that his lack of scientific knowledge could contribute to his phobia. It was a topic they planned to discuss further during their next session. Assuming of course he made it back in one piece.

It had begun with a frantic phone call from one of his biggest clients. As a computer programmer, the nature of his business allowed Patrick to work from home ninety-nine percent of the time. This arrangement had always been a significant benefit to him. Patrick suffered from Agoraphobia and a severe anxiety disorder, which made being around people unbearable. After six years, he had discovered and created an identity for himself in a community of people just like him, shut-ins, people with disabilities, and other Agoraphobics. Together they supported each other, offering life hacks, tricks, and tips that allowed him to control some more difficult facets of day to day life. The second most popular topic of conversation among these groups was which meds people were taking and what side effects they were experiencing. These days, the only time he left the house was to run the occasional business errand and the even less frequent social event. Other than that, you could find him at home. With a gigabit internet connection, four hundred cable channels, Amazon's continued growth, and services like Instacart and GrubHub, it had never been easier for someone like him to avoid what was going on outside. Except for now.

The call had come in early yesterday afternoon. Intertech, one of Patrick's long-time clients, had suffered a critical system error. Their in-house IT guy had tracked the bug and determined an intrusion had occurred. The attack prevented internal access to several of the company's high-security servers, which contained client account data and some of Intertech's proprietary software. Worse yet, it had blocked remote access to the server that housed the operating system. The servers ran on an impenetrable custom OS, designed and coded by Patrick himself. The work itself had been both challenging and entertaining.

He had accomplished all of this from the comfort of his home. Thirteen weeks later, the gold version of the software was complete. He shipped it out to their corporate offices in Boise, Iowa. A video conference allowed him to walk Teri, the company's in-house IT, through the install and configuration. The process went smoothly, and for the last two years, it was a rare occasion that he heard from them. So it shocked him when the call came in. He knew every second a back door was open, was a second that client information was exposed. In their business, that was unacceptable. They clarified that if he wanted to continue doing work for them, he would be in their office tomorrow to get things back up and running. With annual billings of $375,000 a year for various technical services, Patrick couldn't afford to lose that kind of money. Before the phone call had ended, the company had already booked a flight and room for him. He agreed to their terms, jotted down the travel information, and began preparing himself for the flight.

Traffic was on the light side that morning, and Patrick pulled off the exit for Bradley around 10:00 AM. Entering the airport proper, the extra time he had allowed himself had turned out to be a gift. Signs designed to provide travelers with directions were written in an incomprehensible jumble of numbers, letters, and arrows. Which terminal was he leaving from? Where was the line for short-term parking? He spent better than twenty minutes circling the airport, trying to make sense of it all. Soon, all the pieces fell into place, and he pulled up to the short-term lot's gate. He retrieved his ticket from the automated dispenser and followed the "next level" signs up to the third floor. Parking near the exit, he grabbed his travel bag from the passenger seat and slipped out of the vehicle. As was part of his routine, he locked and unlocked the car doors three times to make sure it was secure. He strapped his bag to his shoulder and crossed the walkway into the terminal.

Patrick had always found it challenging to explain to people who don't suffer from Severe Anxiety and Agoraphobia just what his day-to-day life consisted of. The minute he walked through the automatic door, a gush of cold air blew into his face. From there, it was almost too much. He found himself surrounded and overwhelmed by a throng of humanity. People were scurrying to and fro in no discernable order. Carts full of luggage rolled by as passengers raced to meet their planes. His bag had been intentionally selected and meticulously packed, in order to leave no doubt that it complied with all classifications of carry-on, which would allow him to forego the nightmare that appeared to be the baggage check. Familiarizing himself with a long list of potential pitfalls that he could encounter, Patrick had done everything possible to expedite the process. His boarding pass was printed out and tucked away in his wallet behind his driver's license. His bag held no liquids weighing over 3.5 oz, and the contents of his pockets were minimal and easily dropped into a clear plastic tray. In moments he was through security. Patrick did his best slalom, avoiding as much physical contact with strangers as he could while working his way to the departure gate, which according to his ticket was number twenty-five.

He found a row of seats far enough removed from the crowds, while remaining close enough to the gate to keep track of any going ons with his flight. Given his early arrival, Patrick had his choice of seats. He plopped down into a comfortable chair, unscrewed the cap of his Xanax prescription, and dry swallowed two pills. He slipped his noise-canceling headphones over his ears and closed his eyes.

Patrick stirred when he realized someone was tapping him on the shoulder. His eyes popped open, and he found himself face to face with a smiling National Airlines employee. Sliding his earphones off, Patrick looked quizzically at the woman.

"Sir, are you flying with us to Boise today? Flight 533?" she inquired.

"Yeah, I'm supposed to be sitting in row B, seat 2. Is everything okay?" Despite the Xanax, Patrick felt his nerve endings catch fire.

"No need to worry, everything is just fine. We've begun boarding our first-class passengers. It's time to go, sir."

Rising from his seat, Patrick grabbed his bag from its place on the floor next to him and followed the gate's ticket agent. At the end of the skyway, a flight attendant offered him a big smile and asked for his boarding pass. Verifying his first-class ticket, she led him through a heavy blue curtain and to his seat. At first glance, it relieved him. The seat next to him was empty, and if his luck held, it would stay that way. Patrick stashed his bag under the seat in front of him and buckled in. The Xanax's effects still lingered and the seat next to him empty, Patrick tilted his head back against the rest and once again drifted off.

His eyes snapped open by a sudden jostling of his body. His vision was filled with that of a rather portly man dressed in a brown and tan corduroy suit, which looked as if they had made it in the 70s. He was attempting to shove his oversized bag in the allocated overhead bin.

"Sorry about that, buddy, didn't mean to wake you up. Just gotta slide by you here."

The man slid past him and settled into the empty seat next to the window.

"Charles Fairchild, but everybody just calls me Chuck. It's a pleasure to meet you. I mean that buddy, a genuine pleasure.", offering his hand to Patrick.

"Patrick Hunter. Nice to meet you." Patrick grabbed the stranger's hand and instantly regretted the handshake. The stranger's hands were cold and sticky.

"So what brings you to the friendly skies today? If you don't mind me asking, of course."

"Have to go see a client about some hardware."

"You look like a first timer."

"Excuse me?"

"Is this your first time flying? Not to pry, but you seem a little on edge."

"Yes, it is. I'm a computer programmer and work out of my house, but there was an issue with some equipment at their office in Boise, and they made it pretty clear that I needed to come out to fix it."

"Now that is exciting, buddy. I hear computers are going to be the wave of the future. I'm not too worried though, I'm in outdoor advertising myself. You know, billboards and banners and such. I don't know how much customer service you do, but marketing people are a pain in the ass."

Patrick nodded politely. He wasn't sure how much trouble a billboard could cause, but apparently, it was enough.

"Listen, about the flight, it's only natural to be a little apprehensive about flying, especially if it's your first time. As someone who spends half their life in the air, I promise that we'll be fine. The take-off can be bumpy, but once we're in the air, it's smooth sailing from there. Just sit back and relax. We'll be in Omaha before you know it."

"Did he say Omaha?" Patrick thought to himself. A click emanated from the speaker system.

"Ladies and gentlemen, this is your captain, Kerry White speaking. Thank you all for flying with us today. We're just about done with the boarding process. The flight attendants will be around soon to provide a safety presentation. I'll talk to you again once we're in the air."

"I'll tell you one thing, buddy, never try to sell billboards in Omaha. It's right in the middle of frigging Tornado Alley, and the storms just tear the shit out of them. The client calls to complain, we send our local crew out to put them back up, and within a couple of weeks, they're right back on the ground. I keep telling my clients that smaller forms of advertising would serve them better and save them money, but do they listen to old Chuck? Oh no, they want more bang for their buck, no matter how much it costs them. But they pay us to put them up, not offer weather predictions."

There it was again.

"Why do you keep mentioning Omaha? This is the flight going to Boise?" looking over at his row mate. Chuck responded with a sound that could only be described as that of a braying jackass.

"I think you're confused there, buddy. This is the 3:30 flight to Omaha. Isn't that where you're heading?"

Patrick's mind raced. Was it possible he got on the wrong plane?

"What are you talking about?" his voice had raised an octave and had become shaky. "This is the 2:00 flight to Boise, Idaho."

There was no way he was on the wrong plane. The ticket agent had walked him right to the gate and confirmed the flight number and his boarding id, and he was sitting in his assigned seat. This must be the right flight.

"Look here, and I'll show you." Fairchild started removing his wallet from the inside pocket of his coat. The leather looked as worn and dated as the suit its owner was wearing. He removed a slip of paper from inside and handed it to Patrick. It was a boarding pass for National Airlines flight 533 to Omaha, Nebraska. The bond felt odd, and the font used for printing did not match what they used on his pass.

"Yes sir, in just a few scant hours, we'll be setting down in beautiful Omaha."

Patrick's anxiety level shot up from the three or four when he first boarded the plane to a ten. His mind raced, and his body started shaking. Furiously, he smashed his hand on the call button above his head. The passengers in his immediate area pretended they weren't looking.

"God damn it, we're not going to fucking Omaha," he screamed. "This is the 2:00 flight to shitting Boise. I don't want to go there either, but there's not a whole fucking lot I can do about it." His voice continued its rise. He smashed the call button with the palm of his hand.

"Relax kid; there's nothing wrong with Omaha other than the tornados. Some of the nicest people I've ever met live there. You may even like it once you try it."

"Are you fucking stupid?" Patrick screamed at the man in the tan corduroy suit. "I'm not going to Omaha." Patrick could now feel the other passenger's eyes as they fell on him, which did nothing to help ease his anxiety. He felt a hand on his shoulder. It was the attendant.

"Are you okay, Sir? You're shouting, and I need you to calm down."

"I'm fine, but this asshole seems to think that we are going to Omaha. Will you please tell him he's wrong," looking towards Fairchild.

"Mam, I have already shown my boarding pass to our friend here, and it says we are going to Omaha." Chuck Fairchild interjected.

"Sir, are you feeling okay?" the attendant asked.

"I'm not the one with the problem. This guy won't shut up about Omaha."

The attendant disappeared up to the cockpit area. He could see her whispering to two other attendants. After a minute's discussion, one of the attendants knocked on the cockpit door. The door slid open, and one of the staff slipped through the door. She returned with the captain. The man stopped at Patrick's seat and placed a hand on his shoulder.

"Sir, I'm only going to say this once. You are causing a disturbance on my aircraft, and I can't have that. The attendants tell me you have some concern about where this flight is going, is that correct?"

"I'm not the one with the problem; it's this fucking guy right here." Patrick could hear the volume in his voice rise.

"Sir, as the captain of this flight, I am fully authorized to remove you from this plane if you can't calm down. Do I need to call the Air Marshall, or can we handle this between ourselves?"

"I haven't done anything! Why aren't you removing this guy?" He pointed to the seat next to him.

It took the Air Marshall less than five minutes to remove Patrick from the plane. They took him to a small office near the entrance of gate 40 and gestured towards a seat at a metal table. A medium-sized man in a black suit entered the room.

"Hello, Mr. Hunter. My name is Agent Fontaine, and I work for Homeland Security. I understand from the Air Marshall that there was some trouble on the plane. Can you tell me what happened?"

Patrick reported the events that occurred while seated in row B, seat 2, of National Airlines flight 533 to Boise, Idaho. He told the two agents all about the curious little billboard salesperson and how he had told the man about his fear of flying and the insistence of that man, Charles Fairchild he said his name was, that the plane was going to Omaha.

"Mr. Hunter, I'm not quite sure how to tell you this. The seat next to you was empty. We've checked with the airline, and the seat next to you went unsold. There was no one sitting in that seat."

Patrick banged his fist against the table, creating a metallic echo.

"I tell you he was there. His name was Charles Fairchild, and he sold billboards. He told me all about Omaha and how it was a pain in the ass to keep billboards up. He was right there next to me, clear as day."

Fontaine rose from his chair in response to a knock on the door. Behind it stood another black-suited agent. The new arrival whispered something into Fontaine's ear and turned back.

"Mr. Hunter, we have two problems here. As my partner just informed me, the first is that Flight 533 exploded just after take-off."

A thousand thoughts rushed into Patrick's mind. The first being that he should have been on that plane. It should have been him in Row B, Seat 2. He should have been sitting next to a portly billboard salesperson named Charles Fairchild, Chuck to his friends. Patrick Hunter should be a pile of ash right now.

"You said two problems." he croaked out through his suddenly parched throat.

"Yes, I did. We ran the name Charles Fairchild against the passenger manifest for the flight, and as we knew it would, the search came up empty."

"But I swear to you, he was there. I saw him with my own two eyes. We talked about fucking billboards." Patrick's world turned gray.

"We were able to find the name in our database, however."

"Well, thank Christ for that. I told you I wasn't making any of this shit up."

"Charles Fairchild. Date of birth 8/21/1928. Died 12/08/1976 when National Airlines flight 533 crashed five minutes after take-off from Bradley International Airport."

Patrick could not attend any more business meetings or social interaction after that.

Ward C

Furiously, and for the third time that morning, Stevens turned the key in his 1998 Ford Escort; unsurprisingly, the result was the same. The car produced a continual clicking noise, indicating that the battery was, in fact, dead. He slammed his head against the steering wheel. The analog clock in the car's dash read 8:30 a.m., and he had a little less than a half an hour to get to work.

If there were a worse day for Stevens luck to run bad, he would have preferred any day other than this one. Given the infrequency of anything remotely resembling good luck throughout his life, he was unsure why he thought today would prove to be any different. It was the beginning of the month and time for the new duty roster. For the last eighteen months, Stevens had been fortunate enough to find steady work as an overnight security guard at the Silver Pines Sanitarium. It had taken him almost six months to get used to the schedule and to find a level of comfort in his new surroundings. As the new man, they gave him the privilege of monitoring Ward D.

Constructed in 1960 the structure that became Ward D was one of the original buildings when Silver Pines opened in 1961. Over the next twenty-four years, Silver Pines served hundreds of patients suffering from the very worst mental illnesses. It remained in operation until 1985, when President Reagan began shutting down mental health care facilities. For the next 15 years, the building sat unused and had become the subject of many urban legends and a popular location for ghost hunters and paranormal bloggers. Break-ins were common, and the police estimated that between 1985 and 2000, approximately 17% of all calls placed to the station ended up at the vacant property.

Unexpectedly, in the early spring of 2000, new fencing was erected around the former hospital's property line. They strongly encouraged trespassers to stay off the property with the addition of both razor wire along the top of the fence and a pack of Doberman Pinschers now acting as security guards. Shortly after the fencing, several trailers, portable restrooms, and a considerable amount of heavy machinery rolled on to the property. Signage covered the fencing announcing that Voyant Medical Systems had purchased the property and would restore it to its rightful place amongst the finest mental health care facilities in the world. Hiring notices began appearing in both local newspapers and online sites such as needajob.com. Renovations proceeded quickly, and in September 2001, Voyant VP of Operations, Jamie Harris announced that Silver Pines: A Mental Health Facility by VMS would reopen in January 2002. Being in the middle of both a time and financial crunch, Voyant focused the renovation funds on restoring the more recent additions that had been completed prior to the shutdown in 1985. They left Ward D empty and at some point, once their new investment was up and making money, there was a plan to tear the building down completely. Now the only permitted access to Ward D was by security during the regular sweep of the grounds.

Accepting the now inescapable fact that his car would not get him anywhere this morning, Stevens quickly brought up the Uber app on his phone and scheduled a pickup. He might pull this off. His 'five minutes away' driver ended up being closer to fifteen minutes away. Stevens hopped in the back seat, glancing at the clock on his phone, dismayed to see that it was now 9:00 A.M. He was now officially late.

And just in case Stevens thought his luck might actually change for once, a multi-car accident downtown delayed him even further. It was 9:20 by the time he arrived at the front doors of Silver Pines.

Stevens hurried down the hall, seeing his coworkers assembled in the conference room as Mr. Sutton ran down the new shift schedule. Fearing the worst, he took a deep breath and turned the knob.

"Ah! Mr. Stevens, how nice of you to join us this morning. I hate to think that my little meeting here is taking you away from something more important."

"No, sir. I do apologize. You see, my car wouldn't start, and then my cab got stuck in traffic downtown. It won't happen again."

"Let's make sure it doesn't. Now, if I can continue…"

Stevens listened as Sutton continued to explain to his team that due to some budget cutbacks from Voyant, that there would no longer be double coverage in the wards overnight. He went on to explain that while there was no official reason provided by Voyant, Sutton did explain that since most of the patients were sleeping or heavily medicated during that time, he would have to guess that Voyant saw a place to save a few bucks.

A grumbling came from the gathered workforce.

"Listen, I get that this might concern you, but I have been told that they are using this as a test run. The best we can hope for is that the facility director's reports will be enough to change their minds. That's all I've got for you today. Alright, let's get to it, folks. Stevens, if you could give me a minute."

A sigh escaped his lips as he headed over to the head of the long conference table, currently serving as Sutton's desk.

"I just wanted to let you know that you are staying on third shift. It has nothing to do with you being late today; it's just that you are still the bottom man on the totem pole, and given the cutbacks, there's a pretty good chance that you will be staying there for a while. Go home and get some sleep. We'll need you back here at the usual time tonight."

The upside to being stuck on the overnight was that the sleep pattern it had taken him months to get into wouldn't be interrupted. At 4:00 p.m., his usual alarm went off, and he began prepping for his upcoming shift. He turned the T.V. on time for the five o'clock news. Watching the news always depressed him as lately, there were very few stories that weren't about some horrible atrocity being committed somewhere in the world. In his opinion, the world really was going to hell in a handbasket. The lead story on this evening's show was a perfect example of this.

For the last year, a killer had been stalking the small community of Plainfield, Wisconsin. A string of grisly murders had been committed with eight bodies located in the previous six months. Many of the bodies had been found skinned, and the police had exhausted all leads. The media quickly pointed out the similarities between these crimes and those of notorious 1950s serial killer Ed Gein. When

Gein was arrested in 1957, the police conducted a thorough search of both the home and the surrounding property. The search turned up furniture and decorative items made from human remains. The most disturbing of all the discoveries was what appeared to be a suit made out of human skin. While the authorities couldn't confirm what the killer was doing with the skin, the press began to print all sorts of morbid assumptions.

Stevens' third Uber of the day pulled up outside the front steps of Silver Pines a little past 11:00 p.m. His shift didn't start until 11:30, but after being tardy to the staff meeting this morning, he didn't want to give Sutton, or the night supervisor, any more reason to cast an attentive eye his way.

"Good evening, Dave." Stevens offered to an older, heavyset man who was currently entranced by the eight security monitors in front of him.

"Evening Stevens, you're on Ward D again tonight. I'm sure Sutton filled you in on what's going on."

"He did indeed. Speaking of which, I didn't see you at the meeting this morning. Everything okay?"

"Everything is just fine. Sutton and I had this discussion yesterday afternoon. I told him that if I was staying on the overnight, that I wouldn't be attending any morning meetings."

"It would have been nice if he had given me that same choice. I had a complete clusterfuck of a morning and didn't get here until after the meeting had started. Sutton was not thrilled."

"Well, you're on time tonight, so that's all that really matters to me. Make sure you're all set to go when it's time. According to the morning and evening shift logs, it's been quiet all day, and I very much would like to keep it that way tonight."

"Will do, Dave. I'll see you after my first sweep."

Stevens spent the last few minutes before his shift started checking both his flashlight and radio to ensure that both were in good working order and then headed out into the hall.

Being on Ward D duty consisted of two parts. The first, and most time-consuming, was a sweep of the outer perimeter. Silver Pines sat on 5 acres of land, housed several work sheds, an industrial cooling system, and a maintenance garage. The fencing, which at this point was only two years old, had proven to be an imperfect instrument of deterrence. Anyone who was slightly familiar with the layout of the property knew where the cameras were, as well as several holes already cut out for easy access. Once again, the outskirts of the facility had become a regular hangout for the local miscreants. Thankfully, that did not prove to be the case tonight, and he was relieved to find that nothing out of sorts. Relieved to see that everything was in order and that the night may indeed be as quiet as the day, he radioed into the security desk and headed back inside to commence the evening's first sweep.

D's primary issue was that because it was not in use, to say that it was cleaned infrequently would probably be an exaggeration. The entire hallway was filled with discarded liquor bottles, cobwebs as thick as a winter blanket, and the nauseating combination of sweat, urine, and feces. Given the state of things, Stevens was relieved that the sweep of the ward itself was pretty simple. With no electricity in the building, all that was required was for him to check each of the ward's 10 doors to make sure they had remained locked, verify that the windows at the back of the ward were still intact and that the shared entrance between D and the newer Ward C was still chained off. All in all, the entire sweep took less than twenty minutes.

After assuring the secured status of the ten padded and stained doors, Stevens headed back up the hall and to the main entrance. His last stop was the security door between C and D. To his annoyance, he discovered the chains that locked the doors were missing. He scanned the surrounding area with his flashlight to no avail. The chains hadn't just been taken off; they were gone. Stevens picked up his radio.

"Hey, Dave, come back." The radio echoed nothing but static.

"Base, this is Stevens, come back." Once again, nothing but static.

"God damn it." Stevens shook his radio up and down and smacked the battery cover on the back. The static continued. Focusing the beam of his flashlight on the door, Stevens reached out and pushed the filth covered metal bar, opening the entrance to something that certainly didn't look like the newly renovated Ward C. This room was dark and silent as the grave. At the end of the hall stood a heavy metal door.

Cautiously crossing the threshold of the room, the previously steady beam of Steven's flashlight began to flicker. A twinge of panic hit his stomach, inducing a wave of nausea. That was when the whispering started.

An unexpected crackle of static suddenly emanated from his radio, echoing off the walls of the seemingly empty hall. Grasping for his belt, he fumbled the radio, saved it hitting the ground, and attempted to contact the desk.

"Dave, this is Stevens. Can you hear me?"

The static grew louder, and he swore he could hear a voice attempting to come through on the other end.

"Base, this is Stevens. Are you there?"

The static continued to increase in volume before it was cut off completely. The light from his flashlight flickers rapidly before casting Steven's into the blackness of the grave. That was when the laughter started. Stevens felt his pulse rising, and his breaths coming in rapid succession.

He groped for the keyring in his pocket and pulled out a small flashlight.

He moved the light in order to locate the file basket on the door, only to find that it was empty. A quick scan of the grounds revealed a scattering of papers. Gathering up what he could, Stevens began to scan through the pages. The details of the crimes within were eerily similar to those of the murders he had been following on the news earlier that day. Eight total victims were found with the skin removed and two bullet holes to the back of their heads.

Stevens leaned forward and slid the metal plate away from the door and gazed through the window. In the pitch dark, he could make out only the slightest form of a human being.

"Who are you?" He asked through the blackness.

No response came from the cell.

"Are you alive in there?"

Again, no response came from the cell.

"Come on, damn it, give me some sign that you're in there.".

He began banging on the cell door while cursing the mysterious inhabitant inside. Suddenly a guttural scream pierced through the darkness of the cell, and a face slammed into the door, filling the small window.

Stevens knew that face. The eyes, the mouth, the crooked nose from where it was broken when he was three. The face was his.

The small pocket light blinked out, and once again, the dark overtook the ward.

That's when the screaming started.

An All New Yesterday

The last clouds of the afternoon had faded away, and it seemed that there would be at least a little sun before the end of the day. Ralph Emery watched all this happen from inside the visiting room of the Mary Ellis Senior Center. It had been six weeks since Ralph had found himself admitting he could no longer take care of his father's increasing day-to-day needs. At the age of 68, Michael Embry began to forget things. Little things at first. Car keys. Items at the grocery. Where he had left the remote control. From time to time, the older man would walk into a room and have no idea why he had done so. When his father was 70, Ralph received a phone call from the family next door informing him that the old man was wandering in circles through the neighborhood in only an open robe. Fortunately, Ralph arrived just as the cops did. He explained the situation to the officers, who allowed him to take the old man back home. A gracious Ralph went home that night and wrote a check to support the local Police Action League.

Over the next several weeks, the symptoms began to escalate rapidly and in severity. Ralph had started to notice that his father was having difficulty holding a conversation. His ability to recall words had begun to fail. Michael Embry's body had begun to fail, as well. He found himself unable to stand for long periods and had begun to have an occasional fall. The bottom fell out the day Ralph let himself in to check on the old man and just missed being shot. Somewhere down cellar, there had been a box of memories the elder Embry had brought home from the war. Amongst other things, the box contained his field uniform, which still fit quite well, several service medals, and apparently, entirely unbeknownst to Ralph, his service pistol. The old man hadn't even recognized his son, convinced he was a Vietnamese soldier. That was the night the cops had to come and take Michael Embry away. It was no longer possible to ignore what was happening. An extended visit to a Neurologist confirmed what Ralph had long suspected. His father was suffering from Alzheimer's disease. According to the test results, the illness was in its advanced stages. The doctors could offer a best-case scenario was between six and eighteen months, and that for the remainder of that time, the elder Embry would require constant care. Dr. Kisner explained to Ralph that his father would become infirm as the disease continued to spread. By the end, she advised, he would no longer be the man that he was.

The drive home was one of the longest of his life. As he turned down all the familiar streets where he played as a boy, his heart broke inside, knowing that all of those memories were or would soon be lost to his father. All the moments of their life together would drift from the old man's mind. Birthdays, graduations, weddings would all be lost to the disease. The memories of his one great love. Ralph's mother had passed two years prior to the first onset of symptoms, and every day since, he had watched his father fade away. Maybe, in a way, the diagnosis was a blessing. Perhaps the short term suffering and lost memories was a better way to live than being burdened with the knowledge of all he once had.

A tap on the shoulder brought Ralph back to the present. He turned to see the familiar face of Doctor Elaine Kisner. Since the initial diagnosis, she had been working with Ralph, keeping him up to date on all the newest therapies and experimental medication that had shown various degrees of success. He was sure she cost a fortune, but that was for the insurance company to worry about.

"Ralph, how are you doing today?"

He looked back towards the window and watched his father being rolled out to the garden by his nurse.

"Given the circumstances, I'm doing alright. Haven't been sleeping worth a damn. I knew he had been on a downslope since mom died. We'd spend time together, and sometimes it was clear that I was the only one in the room. I just figured he was searching for his place in the world without her. I keep asking myself if there was anything more I could have done. What if I had picked up on the symptoms sooner? Was there anything he could have done that might have avoided this?"

Doctor Kisner placed a hand on his shoulder in an attempt to comfort the man.

"Ralph, we have talked about this almost every day for the last six months. Alzheimer's is one of the least understood neurological diseases out there. There is zero medical evidence to support the argument that the disease is genetic. That leaves a tremendous amount of a gray area to work in."

Of course, Ralph knew all of this. Furthermore, he knew that there was nothing he could have done differently. That didn't mean he wasn't going to continue to beat himself up over it.

"I know, Elaine. I know that everything that can be done is being done, but it just tears me apart, watching him waste away like this. I think it's harder when you know there is no hope. That the path we are on only ends one way." Ralph wiped the early stages of a tear from his eye.

"Well, there is something I wanted to talk to you about. There has been a breakthrough in some recent trials."

Ralph's mind began to race. This was the first time that there may have been the possibility of hope.

"Now, I don't want you to get ahead of yourself. There is an awful lot of information for us to go over, and there is no guarantee that your father would be accepted into the study. Still, given the advanced state of your father's condition, I would feel confident in saying there is a better-than-average chance."

"Okay, then. Tell me all about it."

The two sat down at a table in the corner of the cafeteria, and Elaine laid out the story of Fresh Start Medical. Two military vets founded the company upon returning home from stents in the Second Iraq war. Prior to serving their country, Dr. Helen Morrison and Dr. Greg Wilson had served on CalTech and MIT's staffs, respectively. Morrison's primary field of study was mapping neural pathways in the brain. Her research's ultimate goal was to create functional pathways that would allow for more human movement and sensations with artificial limbs.

On the other hand, Wilson had been a man on a mission since graduating at the top of his class at Yale Medical. Six members of his immediate family had died over the course of two years from a variety of mental illnesses. Greg started every day of his professional life with a silent prayer and promised that he would not stop looking for a way to fix a broken brain.

"The two dove headfirst and without a net. Other than their monthly stipend from the government and whatever fees could be made from speaking engagements, Fresh Start had been operating out of a hole since they opened the doors."

"I trust there is more to the story than that, Elaine…"

"Oh, sorry about that. What Fresh Start had begun to notice during their research with the troops was that for every troop who came home due to a physical wound received on the battlefield, there were six more that should have been sent home due to mental wounds. As we've learned over the last few years, you can't pluck an eighteen-year-old kid from a quiet suburban street who knows nothing of the reality of war other than what they think they know, thanks to Call of Duty and spend the next six weeks turning him into a killer. Then you take this kid, who's never been further from home than a trip to Action Park, and send him thousands of miles from home to kill people he has no real problem with. Of course, he's not actually prepared to deal with the blunt force reality of war. By the time he returns home, he's mentally and physically broken and trained how to kill. Many find themselves with nothing when they return home. No family, no dwelling, no job, and no prospects. Some end up here, some in state hospitals or the VA, but the number of facilities equipped to handle the specific needs of PTSD and the side effects it brings with it far exceeds the amount of healthcare we are able to provide to the ever-increasing number of vets who need our help. The entire system is set up to handle the physical wounds suffered by returning soldiers. There is one, often part-time, psychiatrist available to every five hundred Vets in the system diagnosed with PTSD or other mental health issues. You can imagine the wait time for an appointment."

Ralph sat pondering what he had just been told. Looking back on it now, he did recall an increase in violent crime rates amongst the homeless population. This had all happened within a year after the third Middle Eastern War came to its clusterfuck of an ending. These were young people who answered the call to action after the government had reinstated the draft and served with pride. It's just too bad their government didn't care about the soldiers as much as they did the mission.

"So the plan was to create a medication uniquely tailored for the patient's unique brain chemistry. Since it is standard military policy to perform full MRI scans during the draft board examination, Morrison and Wilson had access to an image of what the patient's brain looked like before entering an active war zone. Any signs of brain damage, especially things like CTE, hemorrhage, or an aneurysm, would immediately disqualify a draftee from combat duty. After a series of aptitude tests, those physically unable to serve were placed in various other positions that would provide needed supplies on the front line. Upon the soldier returning home, they are kept in isolation as a second brain scan was taken. After isolating the part(s) of the brain suffering from injury, the original image is written and stored onto a micro transmitter. The transmitter is then attached to the brain itself, scans for the differences between its memory and the current information. Once the brain is digitally mapped, the transmitter begins to rewrite the sections of the brain that no longer coincide with the imaging of the first scan. While it has a seventy-five percent success rate, there have been some cases of it causing additional damage, resulting in an acceleration of the symptoms. Most failed cases lead to death within one week, leaving the deceased a ranting, drooling mess."

Ralph sat in front of his father's doctor. Over the last six weeks, Elaine Kisner had been with them every step of the way. She was one of the top Neurologists in the tri-state area. That she had dedicated as much of her time as she had was something Ralph would never forget her for.

"So what does all that mean for dad?" he asked, choking up just a bit.

"It means if we can get him into the program, there is an above-average choice that we can reverse the damage caused by the Alzheimers and hopefully, slowly be able to rebuild the damaged tissue."

The answer seemed to be too easy. If this cure was out there, why wasn't it being used around the world? Something wasn't adding up for him.

"Elaine, if this works so great, why hasn't it become a standard medical practice for anyone with a neurological disease? It feels like there's more to this."

"Well, for starters, this is a government project. After Fresh Start's work had begun to show significant results, their money problems were solved by the helping hands of Uncle Sam. The project became fully funded, with resources being offered to them by several of the government alphabet soup agencies for who knows what reasons. I only know what I know because I see a high number of service people who may benefit from such a project. I've known Dr. Wilson for years, so he keeps me in the loop on his work. We have already spoken several times about your father's situation, and he believes he can help him."

For the first time in years, there seemed to be a light at the end of a long, dark tunnel. A way, perhaps, to bring the man he knew as Michael Embry out of the darkness. The man he knew to be a loving husband to Jennifer Embry and a fantastic father to Ralph. Another chance to take a walk in the park or fish off the pier. A chance to listen to the same war stories he'd heard a hundred times before. Right now, he wanted nothing more than to hear one of those stories again. This was a chance to prove that Michael Embry was his father and not a burden.

"So what do we do? What's the next step?"

"There is one thing that we need to discuss before we get started."

Ralph was starting to get a little impatient. He knew that everything Elaine was telling him and how she was presenting it was all for reasons that would all make sense when the cards were on the table.

"I need you to understand how this technology works," she spoke in a serious tone.
Ralph nodded his head and indicated for her to proceed.

"The way they are able to rebuild the damaged brain tissue is by using a previously captured image of the brain in question."

"Yes, and then the tissue is repaired and rewritten with the data from the image."

"Correct."

"Do they even have a digital scan of dad's brain? Where would they even have come up with one?"

For the first time since the initial diagnosis, he saw a sadness pass over Dr. Elaine Kisner's face.

"In 1968, the United States Government made it a requirement for all drafted servicemen to have a brain x-ray. Searching for tumors or damage caused by sexually transmitted diseases like syphilis. Later on, it became an MRI and then so on and so forth, bringing us up to the hand scanners we use today."

Once again, Ralph's brain kicked into overdrive. It still made little sense how this project was going to help his father's condition.

"I don't understand…"

"They have his X-ray in the archives, Ralph. From when he was drafted in 1970."

The world went gray, and Ralph began to slide out of his chair. It was only the quick reflexes of Dr. Kisner that prevented him from ending up on the floor. She carefully slid him back into a sitting position.

"Take it easy there, Ralph; I thought I had lost you. You need to take a minute?"

Ralph took three deep breaths and brought his eyes back up to meet the face of his friend.

"I'm okay. I think I must have misheard you. It sounded like you said that a pair of doctors who specialize in repairing diseased brains have all the tools they need to help my father. Is that what you said?"

"Yes, Ralph, that is exactly what I am saying."

"So, what are we waiting for? What do they need from me to get started? How much is this going to cost?" Ralph realized there were still a thousand questions that he was going to need answers to. It had already been overwhelming, and this could either be the miracle they had been looking for or the wave that washed it all away.

"Ralph, do you understand what this means?"

"Yeah, if it all goes according to plan, I'm going to have my dad back," Ralph exclaimed.

"That's what I've been trying to tell you, Ralph. The damaged tissue is replaced by digital scans taken from the X-Ray. That image is from 1970, Ralph. If we were to use that scan, any memories your father had created in the following years would be lost."

Michael Embry met Jennifer Collins in the Fall of 1972. They were married in May 1974, and in April 1976, Ralph was born. Those were his dad's memories. In 2008, Michael Embry retired with full honors from the Riverland Fire Department after thirty-one years of service. In 2012, Jennifer joined him in retirement, and the two of them traveled the world together. No matter what life threw at them, they could always be found together. Hand in hand. The Embry's against the world. Until June 19th of 2019.

Just like every morning for the last thirty-five years, the alarm clock went off at 6:30 in the morning. Michael rolled over his wife to turn off the clock. He gently shook her awake and headed into the master bathroom. No indication of movement had come from the bed; he shook her shoulder again as he passed by the bed. Her arm was very cold. These were his dad's memories. He looked into Elaine's eyes with a sudden understanding.

"You're telling me he'll live, but he'll still lose everything he is?"

"Yes. He'll live another twenty or thirty years once the degeneration is halted. You'll have more time."

"But he won't know me. He won't remember my mother. He won't remember a single minute of the life we lived together. He'd be a sixty-five-year-old man with the memories of an eighteen-year boy who hasn't existed since 1970. The best I could do is sit by and watch him form a new lifetime of memories. That's not my choice to make. I've got to talk to him."

"You know he doesn't know who you are. He can barely comprehend where he is most of the time. I don't know what you expect to get out of him."

Ralph rose from the hard plastic of the cafeteria chair and headed towards the hallway to the garden. He saw his father, sitting in his wheelchair, a light blanket covering his lap despite the warmth of the day. The day nurse, Ralph, was pretty sure her name was Beatrice, sat next to him on a bench, reading from the pages of a tattered paperback. She turned her head as he walked out into the garden.

"Good afternoon Mr. Embry." the woman offered, raising her hand in greeting.

"Hello Beatrice, how is he today?"

"For the most part, he's doing pretty good. He's a little sharper today than usual. Will you bring him back in?"

"I'll take care of him from here, thanks." he watched the older woman make her way back inside and took her seat on the bench. He placed his arm on the older man's shoulder.

"Dad, it's Ralph. Do you know who I am?"

The elder Embry turned his head up at the boy; a blank stare came over his face.

"You look like my boy Ralph, but you can't be. He died in 1992."

"I didn't die, dad. Why do you think I died?"

"No, no, it wasn't my boy. You're right; my boy didn't die. Where's Jennifer? She would know who it was. She's always been better at remembering those types of things."

All the breath escaped from Ralph's body, and tears filled his eyes as he squeezed his father's arm.

"Your mama must be busy with something. Maybe it's a potluck at the church or something. I haven't seen her in a few days. She knows things. She's always known things."

He didn't have the heart to tell him again she was gone. He had done it three times already, and it broke his heart each time to see the sorrow ripple through the old man.

"Dad, there's a new procedure available that can help repair your memories and slow the Alzheimers. It's experimental, but the results have been positive."

He looked down at his father, who had drifted off as a sliver of drool ran down his chin. He wondered how much of this decision was his to make. Perhaps twenty to thirty years of new memories would bring peace to his ravaged mind.

He picked up his cell phone and dialed Elaine Kisler.

Going Down

"Listen, Rob, Roy, Rick, whatever the hell your name is. I need those invoices processed and on my desk by nine o'clock Monday morning."

Justin Pearce made his way down the hall, Bluetooth in his ear as he continued to berate his hapless assistant on the other end of the phone. Pearce was the model for the successful middle management type. A graduate of Northwestern University's school of business at twenty-one, he was aggressively recruited by Baxter and Marshall right out of college. By the time he was twenty-three, he had risen to the rank of Junior Analyst. At the age of twenty-five, he was a Senior Analyst. By the age of twenty-six, he found himself in a private office on the forty-second floor, and he made his first million by the time he was twenty-eight. If the rumors going around had any truth to them, he was on a shortlist of potential names for an upcoming junior partner spot. Of course, assuming that his assistant pulled his head out of his ass and got those invoices finished.

"I'm sorry, did I somehow give you the impression that I gave a fuck as to whether or not you have plans tonight?" The frustration was almost enough to bring him to tears. What part of this request did this fuckwit not understand?

"Just to make sure there is no miscommunication, let me make this clear for you. Either you get it done, or I will have them find me somebody who can follow simple directions. Do you understand me?"

Pearce shook his head in disgust as he approached the elevator bank. This was the third assistant he had gone through in the last two years. Unlike most of the other departments in the building, Pearce had no in with HR. This meant there was no way to find out who was responsible for this seemingly endless parade of incompetents. Whoever it was, he couldn't shake the suspicion that they were just as useless. He reached out and hit the call button for the elevator.

"Okay, maybe It's me. Maybe it's not clear enough, although I can't even begin to comprehend how that is possible. I will explain this to you one more time. The quarterly reports are due at the end of the month. For me to prepare the outlooks for management, the invoices must be processed so they can be reconciled with the rest of the reports covering the last three months. Now, given that I'm the one with an office and you are the one sitting at a clutter-filled desk, which still smells of your predecessor, who was gone so quickly I don't even remember his name, which one of us do you think is going to get these things done?"

Despite the increasing volume of his voice, Pearce heard the tone that indicated the elevator had arrived. The doors slid open, and he stepped inside.

"Listen dip shit, I'm getting on the elevator and will probably lose you. I don't care how long it takes or how long you have to stay tonight to get it done, but I swear to god if I come in at nine on Monday morning and those invoices are still sitting on your desk, I can guarantee you that by nine-fifteen you'll be sitting on the steps with whatever crap you brought with you in a box. Do we understand each other? Good. By the way, have a great weekend."

Pearce disconnected the call through his earpiece and pressed the button for the level one garage. The doors closed, and the car began to descend. He removed the iPhone from his pocket and began to scan his email. One of the more complicated, and if he was honest with himself, annoying aspects of his job was email. He regularly received between two and three hundred emails a day. Most were just forwards from the different accounting departments keeping him in the loop on day-to-day transactions. Occasionally he would receive something important like market updates or changes to filing procedures. After the screen loaded, the messages began flooding in. A quick scan showed nothing that required his immediate attention. Returning his phone to the inside jacket pocket of his Brooks Brothers jacket, he turned his gaze to the digital readout indicating which floor he was passing. While not the fastest elevator in the city, it moved at a respectable pace. Until, of course, the car came to a screeching stop, somewhere between the twenty-second and twenty-third floors.

"Oh, what the fuck is this?" Pearce said aloud in the empty car.

"It would seem that we've encountered some type of mechanical problem." A voice came from behind him.

Pearce turned and was surprised to see the older man standing behind him. He could have sworn that the car had been empty when he stepped in.

"Just another example of modern convenience, am I right?" The man said.

The mysterious gentleman stood about six feet tall. He had a head of hair the color of cigarette ash with a beard to match. If Pearce had to guess, he would have placed the man around his early to mid-sixties. The unexpected visitor wore a black suit with a pinstripe so subtle it was barely noticeable. His shirt was a sky blue color with a patterned tie. On his feet were a pair of Stefano Bemer shoes, worth easily $2000.

"Sometimes, I wonder if we would be better off just sticking with stairs."

"Hey, listen, I'm sorry for my language as I was getting on. I'm in the middle of dealing with an incompetent assistant and didn't realize anybody else was in the car."

"Apology accepted. The name is Balaam, William Balaam." The man extended his hand. Pearce reached out and shook it.

"So, do you work here in the building, Mr. Balaam?"

"Not exactly, my boy. I'm a consultant for several of the companies here. I usually handle business through teleconferencing, however sometimes things require a bit more of a personal touch. I need to come up and collect signed final drafts of contracts. Even in this wondrous digital age we live in, there will always be, and I truly believe this, a need for a hard copy."

"There always seems to be paperwork. Sometimes I think that it will never end. You sign one form, and then there's three more to verify that the first document was signed. It could drive you to drink. So if you don't mind me asking, what companies do you consult for?"

"That is information that has to stay up here." Balaam tapped his forehead with one fine, slightly extended, manicured fingernail "Confidentiality and all. I'm sure you understand."

"Completely understandable. I swear I've signed more non-disclosures this year than I wrote term papers when I was in business school."

"So tell me, within the bounds of your contracts, what do you do for Baxter and Marshall?"

Pearce paused for a moment, trying to recall whether or not he had told Balaam where he worked.

"Well, right now, I'm a Senior Analyst. It's my job to predict trends in the markets and, based on that information, provide responsible financial planning for my clients."

"Ah, the stock market. Well, that explains it. I had a feeling when you stepped in that you were involved in some kind of finance. How has your year been so far?"

"Not too bad. I'm tracking a seventy-nine percent success rate for my clients. All told, it's more than fifty million dollars, and it's only July."

"That is quite impressive. I would think that if you keep up this pace, that promotion should be all but guaranteed."

Again, Pearce wondered how this unusual old man had knowledge of a promotion that no one in the office had heard about.

"You seem to be on top of a great many things, Mr. Balaam. Nobody in our office even knows about the partnership position opening up yet."

"That is the sign of an outstanding consultant Mr. Pearce. It's my job to know things that other people don't. Now tell me, what would that promotion be worth to you?"

Pearce stopped for a minute to ponder the question. What exactly would this promotion mean to him? If he could make Junior Partner before the age of thirty and keep his nose clean, he would be on the fast track to senior partner before turning forty.

"Well, Mr. Balaam, I'll say this. Receiving this promotion now would probably set me up for the rest of my life. I'm great at my job now, and I know that I would be an invaluable asset to the company as a partner. Of course, all of this is just idle talk since they haven't even announced the opening."

"Let's say, hypothetically of course, I was to tell you that this partnership will be opening up by the end of next month. Do you think there is time to dazzle your bosses enough to secure the position?"

Pearce began to speak but cut his voice off to gather his thoughts.

"To be honest, Mr. Balaam, I'm not entirely sure. I'm very good at what I do, but there are certainly people here who have been here longer than I have."

"Then perhaps, Mr. Pearce, you and I can come to an arrangement."

Pearce looked puzzlingly at his fellow passenger.

"Here is what I propose, you and I will sign a consulting contract. While the contract's language is the usual legalese, the long and short of it is that over the next thirty days, I will work on your behalf to ensure that you will receive the promotion and all the perks that go along with it."

The offer dumbfounded Pearce, but a little voice in his head assured him that this man, this mysterious stranger on the elevator, could deliver just what he promised.

"Well, it sounds as if a partnership with you would be quite beneficial, Mr. Balaam. I have two questions. One, how long would this contract be for, and two, what do you get out of it? I've got plenty of money to pay you for your services. What's the cost?"

"There is no monetary charge for my services. The contract is good for one year, and at the end of that year, I will call upon you and ask for a favor. Once that favor is complete, our business will reach its conclusion. Does that sound fair?"

Pearce had to admit to himself that while some of the details were a little shady, this promotion would change his life.

"Alright, Mr. Balaam, why don't you have your people draft a contract up and send it over to my office on Monday."

"No need for that Mr. Pearce, I despise working with underlings. I have a contract right here in my pocket." Balaam reached inside his suit jacket and produced a contract and pen.

"Feel free to read it if you like, but it is a standard consulting contract. It says if I don't deliver, the contract is null and void. I have thirty days to deliver on my promises, and you have one year to keep up your end of the deal."

Pearce reached out for the pen and paper. He gave the contract a quick perusal. It was a word-for-word transcription of the contract as it had been verbally explained to him. Figuring he had nothing to lose, he leaned the paper up against the car's wall and signed where indicated at the bottom of the page.

"Excellent! I will go ahead and get things moving on my end. It's nice to be able to do business with three generations of Pearce men."

"What? Three generations? What are you talking about?"

"Oh, Mr. Pearce, you are the third member of your family line that I've had the pleasure of working alongside. In 2007, I met with your father James Pearce and signed a similar deal with him. I remember speaking to him about six months in, and everything was going as promised. I was sorry to hear that he passed away in 2008. Who could have guessed that the housing bubble would burst? Suicide, wasn't it? A mouthful of pills and a bottle of scotch will do that."

Pearce stood mouth agape.

"And I met your grandfather back in 1986. Now he was great at his job. When I met him, he had already made $50 million by the time he was 60. He was much more obsessed with financial gain than your father. Of course nobody, well almost nobody, saw the crash of 1987 coming. Your Grandmother came home from the grocery store and found him. Hooked a hose up to the exhaust in the garage if I recall correctly."

Suddenly the car jerked forward, and the elevator resumed its journey down to the garage level.

Pearce turned to face his fellow rider.

"How did you know all those things about my family?"

But the man in the black suit was gone.

A Turn of Events

The throbbing in her head quickly worsened as she struggled to open her eyes. Slowly, the room's details began to fill in, illuminated by the sole source of light in the room. A single 40-watt bulb swung from a loosely wrapped extension cord which ran down the length of an exposed rafter. Sparks spit forth from the rust stained outlet which sat inches from a stack of discarded scraps of paper. The shadows cast from the solitary light did little to improve the agonizing pain in her head and nausea that was now accompanying it. Her attempt to stand was short lived when she quickly discovered she was strapped down. Pain shot forth from behind her eyes, leading to the violent ejection of Karen's stomach contents. For a moment, the throbbing in her head lessened, and her eyes began to clear. As more of her surroundings came into focus, Karen quickly wished she had stayed in the dark.

This space, whatever it was, could only be described as a horror show. Uncured leathers hung stretched across wooden frames. A myriad of mobiles, many seemingly made of bones, rattled as the occasional breeze wafted in through a broken pane of glass. Swarms of flies filled the room, buzzing in synchronized patterns. Karen strained her neck and was able to catch small glimpses of the surrounding room. To her left, tables covered in rust and dried blood lined the walls. The floor was littered with piles of bones and empty discarded boxes of heavy-duty contractor bags. On display, held up with nails on various pegboards, was an array of both power and traditional tools. Multiple unoccupied spaces implied several were missing. Despite her ongoing struggle to remain aware, Karen attempted to create a layout of the area in her head, hoping desperately to locate a way out. Of only slightly less importance was figuring out where she was and just how in the hell she got here. The only thing she knew for sure was that her car had broken down.

Karen Mitchell was a traveling sales rep for Carson International. She had graduated from UWS with degrees in both Advertising and Marketing and was recruited heavily by Carson. Despite their initial enthusiasm to bring her in, two years would pass before any of the people in charge, all middle aged white guys, decided she was worthy of her own route. And when they finally got around to doing so, they made sure that it was one that had failed to be a success for any of her predecessors. Five years later, she found herself on the turnaround of a twenty-day sales trip. This run covered twenty-five towns in the upper part of New Jersey and southwestern Pennsylvania. After five hours of night driving on poorly lit stretches of Route 80, highway hypnosis had begun to set in. She briefly considered pulling over and napping, but the thought of a woman sleeping in her car alone on a dark stretch of highway was not the most comforting. She wanted nothing more than to find a room and get off the road for a while. She was scheduled to return home tomorrow and wanted to be on her way as early as possible.

An additional fifteen miles of darkened, unchanging woods crawled by before the first signs of civilization began to reappear. Her headlights struck the reflective tape along the exit sign's border, which cast a glare that filled the windshield. A moment passed, and Karen was able to make out the sign's contents. The familiar food and lodging icons appeared, and Karen felt a load fall from her shoulders. Her salvation lay just a few more miles down the road. Karen cautiously pulled off the exit and into a blackened turnabout. Approaching the end of the ramp, she rolled to a stop at a four-way intersection. The blinking red and yellow lights of the traffic signal provided a minimal source of illumination. The lack of visibility, however, proved to be inconsequential, as no additional information was to be gained from the intersection. Disregarding any semblance of common sense and ignoring her GPS's last voice direction before it crapped out, she had a choice in front of her. Karen reached up to her rearview mirror, touched her Saint Christopher medal, took a deep breath in, exhaled a quick prayer out, and took a right down the darkened road.

She was twenty minutes off the highway when, from somewhere in the woods, she heard a gunshot, and the car suddenly jerked to the left, catching her left hand in the spokes of the steering wheel, causing a sickening crunching ground. Karen yanked the wheel hard, as hard as her one good hand would allow, to the right. With the assistance of what she referred to as "drunk bumps," she brought the vehicle to a complete stop with no further damage to the machine or the woman behind the wheel. Karen took several deep breaths, bringing a small measure of calm to the situation. Other than the newly acquired throbbing pain, the source of which she was convinced was a broken wrist, she seemed to be in one piece.

A rush of cold September air blew into the car as Karen rolled down the window. With both lanes of blacktop unoccupied, she cautiously exited the vehicle. Dismayed to find the driver side front tire hanging off the rim, Karen reached through the open window and retrieved her cell phone from its dashboard holder clip. The screen of her iPhone showed a full charge and no signal.

"Fuck." she screamed into the dark. Her frustration cut through the silence. In the distance, as if in response, the sounds of birds taking wing filled the air.

Of course, she was no stranger to flat tires. Being on the road twenty plus days a month had motivated her to learn essential car maintenance. Karen had become quite adept at taking care of such things herself. However, that was under ideal circumstances. In the dark, in the middle of nowhere, Pennsylvania, and with a broken wrist was far from perfect. Karen popped the trunk of her car and removed two flares from the roadside emergency kit Tom had insisted she carry. Her ex-husband may have been a cheating piece of shit, but he had always had her safety in mind. She popped the caps off the flares and placed them two feet behind the car. In the distance came the sound of a wolf howling.

A breeze blew past, causing her to shiver as the late September wind began to pick up. In her first stroke of good luck , less than ten minutes had passed before salvation arrived in the form of dim headlights cutting through the black. The flashing yellow lights of a tow truck crested the hill and pulled up behind her.

"Havin' some trouble?" the driver asked as he stepped down from the truck's cab.

As the stranger approached her, Karen stood in awe of his size. Clearly over six feet tall and sporting a massive beard, which reached down to his chest, she could not recall having ever encountered anyone so mammoth. She felt like a toddler when standing in his presence.

"You have no idea how happy I am to see you." Karen offered. "I got lost after getting off the highway, and then my front tire blew. It has not been a great night," she offered a strained smile to the driver.

"That's not uncommon around here. This stretch of road is filled with dangerous dips and potholes. And just in case that wasn't enough from time to time, we have rock slides, and they just leave all kinds of shit everywhere. Couple that with the piss-poor job the state has done with replacing any of the burnt-out lights, and you can see why I spend a lot of nights right here behind the wheel. Tonight, it seems to have worked out pretty well. Wait till I tell my wife that I got to rescue an actual damsel in distress. Listen to me going on and on. Where were you headed?" he asked with a jovial smile.

"I was just looking for someplace to spend the night. Is it far from the next town?"

"It's not that bad of a ride, about twenty miles or so. Let's get your car hooked up, and you and I can skedaddle right out of here."

Another howl from the woods found Karen hopping into the tow truck's passenger side, quickly locking the door behind her. Not that she was entirely sure what good a locked car door was if there was, in fact, a wolf. The cab's inside was filled with a melange of motor oil, coffee, stale cigarette smoke, and underneath it all, cinnamon. From the radio came the voice of a preacher, warning of the dangers of the modern world. The driver climbed up into the cab.

"So, what brings you out to our little neck of the woods?"

"Just traveling for business. I can't thank you enough for stopping Mr?"

"Peacock. Earl Peacock. My friends call me Earl." he offered with a smile stretching across his face.

"Thank you, Earl. I'm Karen Mitchell."

"Well, don't you worry, Ms. Mitchell. It may not be much of a town, but we do our best to make visitors feel at home. I can drop you at the Hanford Inn if you'd like. It's not the Ritz, but the rooms are cleanish, and the rates are reasonable. If you're in the mood to hear a seventy-year-old woman spin a web of bullshit thicker than pancake batter, you're going to love Buzzy. She owns the place now after her husband, Floyd, passed last year. She doesn't see a lot of business these days, so she's been a little bit on the lonely side. If she grabs your ear, you'll never get free." Earl offered over a chuckle. "First thing in the morning, I'll patch up your tire and bring it over to you."

"That sounds great, Earl, and please call me Karen."

They rode in silence as an exhausted Karen watched the miles go by. She found the highway hypnosis returning as the tow truck's lights bounced off the yellow lane divider as it split from solid to double solid and back again. They began to slow down for an approaching traffic light.

As the truck rolled to a stop, she felt a small prick in her arm, then there was nothing.

Karen peered into the darkness, and could just make out a door against a far wall. In an attempt to loosen her bonds, she began to rock back and forth. The rocking intensified, and the chair took a violent tumble to its side. Karen felt her head and shoulder slam into the floor, something from a dark pool splashed up into her face. She opened her eyes and found herself face to face with a half skinned human skull. Now filled with terror, and doing her very best to push back the pain that wracked her body, Karen knew that inaction would lead only to death in this situation.

From her place amongst the carnage covered floor, Karen began to scream.

As time passed and her screams went unanswered, she began to question if there would be a tomorrow and, more importantly, if she would be alive to see it. Tears began to run down her face, and her screams faded to whispers as her throat became raw. The sound of a key sliding into a lock broke the still silence of the room. The lock let forth a scraping sound as rusted tumblers turned inside unoiled hinges. The sound of metal against metal accompanied the opening of a large door.

A sudden influx of light cut a path through the cabin's darkened insides, causing her eyes to squeeze shut. Karen strained against the light, attempting to make out the dark shape now occupying the doorway. All she knew for sure was that she wanted it to go away. As her eyes began to adjust to the unexpected illumination, Karen was relieved to find that it was, in fact, gone. The pungent smell of decay that had permeated the room had now been undercut with a familiar, but at the moment, unnamable smell. The air was filled with something primal. From behind, the pressure from her bindings fell away, and suddenly she was free. A rough hand grabbed her shoulder. Karen felt a warm breath on the back of her neck, and a whisper of a voice said,

"Run."

Unsure of what was happening, and with a head still throbbing from the events of earlier Karen Mitchell bolted out the cabin's front door and ran as if the devil himself was behind her.

Karen did her best to traverse the heavily wooded path, glancing back over her shoulder, doing her best to stay upright. She frantically searched for a path or trail that would lead her out of the dense forest and back to a road. Her escape attempt was impeded by a rolling cloud cover that sporadically blocked out the moon, the pressure in her head, and the continued excruciating pain radiating from her shattered wrist.

Her jackass ex-husband Tom was a horror hound, and because of that, Karen had seen way too many scenarios just like this one. Some big-breasted blonde bimbo goes running through the dark and spooky woods, usually after having pre-marital sex, to flee from some unstoppable killer. Inevitably she trips over a branch, or a rock, or some upturned root. And despite the victim having a running head start, she's inevitably caught by the casually strolling psycho. She would pop up again in the final reel when the victims were laid out in a creative display for the "Final Girl" to discover right before the final confrontation. Karen refused to be a stereotype. Despite the unreal and terrifying situation, she knew she was as good as dead if she lost her senses now.

She had made her way to a clearing and came to a stop. With heaving breaths burning her lungs, Karen squeezed her eyes shut, hoping to clear her head enough to make sense of her shadowy surroundings. In the distance, the sounds of the forest began to encircle her. The breaking of branches was followed by a heavy rustling cutting through the trees. Something substantial was moving quickly, seemingly headed directly for her. Then, just as suddenly as it began, it was replaced with an eerie silence. From behind, an arm suddenly wrapped around her waist, and a calloused hand covered her mouth. Karen was lifted off the ground and began a rapid descent down the mountain and through the woods.

Once, the blur of motion came to a stop. Karen opened her eyes and coughed up a combination of stomach acid and saliva. She felt her knees go weak and soon found herself on the floor. She snapped alert and immediately began to scream.

"Quiet." the blurry man commanded. "You're going to get us both killed."

As her vision finally cleared, Karen became confident that this was not her original abductor. This man was clearly shorter and had not been embraced by the stench of death. Of course, this man had snatched her from the woods, which raised the question of whether or not he could be trusted. She did know that this grimy wooden cabin felt safer than the one she had most recently been a guest of.

"I apologize for the aggressiveness of my ambush. I am not in the habit of playing search and rescue. I do my best to fly under the radar when it comes to the Peacock family and whatever is going on further up the mountain. Our properties share an abutment, so it's been my policy to steer clear whenever I am out here. I leave them alone, they leave me alone, and all is well. I was on my way out for the evening when I saw him dragging you up the hill. It's a rare occasion that I encounter any member of the family. I followed him silently through the trees, eventually making my way to the run-down shack that had sat on the property for over one hundred years. I saw him drag you through the door and strap you to a chair."

The stranger reached into a cabinet above the sink, pulled down a drinking glass, and filled it from a cold water pitcher. He crossed the room and presented the glass to her. Karen raised the container to her lips and felt the clear liquid trickle down her parched throat.

"What else do you remember?"

"I had finished my office visits to Newton, and I was headed towards home. I was three hours into the eight-hour trip back, when I hit the no-man's-land stretch of Route 80. The woods to the right of me had begun to grow thick, while to the left stretched miles and miles of empty highway. With the sun dipping in the west, the length of the day's activities had begun to set in. A sign promising both food and lodging appeared in the distance. I took the exit, and twenty miles further down the road, I did not know where I was, and it looked as if my tire had exploded. I was pulling the spare from the trunk when a tow truck crested the hill. He said he would fix the car and take me to someplace called The Hanford."

"That makes sense. The place is a shit hole, and it also happens to be run by

Buzzy Peacock."

"The tow truck driver told me his last name was Peacock. Earl Peacock, that was his name."

"Yeah, Earl is Buzzy and Floyd's oldest boy. He's what most in these parts consider to be a trapper. That flat tire wasn't an accident."

"What do you mean?"

"Earl has a pair of younger brothers. There isn't enough common sense between them to know when to come out of the rain. They like to hide out in the woods, get drunk, and take shots at cars as they drive by. They're not the best of shots when they're sober, so you can probably imagine that when they're drunk, they miss by a mile, and the driver never has a clue about how close they came to death. But as they say, even a blind squirrel finds a nut from time to time. When they are successful, the car has to pull over on an unfamiliar, abandoned, and darkened road. No cell phone signal, no emergency phones, and no sign of civilization. Then, like a gift from above, Earl and his tow truck come to save the day."

"How long has this been going on?"

"Best as anybody can figure, Peacocks have been living in these woods forever. About two hundred fifty years ago, Margaret Peacock was brought to trial, accused of witchcraft. Her actual crime was being a woman who created a salve that cured a skin rash that had been spreading through the town. At the conclusion of what could barely be called a trial, the court said she was guilty. The townspeople wanted blood, and by order of the town's mayor, they would get it. The sentence was passed, and it was to be burning. Her husband, Jebidiah, had chosen to stand by his wife. In the early hours of the morning, Jebidiah slipped quietly into the jailhouse. Normally, he was not a man prone to violence, but these were not normal times. The only guard was quickly dispatched by a blow to the back of the head. Jebidiah grabbed the keyring from its hook on the wall, he unlocked the cage they had kept her in. The young couple shared an embrace, and stole off into the night."

"And they've lived out here this whole time?"

"That is my understanding of the story. For a long time, no one had seen hide nor hair of the Peacocks. At first, the locals were curious and a bit concerned, but no one came down from the mountain as the years began to pass. The townspeople, not one of whom had ever met a single member of the family, knew the Peacocks were not the type they wanted in their town. It had been decided a long ways back that the family, and the unsettling tales that followed them, were unwelcome amongst good decent folks.

Decades had passed, when one day, two older people in a rusted primer colored pick up came down from the mountain and walked into the First Bank of Pennsylvania. They introduced themselves as Buzzy and Floyd Peacock, and dressed in what was undoubtedly their finest, they sat down with the bank manager to discuss a business matter of great importance. Three days later, the local paper's headline announced that Buzzy and Floyd had purchased the abandoned Bayside Inn from the town and begun preparations to reopen it."

"Is there anybody else living out there that's not related to them? I mean, if it's just the descendants of Margaret and Jebediah, then..."

"It's best if you just don't think about it."

"I left Newton on Monday night. What day is it?"

"It's Wednesday."

Karen felt her throat close up, and she struggled to catch her breath. Wednesday? What the fuck happened to Tuesday?

As he gazed out the front of the window, her rescuer pulled aside a small portion of a filthy curtain covering an even dirtier window. Karen noticed the man begin scratching a spot on the back of his neck.

"I need you to stop and take a deep breath. You'll be safe here. In the twelve years I've been coming here, I have encountered none of the Peacock boys." His eyes peered out through a cracked pane of glass. The woods were quiet and still.

"In the morning, I'll pull the tarp off my Jeep and bring you back to town. You can report your car stolen, and the locals will do their best to help. They're a pretty good bunch, considering all that happens out here." His left eye began to twitch involuntarily.

Karen picked herself up from the floor and walked over to the window. She cupped her hands around her eyes, and pressed her face to the window. The clouds were clearing, and the moon had slowly begun to reveal more of the darkened woods she had spent most of her evening scrambling through. A minuscule beam of light began to penetrate the gaps surrounding the door.

"Please don't think that I am ungrateful, but would you mind telling me what exactly you are doing out here?"

"I'm something of a survivalist and outdoorsman. My grandfather Luthor built this cabin during the winter of 1903. Ever since then, the men in my family have come here to learn to hunt and fish. To live off the land and survive on your wits."

Looking around her haven, she could see this cabin was decorated in the mounted heads of various animals and framed photographs.

"When Luthor died in 1968, he willed the cabin to my father, Dick. He and I came out here together for years. We would stay the winter, hunting, and ice fishing. At times it was a struggle, but that's what made men in my family. We lost Dad in a hunting accident fifteen years ago. It took some time before I was able to come back here. Twelve years ago, I made my first trip up here alone. It was uncomfortable at first. Some of my fondest memories are of times spent here with my family. Still, I knew that generations of my family have prepared for the worst of times right here, and it fell to me to uphold that tradition. Now I make the trek up every September and head back down every March. It lets me get away from society for a while. It really is incredibly peaceful up here. At least most of the time. The muscles in his arms had begun to spasm.

The face of her watch read 1:33 a.m. Several hours remained before the sun started to rise, and he could return her to civilization. A place where you could rent a car, buy a coffee, and perhaps most importantly, a place where your cell phone always has a signal. The interior of the cabin continued to fill with moonlight, and the temperature began to creep up. She rifled through her pockets, coming up empty-handed.

"Fuck!" she shouted. "Where the hell is my phone?"

Her host had moved to the far side of the cabin, busying himself with some unseen task.

"That I could not tell you. Whatever was in your pockets when I found you should still be there."

"Do you have a phone here?" Julia asked.

"As I'm sure you've already noticed, cell phones get no signal out here, and we are way too far in the woods to hook up a traditional landline." As I said, I'm a survivalist."

"What do you do in case of an emergency?" she posed to her savior.

"The first three years I came up solo, I brought a Sat phone with me, but I never needed it. Given how expensive they are to use, I didn't bother after that."

"The solitude is the best part. Being here for six months a year allows me to take advantage of a couple of different hunting seasons. We get a lot of wildlife out here. Squirrels and deer mostly, but two years back, there was a black bear. Word around town is that there is a wolf pack out there, but I'll be damned if I've seen any evidence. Usually, I get one trophy buck a year, and then subsist on the meat for months."

Karen noticed that the man's hands had begun to shake furiously. The last of the dark clouds had finally drifted away, and the powerful light of the full moon now filled both front windows.

The stranger fell to the ground and began to seize. Hair began to push its way through his ragged flannel. His face began to elongate, taking more of a snout-like shape. Foam spewed forth from his mouth as if he were rabid. Karen's mind raced, trying to make sense of what was happening. His eyes, which had gone yellow and catlike, glared into her face.

"Run!" he shouted. Karen turned and ran for the door.

Outside, a wolf howled.

Crunch

Crunch.

That was the sound Phil's right bumper made when his car came to a sudden stop. It had encountered one of the concrete pillars that marked the end of the space in the Home and Garden Warehouse parking lot. It was typical of the way his day had been going. He awoke to the foul stench of water and garbage flowing out of the kitchen sink. It wasn't the first time it had happened. The damn disposal had been on the fritz for the last couple of weeks. Having never owned garbage disposal, he had no idea what was or wasn't a good life span. He supposed he couldn't complain. Like all the appliances, the device had been new when they moved in six years ago. Had it been six years already?

Phil unbuckled his seatbelt and walked towards the front of his car. He could see the broken glass scattered about the pavement. That was going to be another fifty dollars he didn't have, assuming he'd be able to swap the light out himself. Given his recent run of luck, the new bulb would end up costing him three times that. Shaking his head in disgust, he picked up the larger pieces and tossed them into a nearby trash can. He pushed the auto-lock on the key fob, and the car responded with a quick honk of the horn. He turned towards the store's main entrance and headed inside.

"Welcome to Home and Garden Warehouse. My name is Jeff, is there something I can help you with today."

Phil gave a quick up and down of the smiling young man in front of him. His hair was askew and the whites of his eyes were bloodshot. The remnants of his lunch had left a dark grease stain over the GAR section of his apron. Phil had his doubts, but proceeded anyway.

"Well, Jeff, I hope you can. The garbage disposal in my kitchen sink has crapped out, and I need to replace it. Can you point me in the right direction?"

He watched as what was surely a regularly practiced look of confusion set over the kid's face as if he had never been asked that question before.

"Um, I think it's aisle nine, maybe ten, but I'm pretty sure it's nine."

Phil thanked the young man, not wanting to confuse him any further, and headed down the central aisle, scanning the numbers and headings on the signs as he made his way through the store. Surprisingly, it turned out the kid was right. At the end of aisle nine, Phil came face to face with a more staggering variety of garbage disposals than he could have imagined. There was quickly no doubt; he was in way over his head.

He remembered his first time seeing the apartment on Springhill. The two of them had been married for four weeks when they came across the ad online. They both knew it was a good neighborhood with excellent schools and a state-of-the-art hospital all within a quick walk. It was Jessie who reached out and scheduled the original appointment with the owner. It was Jessie who signed the original lease before he had even seen the place. She decided that this was where they were going to live. Looking back on it, she made a lot of decisions like that. The apartment had both a full kitchen and dining room, one and a half bathrooms, and, most importantly, two bedrooms. As a writer, Phil needed a space to build an office that he can work from. Their things were being boxed and moved in before he had even stepped foot over the threshold.

Typically, before purchasing anything, Phil would do his homework. He would spend hours online comparing items and prices, figuring out what store contained the best combination of the two. This time, however, Phil didn't have the luxury. He needed to find a disposal and get back to the house as quickly as possible. The last thing he needed to add to his day was sewage water soaking into and through the kitchen floor. He was reading the back of his third choice when a friendly voice rose from behind him.

"Looking for a new disposal?"

Phil turned, expecting to find another blank-faced young person in a purple smock, He was surprised to see the opposite.

"Yeah," Phil replied. The old one shit the bed this morning. Any advice?"

"Well, there are a couple of ways you can go. If you're looking for a standard unit that will take care of normal food waste, I would recommend one of the Waste King 600 series. They have one-half horsepower and usually run about $150-$175 dollars. From there, you can go up to the Waste King 800 series, which runs about $250."

Phil took one of the Waste King boxes down from the shelf and did a quick scan of the box's back.

"Now, of course, if you're looking for something with a little more oomph, I would suggest the Insinkerator Evolution. It has a full one horsepower and will crush pretty much any food waste you can put in it. Apple cores, peach pits, chicken bones, the Insinkerator will handle it all. It's the one I use in my house, and I have never had a problem. Of course, it's a bit pricey compared to any of the Waste King models, but I swear to you friend that you'll know where the money went."

Phil replaced the Waste King and brought down an Insinkerator. At $350, it was considerably more than he had been planning to spend, but from the way the bearded stranger praised the device, Phil went with his gut and placed the disposal in his cart.

"Thanks for the advice. This does seem like exactly what I'm looking for. The old one just wasn't powerful enough." Phil extended his hand to the stranger.

"Name's Jason Pearson. Pearson Contracting," the man said, accepting Phil's shake. "Hey listen, buddy, do you need a hand with the install? I'm a licensed contractor, and I'm in between jobs on the schedule right now. It shouldn't take me any more than an hour. Let's say a hundred bucks if that works for you?"

Phil paused for a moment to consider the offer. When he had left the apartment a half-hour ago, the smell was truly unbearable. He opened up the windows in the kitchen and living room. Whatever had been sitting in the sink's u-trap must have been there for a couple of days. He didn't really want to introduce a stranger to the vile odor emanating from the apartment. At the same time, however, he did not have the slightest idea of how he would go about actually installing this thing.

"That sounds great," Phil stated. "Why don't you meet me in the parking lot when you're done, and you can follow me over to the house."

"That sounds great, pal. I'll meet you out there in about ten minutes."

As Phil walked to the front of the store, his mind drifted back to Jessie and the apartment.

They had been living there for four years when he started work on his novel. Previously he had made his living writing articles and short stories for a variety of websites and magazines. The pay wasn't great, but coupled with Jesse's work at the clinic; they were able to keep their heads above water. It certainly wasn't the life he had foreseen for himself when he graduated college with a degree in English. Like most young authors, Phil had his eyes set on being a novelist. He was going to write the great American novel and become world renown. The problem with his plan was that to write a book, you first need to have an idea for one, and in four years, he had nothing.

Phil quickly swiped his credit card through the reader, waited for his receipt, and then grabbed the bag containing the new disposal. Phil thanked the cashier and headed out into the parking lot. He looked around but did not see Jason. He leaned against the wall in the front of the store. His mind drifted off again.

He awoke one night in a start, his mind racing with the idea he had spent almost a lifetime chasing. Before he was even fully awake, the names and locations had begun to fall into place. He quietly rolled out of bed, doing his best to leave Jessie undisturbed, he crept down the hall and into his office. The next thing Phil knew it was 4:30 a.m., and he was thirty pages into what would become his novel. Sadly, the rest would not come as quickly.

Out of the corner of his eye, Phil saw Jason step through the automatic doors of the Home and Garden Warehouse, and he met him halfway.

"I'm in the green Hyundai with the broken right headlight. I live at 39 Springhill Ave. Do you know the area?"

"I've got a pretty good idea where it is. I'll plug it into the GPS just in case I get lost. I'll meet you there."

Phil climbed into his car and backed out of the space; his front tires rolled over his headlight's remains, making a crunching noise. Just another reminder of ongoing frustration that was his life. His mind went back to the novel.

Despite the promising middle of the night start, it was nearly two years before Phil was ready to turn in the book's first draft. During that time, the process required the vast majority of his focus. He began to neglect the freelance work that had been instrumental in keeping the bills paid. Jessie had picked up a few additional shifts at work to help make up the shortfall. While she held out hope that they would finally catch a break with the novel's sale, Jessie was a realist and had started to become resentful of the additional responsibilities she had taken on.

Phil had little luck when it came time to shop the book around. His agent, who had been handling all his magazine work, was having a hard time drumming up any interest. The best offer they had received was a deal to print the book with no advance and a 15% royalty on each copy sold. The continued rejections, coupled with their fluctuating financial standing, began to form cracks in their relationship. Years of emotions, both good and bad, had begun to rise to the surface. For the first time in the eight years they'd shared a life together, they had started to fight. Not just the occasional disagreement or minor argument that most couples have. They had turned into voice raising, dish-throwing, door-slamming fights.

Phil pulled into his parking space outside the main entrance to the apartment complex. He hadn't even exited the car before he saw Jason pulling in behind him.

"Hey man, if I didn't say it before, I appreciate you helping me out. I want to warn you that even though I swept and mopped everything up in the kitchen, it was still smelling like roadkill when I left."

"No problem, man. You would not believe some of the nasty stuff I've seen and smelled in my twenty years of doing construction. Lead the way, my friend."

Phil retrieved the front door key from his ring and turned the heavy security lock. They rode up the elevator to the third floor. The smell from the hallway infiltrated their nasal passages the moment the door slid open. They were halfway down the hall when his neighbor, the elderly Mrs. Sloan, stuck her head out from her apartment door.

"Damn it, Phil, what is that god awful stink." the woman asked, short and abruptly.

"I am so sorry about this, Mrs. Sloan. My disposal broke at some point last night and left an awful mess. I'm taking care of it right now."

"We'll make sure you do, or I'll have to call the super." She slammed the door behind her.

"What a ball buster that woman is." Jason chuckled.

"You have no idea," Phil said with a smile. He unlocked the apartment door.

"Good lord, you weren't kidding about that stench, were you?" Jason stepped back, bringing the back of his hand to his nose.

"It's pretty bad. I'll open up some more windows if you want."

"Yeah, why don't you do that, and I'll take a look at the health hazard in your kitchen," Jason responded with a chuckle.

Phil went around the space, cracking the few windows that stayed open on their own. Some of the rooms in the apartment had no functional windows. Some had been jammed shut since they moved in. Others, including the one he did his writing in, had been unfortunate victims of the increasing animosity that his marriage had dissolved into. Once again, Phil found his mind drifting back to the spectacular failure that was his novel.

After six months, there were no better offers for his book. His agent had reached out to everybody he knew in the business and pulled every string he had, but they couldn't avoid the simple truth. The book was a bust. Three years of his life had amounted to nothing. His agent promised him he would line up some magazine work and perhaps even a script re-write for a small indie film. Phil shook the man's hand and told him he would reach out in a couple of days.

When he got home that night, Jessie was raring for a fight. The shit hit the fan the moment he walked in the door. Accusing him of breaking them and making it very clear that she was tired of supporting him. She announced that she had filed for divorce and that first thing tomorrow morning, he would need to find another place to live. Things escalated and then, most regrettably, and for the first time in his life, he struck her across the face. She fell and hit her head on the coffee table. As a thin stream of blood ran from her scalp line, she called him a bastard and slammed the door. Was that just five days ago?

Before he knew it, Jason had finished up the last of the work under the sink and was cleaning up.

"Okay, buddy, you are all set. I've got the instructions right here, and you're going to want to read them through before you dump stuff down there." the bearded man said with a smile on his face.

"Hey, listen, I appreciate you helping me out here. I'd probably be down there the rest of my life trying to hook that thing up." Phil reached into his pocket and removed $100 from his wallet. He handed it to the man.

"My pleasure. If you ever need any help with anything else, don't hesitate to call me." Jason reached his wallet from his pocket, slid the cash in, and retrieved a slightly crumpled business card.

"It's damn hard to keep these cards neat, but the info is good, and you can reach me anytime."

"Again I appreciate everything." He walked the contractor to the door.

"You may need to pick up some strong cleaner to get rid of that stink, though. That Mr. Clean shit you've got under the sink isn't going to cut it. You might want to try something like Room Shocker or Boxie Dog. Either of them will do the trick. They are expensive, but given your current situation, don't skimp out on it."

The two men shook hands one final time. Phil watched as the contractor crossed the lawn to the parking lot, turned back, and locked the door behind him.

Phil sat down at his computer and quickly found the website for Room Shocker. After a quick glance through the reviews, he ordered two bottles of the cleanser, which, as Jason had warned him, was not inexpensive. Phil then paid an obscene amount of money to have them shipped express mail, which promised a two-day delivery. He turned off his monitor, grabbed the user guide for the new disposal, and made his way to the back of the house.

A business of flies clouded the room as Phil pushed his way inside. A small group of them escaped the moment the door was open. Kevin made a mental note to grab a package of pest strips on his next warehouse trip. He walked over and plopped down into the bedside chair. He pulled the manual from his back pocket, crossed one leg over the other, and began to flip through the surprisingly low-quality pages casually.

"There was an awful lot of goddam noise out there, Phil. What the hell were you doing? I don't suppose it had anything to do with finding a job."

"Good news, sweetheart! Everything is going to work out just fine. I met a guy named Jason, and he installed the new disposal in the sink." He explained.

"Well, that's wonderful. And exactly how much did this fuck up cost me?"

"With the install and everything, it was about $450."

"Of course it was. You know if you weren't such an idiot or even any kind of real man you could have done itself. Was the contractor a good looking man? Hmm, I bet he's got the right tool for every job."

Phil took a deep breath. Her animosity towards him had undoubtedly intensified over the last week. She had been cruel to him before, frequently for no reason. Now she was just vile. He regained his train of thought and continued...

"It is supposed to be the top of the line and will handle all of our garbage."

"Our garbage? For one to generate garbage, that person would have to be home long enough to do so. Since I seem to be the only person who is concerned about our well being. It's your garbage, your incompetence, and your fucking mess out there. You do plan on doing something about that stink?"

Again he felt his ire begin to rise. It wasn't like he intentionally broke the disposal. He didn't know it couldn't handle scraps that size.

"I already have. Jason was also nice enough to suggest some cleaning products that will get rid of that awful stink. I know how bad it is. The cleaner should be here in a couple of days."

"The only thing that you seem to be good at is spending my money. Now go find yourself a way to contribute to this household. I just got off an eighteen-hour shift and do not want to be disturbed. Get lost."

A moment later, the room was quiet, and the shrill voice was no longer ringing in his head. Phil reached across the bed and picked up the hacksaw he had left on her nightstand. He pulled one emaciated wrist free from the puddle of congealed blood left on the pillowcase. He began to saw off several finger bones from the rancid corpse lying on his marriage bed. The flesh came off easily, but the bones took a little more doing. He cursed himself for failing to look for something with a little more get up and go during his visit to the warehouse. He was glad when the blood had finally run out. He gathered the scraps and headed towards the kitchen. He flipped the switch next to the sink, and the new disposal roared to life.

"I guess Jason knew what he was talking about." He said to no one in particular as he dropped the skin and bones down the sink.

They fell into the disposal with a satisfying crunch.

Fine Tuning

Willis was not one to stop at estate sales. He was not at all opposed to tag sales, loved a good auction, and from time to time, the occasional storage closeout. In his business, there was a constant need for new, used merchandise to fill his shelves. His only real issue was that the addition of the words "estate sale" usually meant 'hey sucker you're about to pay a twenty percent markup on the price of items.' When profit margins were as thin as his, that extra markup could turn an affordable gem into an unmovable dust collector that would die on his shelves. If he hadn't been returning from a dump run with an empty truck, it was a damn near guarantee he would have just kept driving when he saw the neatly printed cardboard sign attached to a telephone pole.

"Estate Sale Today. 1750 Waves Avenue. 12–6 p.m. 5/16."

A glance at the dash clock informed him it was 1:42. With nothing else on his schedule for the day, he punched the address into his GPS, took a left at the stop, and followed the dulcet tones of Cheryl, his electronic navigator.

The trip, which led him through some of Redwood's more scenic areas, took about twenty minutes. He knew he was getting close when he saw cars lining both sides of the street. It was a Saturday afternoon on a beautiful day in May. On a day like today, a sale such as this would undoubtedly draw a good size crowd. The well-placed signs and word of mouth were bound to bring out the seniors and the lookielews. He drove past the address and found a place to park the truck about a block down.

From the top of the driveway, he could see that the line of cars was not misleading. There were easily twenty to thirty people standing outside a beautiful three-story Victorian that was two hundred years old, if it was a day. He made his way down the winding drive casually browsing the handful of items moved out from the house and carefully arranged to entice possible buyers to come a little closer and see what potential treasures lay inside. Willis had learned over his fifteen years in the business that big house sales usually came in one of two types. The first kind contained hidden gems buried amongst the more pedestrian items like oil paintings of English fox hunters or pseudo-spiritual landscapes. The second kind was often the saddest. Homes that once were the pride of their community had been ignored, purchased on the cheap and turned into pseudo-slums. Each house was then split into multiple apartments, which worked out well for the landlords as often the mortgage payments due on the properties were approximately twenty-five percent of what they were collecting in rent. And with all the units using the same pipes and wiring, it was easy enough to ignore any complaints when claiming that to fix something; simply stating that to do so would be an inconvenience to the rest of the building. They ignored the accusations, and at the end of the year, there was no option to renew the lease. Given the upkeep of the house and the grounds and the neighborhood he was in, he was reasonably sure that he had discovered one of the former, which just might make it worth his time to peruse the scene.

The items displayed on the yard included some beautiful examples of the Federalist furniture movement. While certainly desirable, they were not the types of things that he had room for in his shop. If he were to purchase one, it would require a considerable amount of reorganizing, which would displace dozens of items more likely to sell. These particular pieces deserved to be in someone's home or a much bigger space than Willis could ever hope to have in his hole in the wall.

The furniture was undoubtedly the highlight of the enticing 'come closer and see what's inside' display, so he worked his way down the brick pathway and made his way to the end of the line that led to the house itself. Just ahead of him stood a pair of old hens, if he had ever seen one. They stood, keeping their heads on a swivel to cast a suspicious eye at the surrounding people. They leaned in close, speaking.

"I heard he was involved with some bad people, you know the type I mean, and one day they came to collect him."

"You do have to admit it's strange. Two years ago that author, oh what was her name, I want to say it was Susan something, goes missing without a trace while renting the house, and now Carter goes missing. I don't believe in that much coincidence. Something is not right in that house. I can't wait to get inside."

Willis had heard hundreds of different stories during his time in the business, although two people disappearing from the same house was a new one on him. From weeping widows to shifty-eyed addicts, there was always a story as to why they needed cash. Unexpected health issues, financial hardships. Emotional attachments are stirring up too many memories. Whatever the case, the result was the same every time. He would evaluate the item, make a fair offer, haggle a little bit, and then close. It's how he had made his living for the last fifteen years, and little to nothing surprised him anymore. The line to the house moved quickly, and before long, Willis found himself crossing the threshold and into an immaculate entryway.

It was clear a considerable amount of both time and money had gone into the house's upkeep. Despite being empty for several months, nothing was out of place. The sheen on the floors would lead one to believe it was twenty years old and not closer to the two hundred it actually was. The high ceiling allowed for a grandiose chandelier that could draw the eye from both the floor and as one ascended the sweeping dual staircase. The area rugs and stair runners were spotless. All the woodwork was pristine. Willis found himself thinking that it would be nice to have the kind of money it would take to buy such a house instead of being just another in a line of scavengers coming to pick the meat from the bones.

Willis, having been impressed so far with the quality of what he had seen, began to wander more of the first floor. He was making his way into the study when he overheard several voices discussing a particular piece of art. He entered the room and began casually appraising pieces in his head. A young woman in a sharp gray suit excused herself from the conversation and extended her hand as she walked towards him.

"Hello, sir. Madelyne Sinclair. Howlett, Wade, and Murdoch. We are the firm overseeing today's sale and the distribution of the remaining assets. Is there anything I can help you with today?"

Willis extended his hand to meet hers.

"Willis Sanford, pleased to meet you. I am the proprietor of Days Past over in Hanford. We specialize in antiques and oddities."

"Well, Mr. Sanford, I'm sure that if you stick around and are willing to dig a little, you'll find something that will be just the right fit. Take your time, enjoy the sale, and if you see anything that catches your eye, just let me know."

"Thank you, Ms.Sinclair. To be honest, I rarely attend estate sales. They tend to offer items at a markup that makes it difficult for me to resell for a profit."

"Let's not worry about money right now. Take your time and look around. I can assure you that everything is negotiable."

"If you don't mind me asking, what happened to the owner?"

"Honestly, Mr. Sanford, I don't have the slightest idea. My firm has represented him for years. He was here one day and gone the next. I know that two weeks ago, my boss handed me the file on the sale. He told me we had two days to sell whatever we could and that anything left over would be del, um, destroyed. I know that a contract to purchase the house is ready to be signed once the house is empty. That's why I've got wiggle room on the prices."

"Sounds like a motivated buyer to me. Why don't I go take a look around, and if something jumps out at me that will work for my place, I'll find you, and we'll see what we can work out."

Willis again shook hands with the young lawyer and began to investigate the first floor further.

Every room in the house was just as impressive as the one before it. Decadent furniture filled each room as if it had been specifically designed for it. The brass on the light fixtures was polished to a beautiful shine while forty-watt bulbs helped add to the room's ambiance. Various stone and bronze busts, some of whom he recognized, stood on marble pillars throughout the house. Paintings, some of which were well known to even an art ignoramus like himself. Willis didn't know who the previous occupants were, but it was pretty clear they enjoyed a lavish lifestyle.

Willis had just about given up on finding anything worthwhile when he opened the only closed door. With a twist of the knob and a slight nudge from his shoulder, the door swung open. The inside was stark white, as were the sheets that covered a variety of items of various sizes. Willis pulled back the coverings to reveal, unsurprisingly, furniture that would be out of his price range and occupy way too much floor space back at the shop. The item under the last sheet had finally convinced him that this stop was a good idea.

The item in question was a piano. It was not a grand or baby grand style, but an upright. Upon taking a closer look, Willis saw the manufacturer's mark, Decker Brothers of New York, and even more fascinating was the date, 1886. Willis had taken piano lessons twice a week from the time he was eight until he was fourteen. Some of it had stuck, so Willis pulled out the bench.Placing his hands on the keys, he struck a C chord, and the room with a terrible flat sound.

"Beautiful, isn't she? It's just too bad she sounds like somebody running over a goose."

Willis turned his head to see Ms. Sinclair standing in the doorway and not knowing why he requested a price.

Quickly shuffling through a stack of papers attached to a clipboard, Sinclair removed a single sheet.

"Here it is. 1886 Decker Brothers Upright Piano. Hmm, that's weird."

"What's that?"

"Well, it says here that the piano's last tuning was three months ago, but from what I just heard, it seems like it was a lot longer ago than that. Must be a mistake on the listing."

"Getting it tuned isn't that big of a deal. If the price is right, I'm sure I can turn this around in my shop."

"The listing shows an asking price of $400. I have a rough idea of the cost of a good tuning, I could let you have it for $250."

Willis didn't know what it was about the piece. It was certainly more substantial than many of the items he had already passed on, but he knew he had to have it. Before Willis knew it, his wallet was in his hand. He counted out $250 and handed it to Sinclair. She gave him the clipboard and indicated where to sign. She signed a second copy and handed it over, and just like that, Willis was now the proud, if not the slightly confused owner of a horribly out of tune antique piano. He headed back to the truck, pulled it slowly down the driveway, and loaded his new acquisition into the bed. Ensuring everything was secure, he slipped in behind the driver's wheel and headed back home to Hanover.

His luck continued to run on the right side. He had arrived at the shop, and with the help of his right-hand man Lamont Jones, unloaded the new piece moments before the sky turned dark. A rumble of thunder so intense it rattled the store windows was followed by a deluge of rain that violently slammed into the metal service door that only moments before was wide open. From the inside, it sounded as if a war had just begun in the alley. The two men rolled the piano into the storeroom at the back of the shop, locked the door, and headed out front.

Kit sat behind the register, indifferently flipping through an issue of Time magazine that was already old before she was born. She had been working at Days Past for the last six months.

While Willis did not make it a habit of employing the children of employees, Kit was Lamont's oldest, and he had known the girl since she was a baby. When Lamont came to him and asked if Kit could join the team, he agreed under the condition that it would not affect her schoolwork. Any dip in grades, and the deal was off. All parties agreed to the stipulation, and since that time, she had been both a model student and employee.

"Hey, boss-man. Hey, daddy."

"Hey, Kit. Did I miss anything exciting while I was gone?"

"Nope. Sold a couple of records to that creepy looking guy with the unibrow."

"That would be Stan. He's been shopping here pretty much since I opened the doors. Anything else?"

"Just a box of dusty old books. Most of them were hardcovers by well-known authors. I gave the old lady ten bucks for the box. Even if we get a dollar a book, we still stand to make a couple of bucks on the deal. How about you? Any great finds in the wild?"

Willis flipped through the dusty, water-stained box. Lots of ordinary stuff. King, Koontz, Patterson, a couple of those yearly anthologies from Printer's Ink. The girl was getting smart to the business. Ten dollars for the box was more or less what he would have paid for it.

"Actually, yes. On my way back from a dump run, I came across an estate sale. Not usually my thing, but that little voice in my head told me it would be worthwhile. So now we are the proud owners of an 1886 Decker Brothers stand up piano. It sounds like shit, I'm going to need to find a tuner to come out, but it's a beautiful instrument in excellent condition."

"Let me ask you this oh wise and benevolent leader, where the hell are we going to put a piano?" Kit inquired.

Willis did have to admit that he hadn't thought that far ahead. He still wasn't sure why he bought the damn thing in the first place. It was like it had called to him.

"Haven't gotten that far in the plan yet, kiddo. I know for sure that it needs to be tuned before we even think about making a home for it on the floor."

The grandfather clock in the corner of the room began to chime, indicating that it was now six o'clock, and that meant it was time to call it a day. Kit grabbed the draw from the register and gathered the day's credit card receipts. Every night she worked, she threw a rubber band around the paperwork, placed it in an empty slot in the cash drawer, and put it on Willis' desk.

"Hey man, we're taking off unless you need anything else?" Lamont hollered towards the back of the store."

"No, I'm good. You two get home safe. Lamont, I'll see you tomorrow morning. Kit, enjoy your day off, and good luck with that Trig test."

"Thanks, boss-man."

Willis heard the front doorbell chime, followed by the sound of a key turning a lock. Flipping the switches in the hallway turned off the front room lights and neon signs in the display windows.

He headed down the hall and into his office.

A quick shuffle through the rubber-banded slips of paper, Willis could see what Kit had meant. Some days you payout more than you take in. Today wasn't one of those days, but it was pretty close. In all the years that had passed since he opened Days Past, he had always walked the razor's edge when it came to profits. He knew he would never get rich selling chotskies and people's old prom dresses, but he had thought things would be a little more comfortable than this. Every month when he ran the numbers, it was disheartening. He could keep the lights on, pay his staff, and occasionally purchase an item such as the Decker piano.

"BZZZZZZZZZZ"

The sudden ring of the rear service bell brought him back to the present.

"BZZZZZZZZZ." The door chimed a second time.

Willis reached over to the stack of monitors on his desk and turned on the one for the rear door. He wasn't sure what he was looking at. In the camera frame was a man. At least it looked like a man. It had the shape of a man, but something was blurring the details. Willis clicked the microphone to the on position.

"I'm sorry, sir, but we are closed. We are open from nine a.m. to six p.m. If you want to come back tomorrow, we'll be more than happy to help you."

Willis gave the top of the monitor a good thumping, and for a moment, the picture cleared. He was right about the nocturnal visitor being a man. The character in question was on the short side, heavily bespectacled, and wearing a simple brown suit. He held what appeared to be a suitcase or some type of traveling salesman case in his left hand.

"You misunderstand my intentions, Mr. Sanford; I am not here as a customer, I've come to help you."

"This is getting stranger by the second." Willis thought to himself.

"I believe you are familiar with Madelyn Sinclair. I understand the two of you met earlier today and completed a transaction. Am I correct?"

Willis began to feel unsettled. This man, whom he had never seen before, seemed to have an awful lot of information about the day's activities.

"I believe you purchased a delightful antique piano that is desperately in need of a tuning. My name is William Balaam, and I am the finest piano tuner around in my not so humble opinion. Mr. Sanford, I'm here to help you. Can we talk in person?"

Willis was always cautious when it came to letting anyone after dark. He had been robbed three years prior. No one was hurt, and the robber walked out with less than one hundred dollars. Ever since that day, the policy was once the store was closed; it was closed. Tonight, though, everything seemed different. The gentleman at the back door certainly didn't look like a criminal, and there was no air of menace around him. Willis pressed the buzzer to unlock the back door and headed back to meet the unexpected Mr. Balaam.

The skewed image from the security camera proved reasonably accurate. As the two men approached each other, Willis saw that Mr. Balaam was indeed on the short side. At only 5'10" himself, Willis felt as if he was towering over the man. His glasses were thicker than the camera had let on. The case he held in his left hand was most certainly a salesman's case.

"Thank you for taking the time to speak with me, Mr. Sanford."

"Well, Mr. Balaam, you seem to have me at a slight disadvantage. How exactly did you get my name?"

"That is an excellent question, Mr. Sanford. Allow me to explain. As I mentioned earlier, I am a piano tuner, perhaps the finest in the world. I specialize in antiques. Over the years, I have established a group of contacts that keep me apprised of the sale of certain vintage pieces. Madelyne Sinclair is one of the contacts. She called me early today and informed me you had purchased the Decker upright. A fine, fine instrument and one that I am most familiar with. Can you take me to it?" Willis led the strange little man into the warehouse and to the piano. Willis could have sworn he saw Balaam's eyes light up.

"Ah, the 1886. I haven't seen this beauty in years. Do you mind?"

Willis nodded his head and gestured with his hand to go ahead.

The piano tuner brought his hand down on the keys, striking a simple C chord. The sound that came from the Decker was atrocious.

"That's one sick girl you have there, Mr. Sanford. Very sick indeed. How much do you know about her history?"

Willis explained he knew very little about the piano. He admitted to Balaam that he wasn't even sure why he purchased it. Such an oversized piece was a difficult sell in his shop, but there was just something about the piano that called to him.

"There was one odd thing, though. According to the paperwork Ms. Sinclair handed me, the piano received a tuning three months ago. I'm no expert, but that doesn't sound like three months to me."

"You are quite correct, Mr. Sanford. Based on my knowledge of the Decker Brothers and this particular piano, it is my professional opinion that this poor girl has seen no attention in at least thirty years. She needs some TLC."

"While I appreciate you stopping by Mr. Balaam, the piano's purchase has stripped me of any petty cash. I hadn't planned on getting the work done for at least a few weeks. Can we schedule a time for you to come back once I've got some cash together?"

"Mr. Sanford, again, you misunderstand my presence here. I'm not here to sell you any kind of service. I don't do what I do for money, Mr. Sanford. I have seen many works of art destroyed in the name of commerce. I am here to tune this magnificent instrument—nothing more, nothing less. I ask for no compensation, nor would I accept any. Now then, my watch reads 6:30 p.m. and time's a-wasting.

Am I correct in assuming that Ms. Sinclair did not provide you with the key to open the back panel?"

"No, sir. What you see is what I got. Should there have been more pieces?"

"It doesn't matter. I've been doing this for a long time and have seen this beauty frequently over the years." Balaam turned his back to Willis and opened up his case. The inside was full of various wires, keys, tuning forks, and several things he could not identify. Balaam pulled a key from one of the small drawers and inserted it into the piano's back. It was, of course, a perfect fit.

Upon first meeting the unusual Mr. Balaam, still no first name, Willis felt at ease. His unexpected guest seemed enthusiastic about the opportunity to work on the piano. It was the way he spoke about the instrument that had started to make Willis uncomfortable. He talked about it as if the two were inextricably linked. He looked back to see Balaam removing several additional tools from their tiny drawers.

"Now, Mr. Sanford, I'd like to ask that you leave me to my work. The art of tuning a piano is precise, and any outside noise or distractions can lead to failure. I'm sure you understand."

Once again, Willis felt as if a fog had floated in and engulfed his brain. This man he doesn't know wants to be left alone in the warehouse. Sure, why would that be a problem?

"Sure thing Mr. Balaam. I'll head up to my office. Let me know if you need anything else." Willis turned and headed up the ramp and three stairs that lead into the back office.

Now alone, Balaam began his work. He turned the key to the left and removed the back panel from the machine. Absentmindedly, he reached for the power button on his headlamp, Balaam started to mumble to himself as he began the examination.

Any suspicions Willis might have had about Balaam and his connection to the piano would have been put to rest had he been present to watch the man work. The mumbling continued as his hands moved with certainty and inhuman speed. He knew this instrument, of that there could be no question. After two hours, he slid the rear panel back on, locked it, and called Willis.

"Mr. Sanford, I am proud to announce that this beautiful instrument now sounds as good as she looks. She is tuned perfectly and should need no further assistance for quite some time. As the owner, I would like you to be the first to hear how she sounds." He gestured towards the bench in front of the keyboard.

Willis felt that foggy feeling return as he walked towards the piano. He placed three fingers on the keyboard. The three that make up a simple C chord. He brought them down, and the most perfect C he had ever heard echoed throughout the warehouse. That's when the world went black.

Splash!

Suddenly, Willis was aware that his face was wet. He did his best to pivot his head to get a better idea of where he might be; all he did see was cowboy boots and spurs.

"All right, boy, on your feet."

He felt two hands grab him under the arms and ferociously drag him upward.

"Boy, do you know how truly and completely fucked you are? We'll come back around to whatever you're wearing there, but there is a much bigger issue we need to talk about first."

Willis looked around and, for a moment, could not make his eyes and brain agree about what he was seeing. He was in a jailhouse. At least that's what the rack of rifles and the cells would suggest. The floor smelled like a combination of chewing tobacco spit and horse shit. How did he end up in a jailhouse?

"You gotta name?" was followed up by a sharp punch to his ribcage.

That last shot knocked the wind out of him. He gasped, trying to catch a lungful of air, which just led to more coughing. He felt another fist find the right side of his face.

"You best answer when the Sheriff here asks you a question. Once again, do you have a name?"

"Willis. Willis Sanford."

"Well, Willis Sanford, do you understand how we do things now?"

Willis nodded, doing his best to tamp down the anger that had begun to bubble over. Another fist struck him in the stomach.

"You seem to be a slow learner, Willis. When I ask you a question, you answer. Let's try this again. Do you understand how we do things now?"

"Yes, sir. I understand now."

"Excellent! Now let's have a talk about Annie Wilkerson."

Of course, Willis had no idea where he was, let alone who the hell Annie Wilkerson was, but he did know he didn't need to take any more of a beating today.

"Sheriff, I will be more than happy to talk to you about anything you want, but may I ask one simple question before we get started?"

The Sheriff looked quizzically at the stranger who, according to patrons, just appeared out of thin air at the bar.

"I'll tell you what Willis Sanford, you ask, and I will decide whether or not I'm going to answer it."

"That sounds more than fair. All I want to know is what year is it?"

A rather boisterous laugh escaped from the mouth of the Sheriff. Followed by an actual slapping of his knee.

"Oh, son, you just made my day. You didn't need to go through all that just to ask a question like that. It's the year of our Lord 1886."

Once again, it seemed as if the world was crashing down around him. How could he possibly be in 1886? His head was still foggy from the beating he took earlier, and it hurt to focus on anything. His eyes rolled back in his head, and once again, his world was black.

The silence of his dreaming mind was interrupted by the sound of a piano, somewhere in the distance. As he ran, the music drifted farther away. Quickly running out of breath, he tripped and sprawled face-first on the cold black that he supposed was only a floor because it was how his brain wanted it. As he picked himself up, the sound of the piano returned louder than ever. He looked to his left, and there it was, the 1886 Decker. The black transitioned to blue, and Willis found himself looking out over the sea. A shadowy figure appeared, standing next to the piano bench, opening the lid and producing a pair of oars. He mounted the bench and began to row away. Willis heard a clapping sound and felt the wind on his face.

"Welcome back, son, thought we lost you there." the Sheriff offered snidely.

Willis looked around. He was lying on what used to be a cot, but over the years had become several strips of cloth pulled tight across a creaky frame. He was back in 1886.

"So now that you've rejoined us let's have that chat about Annie Wilkerson. Was this something you had planned out, or was it more spur of the moment?"

Willis was stuck on how to get through this interrogation. He wasn't from this year, let alone this town. He couldn't have picked her out of a lineup if his life depended on it, and he was starting to get the feeling that it just might.

"Well, Sheriff, I wouldn't say that it was planned. I wasn't even in this town two days ago."

"So, at what point did you come into contact with Ms. Wilkerson?"

"I don't think I have. Although I do have to admit, I'm still a little foggy from the number your boys did on me."

"Listen to me you smart ass, unless you want a repeat visit from the welcome wagon, I suggest you start talking."

"Sheriff, I can assure you that whatever happened to Ms. Wilkerson, I had nothing to do with it. The first thing I remember about being in your charming little town was waking up on the floor earlier today."

"You'll forgive me if I don't believe you. Yesterday we found the body of Annie Wilkerson in her home. She had been assaulted and then strangled with a belt.

Now it seems to me to be a hell of a coincidence that less than twenty-four hours after the discovery, you show up in town, wearing some kind of strange dungarees with no belt, I might add. Are you sure there's nothing you want to tell me?"

Willis couldn't admit to the murder of someone he had never met, but he couldn't exactly tell the Sheriff where exactly he had come from.

"I don't know what it is you want me to say, Sheriff? I never met Ms. Wilkerson, let alone killed her. It's just not possible."

The Sheriff plopped down in a chair that had seen better days. He placed his elbows on his knees and his face in his hands.

"You know Mr. Sanford; you don't seem like the violent type to me. I can usually tell when somebody has that darkness in them. I guess it just comes with years on the job. The problem is, I've got a town full of people out there who loved Annie, and they want to see justice done."

Thinking back on history, Willis knew precisely what that meant. Mob justice was quite popular during this period. Usually, it was just an excuse for the town to get rid of undesirables, but they didn't need to make up an excuse in this case. As far as they knew, this stranger was responsible for the death of a beloved citizen. If he didn't figure a way out of this, he was good and truly fucked.

"So you tell me, Mr. Sanford, what should I do in this situation? It's Friday, and the Judge is already gone. I can keep you in a cell until Monday morning and then bring you to court. That, at least temporarily, is the safest option. Our other option is I open the cell door and head into the other room and find some busy work to do."

Willis quickly processed the options that were made available to him. Assuming the Sheriff was telling the truth, he would be safe in jail over the weekend. It was the option that made the most sense. Of course, he could still be living on borrowed time, depending on the Judge's disposition. He clearly could tell no one where he had come from and exactly how he ended up in a town that looked like something out of the movie Tombstone. Taking his chances with a potential lynch mob was equally problematic. Even if he managed to avoid the crowd, he had nowhere to go and even less of an idea how to get back home.

As darkness began to fill his cell, Willis became aware of a low murmuring sound, slowly growing louder as it made its way down the main street. The glow of torches cut through the night, illuminating a path for the lynch mob coming for him.

Taking a look around, he saw the Sheriff was, in fact, nowhere in sight. With a slight push, the cell door swung open, and Willis found himself free. The light of the torches began to cast shadows on the inside of the jail. He was running out of time. A glance around the room yielded both a long coat and a plainsmen's hat. He quickly threw them on and headed towards the back of the building. The door at the end of the back hallway was what Willis had hoped it would be. He threw the door open and was immediately hit in the face with an odor that can only come from an outhouse. Willis covered his mouth and nose with a coat sleeve, and disappeared into the dark. He came to a complete stop when he heard the sound of a piano.

From the outside, he could hear the sound of rowdy drunks celebrating something or another. There were men playing cards and others playing billiards. Above all of that, the one thing that Willis could make out as clear as a bell was the slightly out of tune strains of Stephen Foster. It was his Decker. He was sure of it. He recalled his dream from earlier in the day. The Decker was in that dream, and now, having a moment to catch his breath, he remembered something about the instrument. Something that seemed like it was necessary. He stood up, buttoned his coat closed and walked into the saloon.

The smell of the saloon was better than the one from the outhouse, but not by much. Willis could tell that there had been a whole lot of drunks who didn't quite make it outback. Mix in the smell of stale beer, cigarillo smoke and chewing tobacco made for a rather unwelcoming aroma. Not wanting to draw any attention to himself, Willis found an empty table near the bar's far side and waved over a waitress.

"What'll it be, hun?" she asked. The boredom in her tone indicated she had been doing this for a long time.

"A beer would be great," Willis responded.

After a few minutes, she came back and placed his drink on the table. As she turned to leave, Willis grabbed her by the arm. She looked at him fiercely. He quickly removed his hand.

"Sorry, I didn't mean to grab you like that. I just wanted to know how long the piano player is on for."

The waitress looked up at the clock on the wall. It was 8:30 p.m.

"He should be taking a break in about a half-hour or so. Why do you ask?"

"I'm an admirer of pianos and wanted to inspect that one, but I didn't want to disturb him while playing. I guess I can stick around for a little while. Thank you, and again my humblest apologies." She offered him a quick smile and headed back to the floor. He watched her walk away.

Willis nursed his beer as the slowest half hour of his life ticked by. Uncertain what the piano had to do with the situation he found himself in, he was certain that this was the same piano he had purchased back in 2021. How it was here, however, eluded him.

While Willis sat contemplating his current position, he failed to notice the whispered conversations and over the shoulder glances. Regardless of sound quality, the piano was loud and did an excellent job of drowning out the sound of the approaching mob.

It was 8:45 when the first group came into the saloon. A quick headcount told Willis that there were five of them. They stood at the bar, conversing with the bartender. Willis could hear the mumbling of the crowd through the walls behind him. From the back of the room, the bartender nodded his head and pointed in Willis' direction. He knew they were coming for him, as sure as he knew he must reach the piano. For a moment, the room went silent, and Willis heard a heavenly sound. It was the perfect C. He knew what he had to do, sadly a bullet to the spine prevented him from doing it.

Lamont and Kit sat with their legs dangling off the cargo bay. It had been three months since the last time they had seen Willis. Since Willis had no immediate family, aside from some items named explicitly in a living will, the contents of Days Past were to be sold at auction to pay off the remainder of the lease, outstanding business debt, and subsequent tax liability. The sale was scheduled to begin tomorrow, but a law office had called the store and asked Lamont if he would mind opening the shop a day early for a private viewing. Now out of a job, and with little else to do, he agreed to the request.

A silver BMW pulled down the alley, coming to a stop in front of the cargo bay. A sharp-dressed man who appeared to be in his sixties stepped out from the passenger side, his thousand dollar shoes crunching on the gravel beneath them. On the other side of the car stepped out a stunning blonde, sharply dressed, carrying a clipboard full of papers. She closed the door and walked over to where Lamont and Kit were sitting.

"Mr. Jones, My name is Madelyne Sinclair." She stepped forward, offering her hand to him. "I'm here on behalf of Howlett, Wade, and Murdoch. We are the firm overseeing today's sale and the distribution of the remaining assets. Thank you so much for your time today. Allow me to introduce Mr. Warrington. He's come to look at the piano."

Resurrection of the Worm

It was half-past ten when Erick pulled into the parking lot of the Skid Mark Bar in Amanda. The trip across South Texas took longer than he had planned on, but he was able to hit every stop on his agenda. It had been a productive run, and if this last stop at the Skid Mark proved to be as beneficial, his business would be at an end. He had already arranged for the night's lodging, and despite the lateness of the hour, he had been assured that check in would be no issue.

The vehicles in the gravel parking lot were as he had expected. Throughout the entire trip, he came across one pickup truck after another. The older model Chevys and Fords might as well have been a neon sign. Regardless of make or manufacture, all these trucks had at least one thing in common, bumper stickers. He could count on one hand the number of vehicles that weren't sporting NRA support stickers. The same tired old slogans like "guns don't kill people" and "You can have my gun when you pry it from my cold dead hands." Nothing Erick hadn't seen a million times before, especially traveling through this section of the country. If he only needed one hand to count the lack of NRA stickers, less than one would have covered those missing the big dumb red stickers. The ones that proudly displayed the depth of ignorance and hate in the country. "Trump/Pence 2016" and in second place "MAGA." That, however, was none of his concern. He was here to sell a product, not get into a political argument in the middle of a redneck bar. He popped open the trunk, pulled out his sample case, and went inside.

The sound of honky-tonk music floated out the door as he pulled it open. The inside of the Skid Mark was more or less the same as the last five bars he had visited. The smell of stale beer and even staler urine had mingled together in a rather noxious pot-pourri. There were two gentlemen in the far corner shooting a game of pool, one rather sloppy looking fellow at the end of the bar, and one bartender behind it. It was the old sot at the end of the bar who spoke up first.

"Well, hell, Bill, look at the wetback in that fancy suit. Did you steal that suit, boy? You can tell me, I ain't going to call the police or nothing, I just want to know where a beaner like you gets a suit like that."

"Will you shut up with that shit, Bobby. We don't know the first thing about this young man. Let's see what he has to say."

The goings-on at the bar drew the attention of the two pool players who put down their cues and staggered slightly over to the bar.

"Everything okay over here, Bill? This spic giving you any trouble? Say the word, and I'll bounce his ass right back to that shit stain of a country he came from." The larger of the two, who, according to the stitched name tag on his shirt, was named Willie.

"Yeah, everything is fine. I'm a bit disappointed in the lack of hospitality you boys have shown. I'm sorry for all that noise. My name is Bill Winston, and I own this here establishment. The man offered his hand across the bar.

"Pleasure to meet you, Bill. My name is Erick Sanchez."

"So tell me, Erick Sanchez, what brings you out to our dusty little patch of Texas?"

"Well Bill, I've spent the last week driving through small-town Texas visiting dive bars, honkey tonks, Country and Western joints. If there was a bar in a town, I assure you I saw it."

"That is an awful lot of bars. He was probably robbing them all. Explains where he got the suit from." Bobby offered from the corner.

"Bobby, I swear to god if you don't shut the fuck up, I'll beat you with a club. Besides, he doesn't look like a thief to me." Bill cut in. "He looks like a salesman."

Erick raised his index finger and tapped his nose, indicating that Bill was right on the money.

"Can't slip one past you can I?" Erick offered with a grin on his face.

"Well, mister, I can save you some time upfront and let you know we don't have much need for anything. We have a usual supply chain that provides our booze and such. Napkins, straws, and all that stuff come from a different supplier."

"That's understandable. Out here in the scrubs, there must not be that many options for provisions."

Erick took a glance around the room. The pool players were now sitting opposite Bobby at the other end of the bar.

"I respect that level of loyalty. It's what makes good business partners. I'd like to be partners with you, Bill. I think you'll find that I can provide you with a superior product."

"As I said, we're pretty well taken care of, but since you drove out this way, and the welcome you received, why don't you go ahead and show us what you've got."

"That's all I ask for," Erick said, the grin on his face widening even further.

Erick walked over to the front door, where he had left his case. With one hand, he picked up the case while the other took a glance at his watch. He slid the sample case over to the middle of the bar and popped open the locks. On the inside, surrounded in a nest of custom cut foam, was a single, half-filled crystal bottle.

"Gentlemen, what you see here in front of you is the absolute finest Tequila you will find anywhere on this earth." From the corner of his eye, Erick noticed the nervous glance between Bill and a now much more alert Bobby.

"Well that figures," Willie spoke up, "A beaner selling beaner juice. You say the word Bill, and he's out of here."

Bill dismissed the man with a wave.

"Go ahead, son. I apologize for that big dummy."

"In Mexico, we named this particular batch in honor of my PaPa; we call it "resurrección del gusano" It is a family recipe that dates back three hundred years. I can assure you, gentlemen, you have never tasted a Tequila like this."

"If that's Tequila, where's the damn worm?" Bobby managed almost coherently.

"Actually, my friend, you are thinking of Mezcal. There are no worms in Tequila."

Bobby mumbled something incomprehensible and kept his eyes focused on Bill. He knew better than to make a move without Bill going first.

"Well, that's a mighty fancy story you got there, Erick, but as I said, we're pretty well taken care of."

"I appreciate you giving me your time. Before I go, why don't you set up four shot glasses and a glass of seltzer water."

Bill grabbed four clean shot glasses from behind the bar and a tall glass that he filled with seltzer. Erick removed the exquisite bottle from its case, carefully removing the bejeweled topper, and poured four perfect shots.

"Gentlemen, Nos vemos en el otro lado," Erick offered, raising his glass of seltzer."

"Hey, we don't speak no Mexican in this bar!" Willie spoke up.

"My apologies. All I meant was that I'd see you on the other side."

The four men at the bar slammed down their shots.

"Damn, son, that was just as smooth as the last time I had it." Bill offered. "That must have been about three years ago. That sound about right, Bobby?"

"Should have been a damn worm in it. I told that wetback the same thing last time." Bobby said, sounding more alert.

There was additional praise from the two other men occupying the bar, with more of the same vitriol that he had experienced since walking in.

Erick knew approximately how much time he had left, and he was confident in what was about to occur. He watched as Willie and his partner in crime made their way over to the door. Erick heard the turn of a deadbolt.

"Well, gentlemen, the clock on the wall tells me it's time to hit the road. Gotta get back to the family and all." Erick closed the lid on his sample case and carefully slid it off the bar top. That's when he heard the gun cock.

"Just a fucking minute there you god damn taco head. That's a mighty fine case you've got there and an even finer bottle of booze. Why it looks almost identical to this one." Billy reached under the bar and came back up with a matching container. "Matter of fact, I got it from someone who looked a lot like you. Of course, you do all kind of look alike, so who's to say. He put up one hell of a fight. I'll tell you what."

Erick glanced down at this watch. Two minutes to go.

"Well, boys, let me tell you a story, and then we can discuss when and how I'll be leaving this little slice of heaven."

"Talk quick wetback; you're running out of time." Said Billy.

"You see, in 1720, my family was living in Jalisco. That's in Mexico, but I figure you've already assumed that. For years the family worked the land for a man by the name of Alejandro Ortiz. Ortiz was a good man, and from what I've seen of the family history, several generations of the Sanchez family served the household."

Erick saw Bobby raise his head from the bar top and begin to rub his eyes.

"So in 1770 Ortiz passed, and since he had no immediate family, he set a provision in his will that all properties connected to his estate be passed to his faithful servants. From that point on, my family began formulating a new Tequila from the excellent quality Agave; they had been growing on the land for over fifty years. The technique has been passed down from father to son ever since."

Erick turned his head towards Billy and could see the shotgun he had pointed at him was starting to shake in one hand while the other began scratching at the skin on his forearm.

"This went on for hundreds of years. Every generation of Sanchez men begins by working in the fields. Once they've reached a certain age, they become crop harvesters or in my language, a "jimador." The Agave harvest is one of the most physically intense and demanding agricultural tasks there are. The plants are mature after 7-10 years. Each Agave plant must be dug from the ground by hand, to prevent damage to the fleshy piña. The jimador then uses a unique tool called a coa to slice off the leaves until they are left with a bare, white ball. Once the crop was prepared, it was turned over to the Sanchez women who were the keepers of the family secrets, including the recipe. Once the batch was processed, we distilled it and allowed it to age. The two elders of the village are responsible for the bottle design for each unique batch. We have always distilled in small batches and sold them in bottles like the one you have seen tonight, and the one you stole from my father when you killed him."

Jack and Willie had joined Billy in vigorously scratching their arms. Even Bobby had slid off the barstool and was nails deep into his right cheek.

"Three years ago, my PaPa was just wrapping up his route when he pulled into the parking lot right outside. I know this is true because his GPS records show that this was the last stop he ever made."

Blood started to rise to the skin in droplets as Billy's fingernails had opened up a hole in his arm.

"It's taken me a long time to put this whole thing together. So let me ask you a question, my friend…"

From the end of the bar, Bobby let out an agonizing scream and fell to the floor, pulling out handfuls of hair.

"Get it out of me! Get it out!"

"You see Billy; I wasn't sure what had happened until I walked in the door. Then it all made sense. You see a guy with brown skin and a nice suit, and you automatically assume he's a thief or a conman. Did you even give him a chance to make his pitch, or did you just kill him outright? I'm guessing you didn't do it yourself. I'm guessing these two ass clowns were in on it." Erick said, pointing at Willie and Jack, who were now writhing on the ground as their skin began to flake off in chunks from their arms and chests.

Billy opened his mouth to reply, but all that came out were bits of the esophageal lining and a dark red pool of blood.

"My PaPa was going to be the last in the family line to take up the business. When he went missing, I was away at school, studying to receive my Masters in Infectious Diseases with a specialty in Parasites."

Blood had begun gushing from Billy's nose, and a closeup look into his eyes revealed something was causing them to pulse.

"Thing is fellows; I wasn't exactly completely forthcoming with you before. All Tequila brands available for whole or retail sales do not contain a worm. However, this Tequila right here, well, that's a special batch. It took me two years to get it right."

The shattering of bar mirror glass followed the sound of a shotgun blast. Erick turned just in time to see Billy the Bartender's eyes get pushed out of his sockets from the inside. White larvae followed behind them, creeping down his face, eating away at the ejected tissue on the way down.

Willie began to cough heavily. A deep hacking cough indicated something was blocking his windpipe. With one mighty heave, a stream of larvae exploded in a geyser of blood and teeth. The sides of his mouth puffed out like a squirrel carrying nuts. The effect did not last long as his cheeks cracked open, and a flood of bugs engulfed his already disfigured face and began boring its way through his skull.

Jack was never a believer in the idea of karma, and at the moment that was quite unfortunate, as it might have allowed him to understand what was happening to him. His feet had begun to swell minutes after taking the shot, but as he had high blood pressure, he dismissed the feeling. Now, ten minutes later, he regretted making that choice. Half-blind, he began to tear at his feet, doing everything he could to get his boots off. The pressure that was building on the inside of his boots had cut off the circulation to his feet. His fingers clawed at the laces of the battered footwear, digging in with such ferocity that he lost three fingernails to the leather. Jack's eyes and ears were bleeding, and a stream of the larvae worked its way out of his nasal passages. There was a popping sound, and he found that the pressure in his left foot was suddenly and violently relieved. One last tug at his boot and it finally slid off taking with it a colony of bugs and his foot.

Erick turned to face the last man in the bar, still breathing.

"From the moment I walked through the door, I knew you were involved in it."

Bobby was capable of only primal grunts in response.

"Yeah, well, I'll tell you this much, Bobby, you wanted a worm, and you got it, pal. Say hello to Caenorhabditis elegant, this little fellow thrives in and on alcohol. They're very tiny, and there were probably a couple thousand in that one shot you took. From the minute that you downed that shot, they began a rapid gestation period. Time is a curious thing when you are microscopic. I probably don't need to tell you this, but you're going to die now. It really is too bad you were such a jackass in life."

Bobby grabbed at his throat, tearing it open as the bugs made their way out.

Erick grabbed his case off the bar top, turned off the lights, and headed out the door.

Central Monitoring

He reached the door in the middle of the third ring. Despite the distortion caused by the beveled glass on the front door, it was clear that his visitor was a young man in the dark blue jumpsuit often associated with field service workers. The embroidered patch on the left breast pocket confirmed that this particular young man was a representative of Rampart Security Company. On the opposite side of his chest, a smaller and less impressive patch revealed that the kid's name was Tommy. He was here to install the new security system.

The previous Tuesday, as he was leaving the house, he found himself face to face with the affable Debbie Richards, local sales representative for RSC. She approached with her hand outstretched, a business card tucked away in her palm.

"Hi there! I'm Debbie Richards and I represent Rampart Security Company. I've been going door to door, talking to your neighbors and really getting a feel for the needs of your community. This is a beautiful home you have. If you don't mind me asking, how long have you been living here?"

Robert paused for a moment, the mathematical gymnastics going through his head.

"Not terribly long, as a matter of fact. My family and I just moved in a couple of months ago. My name is Robert Revell, it's a pleasure to meet you. Would you like to have a seat?" He gestured towards two empty rockers sitting on the front porch.

"Iced tea?"

One hour and two glasses of iced tea later, Debbie left with a down payment check and a scheduled appointment for the following Wednesday. That was today. He opened the door.

"Hello, are you Mr. Revell?" The young man asked, flipping through papers on his clipboard.

"Yes, I'm Robert Revell, are you from Rampart?"

"Yes, sir. My name is Tommy. I've got an order here for a full house installation, is that correct?"
Revell reached into his back pocket and came out with his copy of the contract he had signed with Debbie.

"Debbie sold me on this package. She said it was the best one on the market." He handed the paperwork over to Tommy, who gave it a passing glance. He had seen the sales flier dozens of times.

"Everything looks to be in order. Let me grab my gear and I'll get started,".

"That sounds great. How long do you think?"
Tommy looked at the clock on his phone, hard, like the math was difficult for

him. Revell could see the wheels spinning in his head.

"A couple of hours, three at most. I install a lot of these systems." Tommy offered as he headed back out to the driveway. Moments later he returned, pushing a handcart full of boxes of various sizes, each stamped with a logo identical to the one on his breast pocket. The sheer volume of equipment that was to be involved surprised Revell.

"That can't all be for me? It seems like an awful lot of gear."

Tommy double checked the work order and confirmed the batch numbers on the form to the boxes. Everything was in order.

"Yeah, this is all you. The order is for a full home installation. Is that a problem?" Tommy inquired.

Revell ran through the scenario in his head. It was now one o'clock. He was due at work by five-thirty, meaning he needed to leave by five. He explained the time frame to Tommy, who once again assured him he would be done and cleaned up before Revell needed to leave.

Revell was the type of customer that installers absolutely hate. He followed Tommy through the house, harping about the camera placements, many of which were unusual. "They need to be well hidden, or my kids'll freak out."

"Nice parenting," Tommy thought. But he didn't care. He had two things on his mind: He had a joint packed with the finest bud in Hanford, and his mom was making breakfast for dinner tonight. He had zero interest in postponing either longer than necessary.

"So if you don't mind me asking, what made you decide on the 'Safe Space' package? It seems like a lot more security than a house this size requires."

"Truth be told, Tommy, we just moved in last month. My wife was having some issues with a former co-worker, and it turned into a rather nasty stalker situation. There were a couple of break-ins, unwanted packages, phone calls at all hours. All of which made staying in that house quite complicated. We just want to put it all behind us and start a new life here in Hanford."

"Wow, man, that's pretty fucked up right there. Oh, shit my bad."

"Don't worry about it kid, everybody says fuck every once in a while." Revell did his best to stifle a chuckle. The next hour went by quickly, without further inquiries from either man. Tommy found Revell sitting at the kitchen table.

"All right, Mr. Revell, everything is up and running. I'm sending you a text with a link to follow to complete your setup." Tommy handed Revell a rectangular box. "In here is your user guide, warranty information, window clings and a lawn sign. I don't know if Debbie mentioned it, but if you leave the sign up for a month, the company will give you $25 for every customer who signs up using the unique QR code in the lower left-hand corner. Never hurts to spread the word, I guess. Anything else I can do for you before I get gone?"

Revell shook his head and handed the signed paperwork over to Tommy. He walked the young man to the door, thanking him for his hard work. Revell watched as the young man climbed into his van and drove down the street.

The clock on the wall read 4:45. Revell ran through the final installation process on his phone and verified that all the cameras were active and that they covered 98% of the home. Satisfied with the job, he grabbed the box Tommy had left from the kitchen table. Revell headed out the front door, stopping long enough to lock up. Using the remote starter, his car sprung to life. Revell approached the rear of the vehicle, tossing the box into the trunk. He came around and climbed into the driver's seat. Moments later, the car was out of sight.

At 5:25, Karen Williams pulled into her driveway. With a client buzzing in her ear, her arms filled with files and her two children running in circles around her feet, she missed not only the muddy size twelve boot prints on the entry room runner but more importantly she missed the dim green light leaking from the side of a framed picture on the wall near the front door. It was the light that showed someone had activated the security system.

Car Note

Monday.

  Kirk Williams had no reason to dislike Mondays. He wasn't a lasagna eating cat, nor had he ever 'had a case of the Mondays.' For him, it was just the start of the work week. Between moving to the city and starting his new position with Howlett, Wade, and Murdoch, his weekends were being used to familiarize himself with his new clients. That and the ongoing promise that this would be the weekend he ultimately finished unpacking. Well, there was always next weekend. After three months, he had dug himself into a nice little rut, and it kept his life simple.

  This Monday, however, was peculiar. He had traveled to see his folks back home for the weekend, only to have his car break down en route. Because of his location and the poor cellular service, it was more than an hour before a tow truck arrived. Once they pulled into town, he called his folks to let them know what was happening. His father offered to come get him, but the sun was going down, and he knew his old man shouldn't be behind the wheel after dark. He told his dad to stay put and that he would be there directly. The mechanic informed him he would have to go over to the next town to pick up the parts he required. He would have to go in the morning, as the parts store had already closed.

  Further adding to the shit pile his day was becoming, the mechanic came out and brought with him an estimate for $2200. Since he couldn't get by without his car and since there was one mechanic in their little town, $2200 it was. With a swipe of his credit card, he paid the mechanic $1100, half the total balance, signed the slip, grabbed his overnight bag from the trunk, and walked the four blocks from the garage to his parent's house.

  Saturday had been going remarkably well until the mechanic called. He was still waiting on the parts, so the job was going to take longer than forecast. His car would not be fixed until later on Sunday afternoon.

  This disclosure was the absolute last thing Kirk needed. If he didn't get his car back until Sunday afternoon, he wouldn't get back to the city until late. The delay was going to wreak havoc on his morning program. Sometimes the best of intentions led to a string of unavoidable calamities.

  Despite his late arrival home and what was shaping up to be a busy day, he held no negative feelings towards this Monday. His morning had been a steady stream of phone calls and scheduling meetings with clients. It was closing in on 2:00 P.M. when he finally had a moment to breathe. He pondered going out for lunch, but with clients coming in at 3:30, it made more sense to grab something from downstairs and get back to his desk.

  He was glad he did, as his 3:30 meeting became a three-and-a-half-hour-long shouting match between two grown adults, one of whom was his client. In the end nothing had changed except for the number of hours he was going to end up billing this month. Kirk rewound the meeting's recording, wrapped it in a note, and left it in Delores's inbox for transcription. These delays were why it was close to 8:00 P.M. by the time Kirk made it down to the level three garage. He used his remote to start his

2011 Sentra. Replacing the car was what that $2200 had been set aside for. A lawyer at a respectable firm, even the lowest associate, wasn't driving around in a nine-year-old Sentra. He now had a professional reputation to consider. Keith had enjoyed a lot of great times with that car, but times had changed. Kirk approached the driver's side door, and there, centered in the window, was a bright yellow square. It simply read…

"Are you enjoying living at 2400 Golden Hill Apt 1C?"

Kirk looked around the structure. There was no sign of anyone in the area, including the security patrol. On the far side of the level was a blue sedan. From this distance, it could be anything from a Chevy to a Mercedes. After jogging across the otherwise empty structure, he was right about the vehicle being a Chevy. A Chevy decorated several orange parking violation stickers that had been there a while based on the three inches of dust and dirt covering most of the vehicle. And if this did not indicate just how long the car had been sitting in the lot, the boot on the right front tire drove the point home. He returned to his car, pulling the strange note off the window, tossing it out. He slid into the driver's seat and keyed the ignition. As he prepared to back out of the space, he saw the black side of a Polaroid hanging from his rearview mirror. He pulled the obstruction down and flipped it over. It was a shot of the front of his apartment building. Disturbed, he tossed the photo on to the passenger seat, pulled out of his spot, and headed for the garage door.

Tuesday

"No, Sir, no, I don't think that we should settle just yet. I know it sounds like a lot of money, and it is. Still, given the damages your property sustained, coupled with them not having the proper permits to be excavating on that site, especially given the geologist report's findings, I assure you that if we hold off just a little longer, one of two things will happen. Either their offer will substantially increase or we go to court, and the judge will find in our favor. Either way, we get everything we wanted. Well, yes, I do. That's terribly kind of you to say. Just bear with me a little longer. That is outstanding news, Mr. Jordan. We'll speak again soon."

Kirk was just finishing updating the Jordan case notes when there was a quick rap at his door. He looked up, shocked to see Susan Wade standing in the open doorway. In the three months since he started with Howlett, Wade, and Murdoch, he had met none of the partners. They weren't the most prominent firm on the block, but they were constantly busy and practicing the kind of law that leads to actual change. Kirk rose from his desk to meet his boss halfway across the room.

"Ms. Wade," he extended his hand, "It is so great to meet you. Thank you for this opportunity."

Veronica Wade met the offered hand with an enthusiastic handshake.

"I apologize for this taking so long, Mr. Williams. As I'm sure you've noticed, things can get a little crazy around here. I've been out of town for the last six weeks, and I have no idea how long Lawrence will be gone. He's tied up with what was supposed to be an open and shut case. Anyway, I'm stopping by because I have a personal policy to have lunch with any new hires. Of course, that regularly takes place much earlier than this."

"Was she asking me to lunch?" he thought to himself.

"My apologies for the brevity of the situation. I'm back on the road tomorrow, and this was the first time I've had a chance to come and meet you. I know we keep you pretty busy around here, but I assume you can spare an hour to have lunch with your boss."

"Most assuredly, Ms. Wade."

"Do you have a preferred place to eat? What's your favorite?" she pried.

"I've only been living here a few months and haven't had time to explore the local cuisine," he admitted to her.

"Sounds like you need to get out more," she offered with a smile. "Why don't I just text you the address of a great place near here. How does 1:30 sound?"

"That sounds great. I'll keep my eyes open for that text, and I'll see you this afternoon. Thanks." and just like that, Veronica Wade had vanished from his office.

The rest of his morning went pretty smoothly. At around noon, the text from Ms. Wade had come in, and he traced out the route to a place called Ruby's. It was about a fifteen-minute drive from the office, so Kirk ensured all the files for his 4:30 P.M. conference call with Judge Greendyke were in place. The call was another in an already dragged out property dispute. This time it was so he and opposing counsel could update the court on the delayed status of discovery. He thought that Howlett, Wade, and Murdoch lacked a real estate lawyer, and his minor in just that subject may have played a part in his current employment. Of course, the why behind it wasn't that important. The clock on his desk read 1:00 P.M. It was time to leave for lunch. He made his way from his office to the elevator. He pressed the 3G button and headed down to the garage.

Unlike his journey to level three the night before, there were plenty of other vehicles during the day. Still no sign of the security guard, but perhaps they shared the same lunch hour. Still mildly disturbed by the strange occurrence from the night before, when he arrived that morning, he parked on the lot's far side. If somebody was fucking with him, he wasn't going to make it easy. As he approached his car, he could see that this plan had already failed. Kirk could see the neon green square stuck to the driver's side window even from this distance. He yanked the note from the window. It read...

"Howlett, Wade, and Murdoch. What an interesting choice."

A glance through the passenger side windows, Kirk saw another Polaroid hanging from the rearview. The flash had overexposed everything in the shot except for the security booth. Inside, although the poor quality of the picture marred this, was a large person wearing a blue uniform.

"What the fuck." Kirk uttered to himself. The alarm he had set for lunch went off, and just like that, he was late to his first and perhaps only lunch with a partner. Given his options, he tossed the note and picture into the back seat and made a fifteen-minute drive in five.

After apologizing profusely, the lunch went extraordinarily smooth. The two discussed the history of the firm and its accolades it had achieved. At 2:30 P.M., an alarm went off on Wade's phone, informing her it was time to leave. She thanked Kirk for coming and advised him to call if he required anything. The two shook hands, and she rushed out the door. Kirk finished the last of his drink and headed out. With the car parked on the same side of the street as the restaurant, the neon orange note on the passenger side window was difficult to miss. There was no message on this one, it was just a red thumbprint. Kirk had to assume it was blood. The newest Poloroid confirmed this with a picture of a hand with no thumb, sitting in a congealed pool of blood. Hurriedly, Kirk threw open the car door, and vomited on to the street. This situation, whatever it was, seemed to be intensifying. He called into the office and had them assign another lawyer for the afternoon conference call. After that, he headed home, smoked a bowl, and went to bed.

Wednesday

"And in local news, it's been two days since the disappearance of Michael Collins. Mr. Collins, 54 years old, has worked for Simmons Security for almost thirty years. His most recent assignment was as Supervisor at the Templeton building on Cross street. Mr. Collins, who has no immediate family in the area, was reported missing by his employer after failing to report for work. Bill Simmons, head of the company, had this to say…"

"Michael Collins is one of the best employees we have. For him to not show up for two consecutive shifts tells me there is something wrong. He's been with the company for roughly thirty years and is a part of our family. Simmons Security is offering a $10,000 reward for any information that will lead us to Michael. With the help of the police, we have set up a tip hotline. If you have any information, please contact us at 888-555-0411."

The coincidence of two missing security guards barely registered to Kirk. He was preoccupied with the increasingly bizarre events of the last two days. Sitting at the edge of his bed, Kirk was still feeling less than calm after yesterday afternoon's gruesome revelation. He contemplated taking the day off, but a quick look at his calendar put the kibosh on that thought. His schedule was full, and a lot of it involved cases only he was familiar with. At 7:30, the coffee maker turned on and began its cycle. He stepped into the bathroom and set the control dial in the shower. He passed through the bedroom and out into the hall. As he approached the kitchen, something foul overpowered the coffee pot's aroma. His curiosity led to a grisly discovery. Hovering above his kitchen table was a swarm of flies. Underneath those flies was a human thumb and stuck to the back of the front door were four multi-colored sticky notes, each displaying a bloody fingerprint. For Kirk, this had now passed the point of concern and crossed into scary. He then made two phone calls. The first was to the firm. Without going into all the details, he informed them there had been an emergency, and he would keep them up to date on the situation. The second was a call he should have made two days ago. This call was to the police.

Within the hour, his apartment became overrun with law enforcement. Plain uniforms, CSI, detectives, all making their way into every nook and cranny of his apartment, gathering anything they construed as evidence. There was no sign of forced entry at the door or windows. A cursory search of his car found no evidence of blood or human skin. There were no fingerprints other than his own. CSI technicians removed the notes and pictures from the last few days, bagging and tagging them as evidence. They impounded the Sentra to allow for a more thorough investigation. For the better part of sixteen hours, Kirk sat and watched as strangers pawed through his belongings, all the while answering the same questions repeatedly

Thursday

Kirk was able to get to bed before the sun came up, even if it wasn't even his bed. He had no choice but to go into the office today. Yesterday had been too busy of a day to miss, but given the situation, contacting the police couldn't have been delayed any further. He had assumed the first note was a joke. Perhaps a little razzing of the new guy in the office. That assumption didn't last long. The disturbing notes and photos, not to mention the thumb left in his kitchen yesterday, had pushed things way past pranks. He ran through a sped up version of his morning routine, limited by his unfamiliarity with the hotel's amenities. Washed, dried, and dressed, Kirk scheduled an Uber, grabbed the to-go bag, and headed out of the room. Stuck on the door, placed to cover the peephole, was a black and white square. On the back, written in a silver marker, was the message…

"We'll leave the lights on for you."

The front revealed a picture taken the night before. They took it from inside the room while he slept. An icy shiver ran down his spine as the Uber pulled up to the curb. He slipped the picture into his pocket and opened the rear passenger side door.

In a bit of good luck, traffic was lighter than usual, and he arrived at the office at 7:45 A.M. Doing his best to set aside the events of the day before, Kirk hit his desk, which was overflowing with work from yesterday, and took off running. He appreciated the extra work. It kept him focused on the task at hand and not the still uncertain events of the night before. All was moving ahead smoothly until 10:30 when the phone on his desk rang. He brought the receiver to his ear.

"Kirk Williams, here, how can I help you?"

"Mr. Williams, this is Detective Li. We met last night at your apartment."

"Yes, Detective, I remember you. What can I help you with?"

"I was calling to inform you we've identified the owner of the thumb you discovered. His name is Michael Collins. He's 54 years old and lives on Concord St here in the city. Here's something you might find interesting. He was employed as a security guard at the Templeton Building. Say, isn't that where you work?"

Kirk did not care for Detective Li's tone. He couldn't recall ever having met Mr. Collins, let alone have anything to do with his disappearance.

"You know very well, that's where I work, and I do not appreciate your implications. If you know where I work, then you know what I do. Let's keep this civil, shall we? Has anything else turned up in my car, and when can I expect to have it back?"

"Shouldn't be more than a day or two. Your insurance company should be able to provide you with a rental. If they don't, or there is a percentage they don't pay, the department will reimburse you the rest. That is assuming, of course, that the car is clean."

"Thank you for that information, Detective. Listen, I don't know what the hell is going on, but I'm as much of a victim of this person as Mr. Collins is. I assure you I am here to help in any way I can."

"I appreciate that Mr. Williams and I apologize if I offended you. You are not in any way considered a suspect. I'll be in touch soon, and I'll see what I can do about speeding up your car's sweep." The other end of the line disconnected.

Kirk felt a little better. He knew he was never a suspect, but it was nice to hear that from the police. Taking advantage of the distraction, Kirk made the call to the car rental place. After a quick search on his cell, he found the number for By the Mile Car Rental and auto-dialed.

"By the Mile Car Rental, this is Greg speaking, how can I help you today?"

Kirk quickly described to Greg how he could help him. After exchanging relevant information, Greg verified his insurance company offered one hundred percent coverage on rentals. They agreed on a seventy-two rental contract. Based on what Detective Li had told him, he should have his car back by then. Greg emailed him the agreement, which was digitally signed and sent back. The only snag in the entire process was the delivery window.

"I apologize, Mr. Williams, but there is no way we can get a car out to you today. The very best I can do is have it dropped at your home first thing tomorrow morning, which according to the schedule, would be at 7:15. Because you've already paid and signed, we can leave it in the driveway and place the keys under the mat. I'll also waive the return fuel fee when you bring it back."

The whole arrangement sounded very reasonable to Kirk. As long as the car arrived in time, he would have no trouble getting to work. Greg appeared to be excellent at his job. The clerk had placated him before he needed to be.

"That all sounds great, Greg. Thank you for all your help today. If you have some kind of satisfaction survey, I'll be more than willing to take it."

"Thank you for those kind words, Mr. Williams. We do our best to make sure our customers don't have to take an inch because we already gave them the extra mile. Have a great day."

Well, Kirk was uncertain about having a great day; at least that part of things was painless. He looked at an increasing stack of folders building upon his desk. It looked like it was going to be another late night. If he was honest with himself, it was a relief. He wasn't looking forward to being by himself tonight. And while he couldn't sleep at the office, he could stay later than usual.

Friday

The clock on his microwave read 3:24 A.M. as he dragged his sleep-deprived body through the door. It had been three days since the last time Kirk had gotten a good night's sleep. He had wondered if another version of the "burning the candle at both ends" idiom might offer a better explanation of the events of the last four days. He dropped his coat on the kitchen floor, made his way into the bedroom, and face planted into his bed.

The ringing of his cell preceded his alarm by less than a minute. Blurry eyed, he swiped at the screen. It was a recording from the rental car company. The message was to inform him that his rental vehicle was in the driveway, and the keys were under the mat. A six-digit unique identifier has been sent to the phone number provided. This code will remain active for the length of the contract term.

"Thank you for choosing By the Mile Rental Cars, where our customers don't need to take an inch because we've already given them that extra mile."

Kirk swiped left to disconnect the call and then again to silence the alarm. Four hours. He had been asleep for four hours. Once again, this was problematic. It was going to be an endless day at the office. He had two client calls scheduled this morning, and an all-hands meeting this afternoon. He had two options in this situation: get cleaned up and go to work or be fired. The decision came relatively quickly. Besides, it was Friday, he could get back on track over the weekend. He looked out the front window and saw a black Lexus parked in his spot.

"Sweet ride. Way to go, Greg." Kirk thought to himself as he headed out the door. He was halfway between the building entrance and the rental car when he saw a neon green square stuck to the trunk. His blood ran cold. As he moved closer to the Lexus, he heard a muffled sound coming from the car. He plucked the note from the trunk. It read…

"DO NOT ATTEMPT TO OPEN THE TRUNK."

"Fuck you!" He screamed into the morning sky. It was then he realized the point of origin of the noise. Something was banging around in the trunk. He ran to the driver's side door and pulled up on the handle. It was locked. He grabbed his cell from his pocket and desperately searched for the unlock code text from the rental place. The sounds coming from the trunk had increased. Several terrifying thoughts ran through his mind. Did he lose the message? Did it ever come through? Relief washed over him as the message finally appeared on his screen. Hands shaking, he entered the six-digit code on the keypad, and the door unlocked.

Unfamiliar with the rented car, he scrambled to locate the trunk release. Checking all the usual places the lever might be, he looked to his right and grabbed the glove box's handle. Kirk tugged on the handle, and the top half of the split storage space popped open. A black and white square, identical to the ones that had recently become a daily staple in his life over the last few days, slid out onto the passenger seat. Kirk snatched it up. The back also contained a message written in silver marker. This one read…

"I told you."

Kirk flipped the picture over to the image side and drew back when he saw it. The shot was a pair of green eyes looking into what appeared to be a rearview mirror. Kirk flipped his eyes to the now unobstructed mirror. The last thing he felt was the cord wrap around his neck.

"Recapping tonights' top story, the body of missing security guard Michael Collins was discovered earlier today. According to a spokesperson for the Police, Mr. Collins' body was found garroted in the front seat of a rental car. The vehicle in question came from Buy the Mile Rentals. When asked for comment about the rented vehicle, Buy the Mile Head of Public Relations Ainsley Wells stated the company does not release customer information to the public. However in a WTWR exclusive we have obtained a copy of the rental form. The car was rented to Kirk Williams, an associate at Howlett, Wade, and Murdoch. The police have no leads at this time. As always, we will do our very best to keep you up to date. This is Beverly Clawson with the WTWR news team saying good night."

Eight Hours

12:46 P.M.

> "Get your motor running. Get out on the highway."
> Steppenwolf
> "Born to be Wild"

    For the first time in four days, Jack Wilson was finally able to think about something else. For the first time since leaving New York, Jack enjoyed a moment's peace when he wasn't thinking about his wife for just a split second. Or his business partner. Let alone the position he found them in at that dive motel in Paramus. For the first time in four days, Jack Wilson was able to see the world around him in a new light. There was a classic American driving song on the radio. His 1965 cherry red Ford Mustang was a classic American car. This mostly empty stretch of road, which seemed to go on forever, made him feel like an early American pioneer. In that perfect second, Jack Wilson knew that his life was going to be okay. It was in this euphonious moment of understanding and acceptance that, at 70 miles per hour, he passed a sign which read…

Last Gas For 150 Miles

2:04 P.M.

> "When you're driving through the desert, and your car runs out of gas,
> Lotsa luck, pal, Lotsa luck."
> Allan Sherman
> "Lotsa Luck."

    A quick check of the time showed Jack that he was running about two hours ahead of schedule. After his speedy exit from New York, his first course of action was to reach out to Congresswoman Kim Hoggard from Arizona's fifth congressional district. Jack and Kim had known each other for close to thirty years, having first met in 1992 while attending a Bill Clinton campaign rally at Joyce Kilmer Park in the Bronx. As it turned out, both would be attending Manhattan College in the fall. In school, both majored in political science and graduated in the top ten of their class in 1996. After graduation, the pair had dedicated endless hours to the Clinton re-election campaign, where they established themselves as stars on the rise in the local political scene. When Kim had first decided to throw her hat into the ring in 1997, Jack ran her campaign, and it would become the first of many successful campaigns. Now, almost twenty years later, Kim Hoggard was running for a U.S. Senate seat, and Jack Wilson was an out-of-work political advisor whose wife was cheating on him. When he had decided to call Kim, it was only to let a friend know what was happening in his life. Kim broached the subject about bringing him on to the campaign, based on their previous success, and Jack's sudden abundance of free time. With nothing keeping him in New York, Jack told his friend that he would see her in five days.

    Now four days into his drive, Jack was finally closing in on his final destination. If he were lucky enough to keep his current pace, he would be in Scottsdale by tonight. He had never been to Scottsdale, but according to forty-nine Yelp reviews, the Gainey Suites was the very best hotel in the area. After two nights of interrupted sleep in crappy roadside motels and one chiropractic nightmare in his car's back seat, Jack was looking forward to sleeping in the best-rented bed you could find in town.

The details of the desert flora had begun to come alive as the car started to slow down, and the engine began to stutter. Taken by surprise, Jack frantically began searching the car's dash to locate the cause of the problem. His eyes finally fell on the gas level gauge and saw that the little white needle had gone past the empty indicator's end. He slowly turned the steering wheel to the right, verified through the rearview that the road behind him was empty, and drifted the Mustang into the breakdown lane. The door swung open and Jack stepped out of the car. He gazed out over miles of deserted highway and the desert's vast expanse all around him. He removed his iPhone from his front left pocket. There was no signal.

3:10 P.M.

> "I'm feeling numb and hopeless, into a desert I still stay.
> The sun burning in the sky, and no one's there for me, oh no."
> Evershed
> "Walking Down the Road."

The dashboard thermometer in the Mustang read 112 degrees. On the East Coast, he was always told that the southwest's heat was dry. And while it was nice to be able to breathe without feeling waterboarded, 112 degrees, especially when stranded on the highway in the middle of the desert, was hot. Over the last hour, Jack had not seen a single vehicle pass by on either side of the road. Coming from New York City, Jack had never seen a more infrequently used stretch of asphalt. He glanced down at the screen of his phone from time to time, hoping that something would change. Jack was hoping to see any kind of signal. Nothing had changed in the five minutes since he had checked the last time. The phone was without any type of signal. Clearly, a thousand dollars well spent.

"I guess Verizon couldn't dig up enough interest to provide cell phone coverage in the middle of nowhere," he thought to himself.

For the first time, it occurred to him he had become a slave to the welcoming glow emanating from the LCD screen. It was another entry in the rapidly progressing race to provide humanity the ease of simulated social interaction while, by their very design, encouraging significantly less actual physical, social interaction. The little screen had come to take up at least every third thought in his mind. Any answer to any question was simply a swipe away. As his magical wonder screen sat useless on the passenger seat, he desperately began looking for something that might create some kind of shade to protect himself from the relenting rays of the mid-afternoon Arizona sun. He had come to realize that digital tools will never completely replace the actual physical ones. With no phone signal or Wi-Fi access, the only function this marvel of modern technology served was to provide the time, and even that would only last as long as the battery held a charge.

4:13 P.M.

> "A burnin' hot sun a cryin' for water, black wings circle the sky."
> Johnny Cash
> "Lost on the Desert"

Jack was pretty confident that he had lost some time. To the best of his recollection, he had left the car around 3:30 P.M., but now the increasingly dim screen on his phone said it was 4:13 P.M.

"The heat must be fucking with my head," he thought to himself. "I swear it's hotter now than it was an hour ago. How is that even possible?"

When the second hour was coming around, and Jack had still not seen a single traveler, he decided to start walking and try to find help. The heat inside the car had reached a level where you could have baked a chicken, and Jack did not want to think about himself being the chicken.

With no idea what was in front of him, he decided to head back in the direction that he had come from. He racked his brain, trying to remember if he had passed anything. Nothing was coming to mind. He didn't recall seeing a gas station. Had there been a house of some type out in the desert? He was pretty damn sure there wasn't. No one was building homes out here in the middle of nowhere, Arizona, were they? Jack was pretty sure that was the case. No need for cell phone towers if nobody was out here to need them. Being right, however, did not make him feel any better. And as if to make matters worse, his head had begun throbbing, the intensity rising with each step he took. Bolts of pain shot through his forehead, and into the back of his eyes. He began to wonder if this was what heatstroke felt like?

Jack's brother Ross had served in the first Gulf War. When he came home, he explained to Jack that heatstroke was common in the desert, and the one thing that was stressed more than any other from the time he had arrived was to stay hydrated. During most of his time in the Middle East, the average daily temperature was 119 degrees.

"A soldier carries a lot of weight between fatigues and gear, and a good part of that weight is water. It's probably the most important, non-combat related gear we carry. I hope you never have to spend any time in a hot spot like that, little bro. I wouldn't wish that on my worst enemy."

For the first time in several years, Jack missed his brother. The last time they had been together, Jack's engagement to Becky had led to an awful argument. Ross hated her from the beginning and did everything he could to get Jack to see what he saw. Of course, a boy in love was a boy in love, and Jack turned his back on his brother. Right now, he'd give the world to have Ross here with him. Saving the day like he always did.

Then three things happened in rapid succession:

• A broken piece of pavement in the breakdown lane crumbles and falls away from the side of the road.

•Jack's ankle twists on the newly created divot, his knee smacks the safety rail, and he tumbles over the side.
•Blackness sets in.

6:27 P.M.

> "In the desert, you can remember your name,
> 'cause there ain't no one for to give you no pain."
> America
> "A Horse with No Name"

Jack was awoken by a sensation that he could not recall having felt before. It was a sharp little jabbing pain. Similar to the way a needle feels when you are getting tattooed, but more random. He may not have known what was causing the pain, but he knew that it was proliferating. He threw his eyes open and found himself face-to-face with a vulture. Well, face to the back of the bird's neck as its head was currently bobbing up and down as it dug at a hole it had picked into the flesh of Jack's leg. A scream escaped his lips as he ferociously flailed his arms towards the scavengers. In less than ten seconds, Jack was able to redefine his definition of pain. As the last of the black feathers disappeared, one look at his leg led to an immediate, dehydrated foamy projectile from his mouth. The tibia of his left leg was no longer attached to the fibula. It was, in fact, sticking out of the left leg of his jeans. He felt the world spin around, and then blackness came flooding in once again.

7:36 P.M.

> "Does anybody really know what time it is?"
> Chicago
> "Does Anybody Know What Time It Is?"

Jack looked out over the ocean and watched as the sun began to set. A cool breeze swept in from the east, and a young man in a snappy pair of shorts with a canary yellow polo shirt brought him a rather large bottle of water. A little further down the beach, he saw Becky lounging and keeping a half an eye on a small child stumbling through the sand in the way only those new to walking can. She was still as beautiful as the day they were married. He palmed the waiter a five and strolled down the beach. He would sit in a folding chair next to the woman he loved, wriggle his toes in the sand, and enjoy the spectacular end to this magical day.

As he walked from the sidewalk to the sand, he heard the sound of wings and noticed large shadows on the ground. He looked into the sky and saw nothing but the rising moon. As he continued to move forward, the shadows circled just one step ahead of him.

As he approached his wife, he was able to see the child at play more clearly. It was a little boy who looked nothing like him. He increased his pace through the sand and reached the back of the folding chair. Taken aback in shock, he could see the other chair was, in fact, occupied. It was Foster Lee, his occasional business partner and the best man at his wedding. The two were holding hands and laughing over some joke not heard by Jack.

"Becky? Foster? What the hell is going on here?"

"Well, you might as well tell him now, Becky. Honestly, I'm surprised it took him this long to figure it out."

"Becky? What is he talking about?"

"This marriage of ours is over, Jack. You can't expect me to stay with someone who seems to have no ambition in life. It's been three years since the last campaign. Your side lost. To be honest, I'm not even sure why you were working for that dumb bastard anyway. He never had a chance of being Governor. What are you going to do with your life, Jack? I've already decided what I'm going to do with mine."

"Listen, Jack. I just want you to know that I understand what you're feeling. We didn't plan for this to happen. It just kind of did."

Jack had heard enough. He fought off every urge telling him to punch that prick in the head until his hand broke; he wouldn't give them the satisfaction. He would be the bigger man, and even though his wife was leaving him for his now-former best friend, he wasn't going to let it ruin his trip here in paradise. Nothing either of them could do would take that away from him. He went back to the patio and motioned for the waiter to bring him another bottle of water. He tipped the boy a second five and let the crisp, clean water flow over his lips and down his parched throat. Even the shadows had gone away. It was a perfect evening.

7:58 P.M.

> "Does anybody really care?"
> Chicago
> "Does Anybody Really Know What Time It Is?"

Jack's head snapped back, and his eyes fluttered open. Displayed in a panoramic view in front of him, was the blessed sight of the sun setting behind the mountains. It had finally occurred to him he would never leave this crater. If this were the last day of his life, at least the night would come, and with it blessed relief from the blistering sun that had brutalized his body and mind all day. His eyes once again began to feel heavy.

"How cold does the desert get at night?" he pondered to himself. "Were vultures night feeders?"

8:45 P.M.

The first of the coyotes howled.

Worth A Thousand Souls

1

"Excuse me, miss…"

"Pardon me folks, if I could just have a minute…"
"Good afternoon ladies, you're a fun-looking group…"

    Kevin slipped his pen into his shirt pocket, and turned, dejected, back to the sad little kiosk in the middle of a mall that had seen better days. It seemed to him that in the three months he had been working for Above the Skin, Beauty and Glamor Shots, at least four independent stores had closed their metal gates for good. The anchor stores, Target, Lord & Taylor, and Macy's, seemed to be in it for the long haul, but even they knew the day and age of big box brick and mortar retail was coming to an end.

    This, of course, was not what Kevin had in mind a year ago when he graduated from CalArts. After four years, and a lot of hard work, he left with a double BS in Photography and Graphic Design, and somewhere in the neighborhood of a quarter of a million dollars in student loan debt. His student project, a black and white collection of candid shots of disenfranchised Los Angelinos and the neighborhoods they lived in, had been selected by the Alumni board, which just happened to include the Deputy Mayor, to be placed on display in the Atrium at City Hall. During that summer, Kevin Collins enjoyed his fifteen minutes of fame. His daily email doubled in number. His inbox overflowed with offers to shoot weddings, bar mitzvahs, retirement parties, and birthdays. No doubt from people who saw his work on display. While some of these offers were more than generous, none were the type of work he desired. Then again, $250,000 was a lot of money and on top of the debt, he had day-to-day bills that required his attention. So that Fall, Kevin spent his weekends coaxing smiles out of families who in most cases clearly had no desire to be that close to each other. He found those shoots were only slightly more entertaining than spending a Wednesday afternoon taking pictures for non-denominational corporate holiday cards. Twenty stiffs in suits gathering together as awkwardly as possible while attempting to look as professional as expected. Truth be told, almost every single one of those sessions could have been exchanged with another, and he guessed some people wouldn't even notice. Sure, there was the occasional minority or woman, but ninety-nine percent of the time it was twenty white dudes all wearing the same suit. By the first week of December, however, the well had run dry. Despite excellent reviews across his social media presence, Kevin was learning the ups and downs of the independent photo business, and the first lesson he learned was that winter could be very lean for a freelancer.

    By the middle of January, things had begun to get desperate. He had paid his rent, phone, and internet bills, but all the rest were now a month behind, and according to his calendar, he had one job scheduled for the month of February. By this time next month, he was going to be unable to make his rent. He hated to think about it, but it was becoming clearer each day he was going to either find a non-photography way to support himself or suck it up and start applying to those awful kiosks in the malls or those "photo studios" in strip malls. The ones with the broken lights and holes in the wall.

"So much for the Pulitzer." Plopping down on the sofa, he grabbed his laptop and headed to needajob.com.

2

The first few days of the job search had proven fruitless. As far as he could tell, there were jobs for three kinds of people on the website. Jobs for people who have worked for a company for years and were looking for a change. They have the experience and most of the time would make a good candidate. Jobs for people with no experience, kids right out of college, or guys who had just finished paying their debts to society. Mostly manual labor, some legitimate, some not so much. The third type was made up exclusively with traps for idiots. Get quick rich schemes, earn some ridiculous amount of money as you work part time from home, secret shoppers, things along those lines. In this third category, there was something for everyone. Everyone but Kevin.

On the fifth day, a most unusual thing occurred. After logging into needajob.com, Kevin's attention was drawn to a flashing yellow envelope in the upper right corner. He paused for a moment, considering the possible ramifications of clicking the icon, he brought the pointer to rest over the envelope and left clicked. His concerns were immediately assuaged when he saw the contents of the message.

Mr. Collins,

We came across your resume on needajob.com. We are quite impressed by your educational accomplishments and even more so by your eye. Your display in the Atrium was truly inspired. While we do not have any specific employment opportunities at this time, what we do have is a rather unique situation we would be interested in speaking with you about. No need to schedule an appointment. Just show up at the Above the Skin kiosk at the Galleria and ask for David, he'll get you started. When we think you are ready, our man will come to you. Good luck, Mr. Collins, I look forward to working with you in the future.

Madelyn Sinclair
SVP Talent Acquisitions
Above the Skin, Beauty and Glamour Shots

A photo kiosk in a mall. On the career path of someone with a CalArts degree in Photography, a mall kiosk shouldn't even be on the list. It was like graduating from a high end culinary school only to be hired as a dishwasher. A quick look at the stack of bills piling up went a long way in making the decision for him. The thought of having to return home with his tail between his legs was not one he wished to entertain any more frequently than usual. Taking a quick look at his watch and realizing the rest of his day was free, he threw on something slightly nicer than his usual unemployment attire, plugged the Galleria address into his phone and headed out the door. As he backed out of the driveway, the strangest thing occurred to him. He didn't have a resume on needajob.com.

Madelyn Sinclair could often be found frantically pacing around her desk while yelling at some unwitting nimrod on the other end of the line. It was hard for Ballam to make out exactly what this one had done. Standing outside the closed door of her office, he wondered if there would ever be a change here at AtS. Some days, it felt as if he had been here his entire life. At some point, and honestly couldn't remember exactly when it was, he was promoted to SVP of Special Technologies. Like Madelyn, William Ballam only answered to one man, and the less they saw of him the better. His primary responsibilities involved creating new photographic techniques and equipment that would turn even the most unpleasant person into something desirable to someone. He was good at his job, very good. Throughout his lengthy career, Ballam had pioneered technology that would go on to become industry standards. William Ballam's name carried considerable weight in the world of photography. From advertising one sheets to still pornography and everything in between, if you worked as a professional photographer you knew the name William Balaam. Looking through the window, he saw Madelyn slam down her headset and drop into a chair in the middle of the room. She waved for him to come in.

"Well, that sounded like it was twenty pounds of fun in a ten-pound hat." Ballam offered, doing his best to push a smile on his face. It would come to no one at the company that Ballam was not a fan of Sinclair. It had long been his opinion that the only reason she had received her promotion was because the team behind her was brilliant and they made her pop to the boss.

"How long have we been doing this, William? I have not come across a single employee mentally capable enough to handle this project. Somehow we've surrounded ourselves with thieves, feebs, and incompetents. I wouldn't trust any of them to walk my dogs, let alone step up for this project."

Ballam took the seat across from his colleague. He understood her frustration. He himself had been sitting on a brand new piece of camera equipment for the last five years, and during that time and all the interviews, of which there were many, he had failed to turn up a qualified candidate.

"It's just the way of the world now. Most of these kids have no real responsibilities, so mostly they don't need jobs. Couple that with a generation who is not used to being told no, and your options become very slim. The person we're looking for should be older, but not by much. Think twenty-two or so. Experience would be great, but not a requirement. I don't think we could be so lucky, but a degree in anything would be a blessing from above."

Two days later, one of the gals from H.R. emailed both Sinclair and Ballam a copy of the resume belonging to one Kevin Collins. Despite their offices being on the opposite ends of the building, the reaction was simultaneous and, when later discussed by their fellow co-workers, remarkably similar. Madelyne had her secretary send out the inquisitorial email immediately. In less than one hour's time, the email had been received and opened, and she was on the phone with Dave from the Galleria kiosk. Mr. Kevin Collins had shown up and was being shown the ins and outs of the location. A one hundred-year-old bottle of champagne from a winery that ceased to be during the events of World War II was popped open and celebrated with both Mr. Ballam and Katie, her assistant. Arrangements were also made for Jackie in H.R. to receive a bonus for being on top of things. After all these years, this could be what they had been waiting for.

3

In the beginning of things, Kevin had to admit to himself that this job wasn't the utter horror show he thought it was going to be. His co-workers, the few of them that there were, all seemed to be affable enough. They were, in his opinion, perfect examples of a generation who received awards just for showing up. All except for Lyndsey. She differed from the others, and not just because she was the only female on the staff. You could tell just by the way she carried herself.

This was a young woman who had bigger plans for her life. Just like Kevin once had.

It was his boss that he couldn't wrap his brain around. When the two men first met, he introduced himself as David Nelson. Somewhere in the back of his mind, Kevin knew that name. After their initial meeting ended, Kevin dropped the name David Nelson into the search engine on his phone. Within seconds, hundreds of thousands of results came back. It was the first picture that put it all together for Kevin. David Nelson had been one of the most awarded photo journalists in Los Angeles during the nineties. Many of the most notorious images of the civil unrest in Los Angeles during that time were captured by Nelson. He was a legend. So what the hell was he doing running a photo kiosk in a crap mall like the Galleria?

The first two months went relatively smoothly. For the most part, his customer base consisted of newly engaged couples, children of all ages, and the occasional graduation or anniversary shoot. For the most part, they were interchangeable. Look at the camera, everybody smile, on three, blah blah blah. It wasn't even really a camera. Sure, it functioned as such and was capable of capturing quality images, but it was essentially a computer with image capture technology. This kind of equipment was an affront to real photographers. There was no easy way to change the angle you were shooting at. No rewinding of film, hell there was no film. Just digital images sent to a printing house somewhere downstate. One week later, they were back, printed on glossy paper and ready to be brought home and framed, preferably according to his boss, in frames purchased right there at the location. These precious moments can be yours for only $29.99. Not a bad deal for a lifetime of memories. Kevin began to wonder if he was too young to be that cynical.

The only thing that made the job tolerable was every Wednesday and Thursday when the closing crew consisted of himself and Lyndsey. The first couple of nights were a bit awkward, as Kevin had only ever been in charge of closing twice and Lyndsey had never done it. When he closed with David, they were usually ready to go by 9:20. If it was a slow day, they could be out by 9:05. There had been a lot of 9:05 nights lately. The clock had crept closer to 10:00 by the time Kevin was locking everything down for the night. Not that it had been a particularly busy day, there had only been two sessions booked, and they were earlier in the day. It was simply a matter of taking his three months of experience and combining in with the two possessed by Lyndsey, and the sum of the equation was that they were fucked. It was just after 10:00 as the two tired clerks made their way from the Above the Skin kiosk, on the second floor down to the garage level.

"See you next week, Kevin." Lyndsey offered, while sliding the door key into the lock of her 2004 Toyota Corolla.

"Sounds good to me." he offered a wave. He paused before opening his car door. "Hey Lyndsey…"

"What's up, Kev?"

Before he was able to say anything stupid, his brain kicked in.

"Nothing. See you next week." He hopped into the driver's seat and waited long enough to see Lyndsey get out safely. He backed out of the spot and headed back to his crappy apartment for another night of Kraft dinner for one.

4

During this time, Kevin's work began to draw the attention of the two SVPs at Above the Skin. It was accepted from the beginning that nothing Kevin did with a kiosk camera was going to match the quality of his previous work. That being the case, he was adjusting to the digital media, and his customer response cards had been top notch.

"So what do you think, William?"

"The young man does have potential. According to the cards, people really seem to like him. The most common comment left by far was how easy it was to work with him. Especially with children who, as I'm sure you know, can be the most difficult group."

"Well, that's great and all, William, but is this kid the one we need to pull this off?"

"He definitely seems to meet all the criteria we've been looking for. He has exceptional talent with real equipment, and we've got that covered. Look at it this way: either he is able to complete the task at hand or he ends up like Nelson. It's a win/win situation for us."

Madelyne Sinclair flipped through the proof sheets and customer comment cards that had come in over the last two months on Kevin Collins. She had to admit that the numbers were very positive.

"Okay, let's give Mr. Kevin Collins a try, but know this Willam, if this goes sideways, like last time, I am not taking responsibility for this one. Do we understand each other?"

"Oh, I understand you perfectly, Madelyne. Crystal clear." a slim smile crossed over his lips.

"When can we get this thing started?" she inquired.

"No time like the present. I'll pop down there tomorrow afternoon right around lunchtime and have a chat with our new star."

Once upon a time, the food court at the Galleria was a sight to behold. There were six pick up and go snack carts, three middle range sit down family-style restaurants, and a dozen or so representatives from the major fast-food chains. There really was something for everybody. At its height, it was ground zero for teens and families alike. Starting in 2009, the mall would allow extended hours in the food court hours to coincide with the addition of the movie theater. Of course, that had been a while ago. By 2016, however, regular and increasingly violent acts plagued the theater's nighttime hours, and due to insignificant ticket sales to justify a day shift, the decision to close the theater was a one-sided affair. The owners would not continue to dump money into a pit, and in 2017 the doors were shuttered. The move left the mall with a massive two story eyesore. Despite shuttering all entrances from the inside with steel gates, the outside windows and doors were simply covered with plywood. According to the security camera footage, the wood lasted less than two weeks. Subsequent attempts to replace the boards were met with similar responses. After the first year, management accepted the inevitable and ordered Jersey barriers placed in front of all the doors. It wasn't going to keep everybody out, but it was at least a token gesture to placate the city offices who had been receiving an increasing number of complaints. The space quickly became a hangout for both the local youth and junkie populations. As one group quickly surpassed the other, violent acts once again became an issue, and because now it was white kids whose parents just happen to hold positions of influence, the cops were called in to clear the place and secure the entrances permanently this time.

On August 23rd 2018, StarCase cinemas, a theater chain out of Canada with over 1,300 screens throughout the country, released a statement to the press stating that they would be extending their business into America and their first project would be to restore the Multiplex at the Galleria . While the announcement was light on details, it did provide an opening window of January 2021. Six months later, it was more quietly announced that due to fluctuations in currency values, StarCase would be pulling out of the Galleria project.

With the departure of the theater, the mall reverted to standard operating hours for the remaining businesses. This led to a further decrease in business in the food court. Within a month of the announcement, all but one of the snack carts and two of the three sit downs were gone. In 2018, the smaller independent stores started to leave thanks to a decline in foot traffic and increased rent. A decrease in retailers led to a decline in both the quality and quantity of employees. This, of course, led to a decline in customers, who found it less of an annoyance ordering everything they needed online. The overall decline in business was devastating to the remaining eateries. By 2020, the once bustling hub of activity had been reduced to a newsstand, whose sole purpose was to sell overpriced cigarettes to mall employees who forgot to stop at the gas station before coming in, and three counter service places. Every day, the options were the same. Chicken Shack, known for its delightful biscuits and secret recipe chicken, a McDowells, home of the Big Mic, and last and certainly least a Run for the Border, which is mall Mexican food so there was little to say about that. Every day for the last two-and-a-half months, right around one p.m. Kevin would make his way upstairs and decide which of these culinary delights was going to cause him the least amount of gastronomical inconvenience later in the day. The contents of his pocket went a long way in helping to form his decision when he came out with three crumpled dollar bills and a small variety of change. Chicken Shack it was. A drumstick, biscuit, and a drink for $2.99. Still the best deal to be had around here these days.

After paying for his order, Kevin looked across a sea of empty seats and tables. Based on a quick, but fairly accurate count, there were ten other people occupying a space that was designed to sit hundreds. He found a table reasonably far away from anyone else and began to unpack his lunch. As always, the first bite of Chicken Shack was a delight. He knew he would pay for it later, but at the moment it was his menu for the day and he was set to enjoy it.

Kevin was just wiping the last of the biscuit crumbs from his beard when he noticed the small man in the crisp black suit. He was one of those men that could have been fifty or ninety. Despite his size, the curious stranger cleared the space from the escalator and Kevin's table surprisingly quickly. A black attaché case swung by his side with each step. He came to a stop at the opposite end of the table.

"Kevin Collins, I presume?" the man stated, offering his hand in greeting across the remains of the Chicken Shack lunch.

Kevin rose from the table and took the stranger's hand.

"I believe you have me at a disadvantage, sir."

"You are quite correct, Mr. Collins. My name is William Balaam and I am the Senior Vice President of Special Technology for your employer Above the Skin."

Kevin's mind began to race. He tried to remember if anything had happened during the last two-and-a-half months that would require an unannounced and private meeting between himself and a Senior Vice President. The worst thing he could recall happening was when this woman named Karen freaked out on David for not having Easter backgrounds in June. Whoever said the customer is always right didn't work in a mall in 2021.

As if he was reading his thoughts, Balaam looked and smiled at Kevin.

"Don't worry, young man, you're not in any kind of trouble. As a matter of fact, it's just the opposite. I'm here today to discuss an interesting possibility that has come up. What do you say to a real lunch? You know, somewhere outside this shithole."

"Well, my lunch break is almost up. I should get back and help Dave out. Perhaps we can do this later today?"

"Don't worry about Mr. Nelson, I've already informed him of the situation and traffic at the stall is non-existent. We've got all the time we need. Follow me out to the car."

Since there was no reason not to take the man at his word, after all who would claim to be a SVP from a crap photo company that operated out of malls, Kevin deposited his garbage in the nearest bin and followed Balaam out the door.

Sitting against the curb, engine purring, despite the lack of a driver, was a classic 1976 Corvette StingRay in a dark red color Kevin had never seen before. It was similar to the cherry red color from the fifties, but there was something more sinister about it. The door opened as he approached it, causing quite the startled reaction.

"Nothing to worry about my boy. Little tricks here and there, but nothing dangerous." Hallam assured him. The two men climbed into the car and headed north on Main St. And it may have just been a trick of the eye or bad angles throwing distorted shadows, but Kevin wasn't completely sure that Hallam was driving.

"If I may ask Mr. Hallam, if you have no problems with my work, what brings you to the Galleria?"

"To be frank, your talents are being wasted in that dump." Hallam responded with no hesitation.

"While I appreciate the compliment, I do work for your company, sir. Seems a rather harsh observation of one of your properties." Kevin offered.

Hallam chuckled at the protective tone found in the young man's voice. Hallam knew then this was who he had been looking for. They took a left into what as far as Kevin could see, the only parking spot in front of a solid matte black building. Hallam opened the car and began to step out.

"Come on, son, nobody's going to open that door for you."

Still quite confused about what was going on, Kevin opened the car, doing his best not to nick, ding, scratch, or in any way damage this pristine vehicle. With that task handled with great care, Kevin crossed over to stand behind Balaam, who had walked up a short flight of steps that Kevin hadn't even seen. In front of the door, a small slide window, reminiscent of a 1940s era gangster picture, had slid open. Words were exchanged in whispers, and Balaam pointed back towards the car. More words and then finally Kevin was waved over to the now open door.

"Before we go in, there are a few things you need to know. First, don't talk to anyone. Don't even talk to me until we reach our table. I called ahead and placed our order for lunch. The staff will bring it out to us one course at a time. Again, do not talk or respond to them in any way. While you're at it, try not to listen to anything said or directly asked of you. I know this is a bit on the confusing side, I can see that by the look on your face, and I'll be more than happy to answer all of your questions once we're settled in. Don't worry, just follow my lead and you'll be fine." Balaam took the three stairs leading up to the door and headed in, with Kevin in lock step behind him.

Kevin sensed that something was off the minute he walked through the door. The inside of the building was at least ten degrees warmer than the temperature outside. He could feel his mouth drying out while the first drops of sweat began to bead on his forehead. The climate changed from the aridity of a desert to the suffocating humidity of a rainforest. They walked for what felt like an eternity through the blackened halls of the mysterious building. Just as Kevin was feeling he had come to the end of his rope, they arrived at their table. Parched beyond any thirst he had ever known, Kevin grabbed the first glass of water he could find and emptied it in three big gulps. He looked desperately at the glass sitting in front of Balaam.

"By all means." Balaam offered, waving his hand in a gesture to inform him to proceed. Kevin grabbed the second glass and guzzled down the ice cold water until he began to choke.

"Take it easy there, boy. I would hate to lose you now. We haven't even gotten to the good part yet."

Kevin placed the glass on the table and sat back, doing his best to catch his breath and regain his composure. Slowly, his face returned to its normal color, and he could breathe again.

"Feeling better, are we?"

Kevin shook his head in response.

"Good. Now then, the first course will be here any..."

An eerie stillness filled the air and, as if on cue, a server dressed in a black on black tuxedo, face covered by a matching mask, arrived at the table laying out a bowl of soup in front of each man. The figure waited long enough for Balaam to taste the soup, receiving any commentary that might need to be passed along to the chef. Balaam reached into the inside of his jacket and came back out with a leather pouch. Undoing the zipper, he removed a six piece set of Obsidian eating utensils. Selecting the larger of the two spoons, Balaam placed the ebony soup spoon into his bowl, approved of the dish and then dismissed the server with a wave.

"Mr. Balaam, I don't want to overstep my bounds, but can you please tell me what the hell is going on here?" Kevin exclaimed, his voice creeping into the hysterical range.

"That is certainly understandable, Mr. Collins, and I do have to say that you have been a good sport so far. Why don't you get started on your soup and I will do my best to answer any questions. But I think it's best if I give you a little background into ``Above the Skin."

Kevin did his best to keep track of what Balaam was saying, while enjoying what very well could be the best bowl of soup he had ever had in his life.

"The first thing you should know is that the Above the Skin you work for is a miniscule part of what we do. In the late 20s and early 30s, my boss was an early pioneer in photo booths. You are familiar with photo booths, correct?"

Kevin nodded his head. He spent his summers in arcades on the Jersey Shore and had spent an embarrassing amount of money on them in his lifetime. Sadly, most of them were solo shots.

"In the early 80s, when malls were still a new thing, my boss began to invest in a bevy of new technologies. The most successful of which allowed for the creation of high quality prints in a variety of sizes in the same time it took the photo booths. After a corporate buyout and six weeks in the lab, the technology worked like a charm. In 1982, he opened the first Above the Skin Beauty and Glamour Shots. To say it was a success would be an understatement. Within the first week, all appointments for the following six months had been booked. And AtS was not just a photo studio, the shop offered the works. Complete hair care, make overs, mani/pedis, everything a go go woman of the 80s would want. By 1987, we were fifty locations strong in malls across the country. Five years later, we had tripled that number. Business was booming and so were the profits."

"So what happened?"

"Things continued on a rocket ride through the end of the 80s and well into the following decade. The amount of money that was made is almost embarrassing to talk about. At the turn of the century, however, we became aware of some troubling industry predictions. Research studies completed by several of the top economists in the country revealed that by 2010, thirty-seven percent of non-grocery shopping would be conducted online. They were off by two percentage points. It didn't get any better from there. Further financial predictions showed further decline, with numbers increasing from thirty nine to sixty-four percent between 2010 and 2020. During that time, foot traffic in both shopping centers, and standalone big box stores began to decline. By 2030, if the predictions are correct, there will be no malls in this country. The number of major retailers still occupying physical space, some of which had been venerable institutions that had survived for centuries, will crumble and before long be nothing more than a memory for its staff and customers. Online sales numbers are expected to reach as high as eighty-three percent of all transactions. There are always services that, by necessity, will require a physical presence. Restaurants, many of whom were also taking full advantage of the rapidly evolving food service delivery industry, were still more than happy to welcome people through their doors. Grocery home delivery had been a thing for decades, but someone would always need a quart of milk at nine o'clock at night. The two versions of commerce will eventually learn to co-exist, but it will take a while."

Kevin stood, mouth agape, staring at the strange Mr. Balaam. He was at a complete loss for words.

"I know it's a lot to process all at once, but I can assure you that our economists are rarely wrong."

"So what happens to all the people who need those jobs?" Kevin inquired.

"That's not a concern at the moment. Just because the numbers don't lie doesn't mean there aren't a lot of moving parts behind these things. Now let's get back to you, shall we?"

Still slightly chilled from the ominous information he had just received, Kevin slowly nodded his head.

"Just to make sure you understand what's going to happen here today, there are a few things you should know. For starters, this is not a job interview. You already have a job with this company, so we can skip all the preliminary bullshit. Second, I've already seen your work. Your display in the Atrium last year was stunning. The work you have done for us, though lacking the creative spark of your personal work, has been stellar and your customer response cards have nothing but positive comments. So I already know you can do the job. What I want to know is how dedicated you are to your craft?"

Kevin paused for a moment, mulling the question over in his mind, all the while trying to get a read on Balaam's body language.

"Mr. Balaam, I have loved photography since I was old enough to hold a camera steady. It has been my entire life. When I graduated from CalArts, I knew that someday I would be creating great art. It happened with the City Scapes show, but since then, that dream has been put on the back burner so I can pay my bills. Please don't think that I'm unappreciative of what I've got here, it's just not what I saw myself doing after I graduated."

"One of the things I like about you kid is that you know when to keep your head down and do the work. Your time really is being wasted at the mall. You are a far better photographer than not only your fellow employees but most of the employees working for AtS across several of our divisions. You have a tremendous depth of knowledge and a god given skill that can't be taught, but the best part is you'd never know just by talking with you. For someone who possesses a level of talent as yours, I've not heard a single complaint about you having an ego problem or feeling superior to your co-workers. That's an admirable skill to possess."

"I was told growing up that nobody enjoys being told they're stupid. It's always advice I kept with me. I know I didn't finish third in my class at CalArts because of dumb luck. I know how good I am. I know that one day soon I will find the opportunity I've been looking for and that before I'm twenty-five, I'll be doing what I've always wanted to do."

"And what's that, Kevin? What have you always wanted to do?" Balaam spoke up.

"I want to create perfect art. The kind of art that can touch everyone who sees it. The kind that you can't look away from. Art, that means something different for you than it does for me. What do I want to do, Mr. Balaam? I want to capture images that will become history."

A smile found its way across Balaam's face. He now knew that his pick had been the right one. This lad possessed all the qualities that both he and Sinclair had been looking for. The silence around the table had returned as the next course was served. A tossed green salad with a near invisible but delightful smelling dressing. The air cleared as the server walked away. Just like the soup before it, each mouthful of salad was better than the previous. He wasn't sure where he was, which was unfortunate because so far this was the finest meal he had ever had. He couldn't shake the feeling that this was a one time thing.

"Well, Mr. Collins, it seems that you have a rather clear plan for your future. We at Above the Skin want to encourage that dream. We want to give you the time and equipment you need to accomplish that goal."

"No offense, Mr. Balaam, but I just don't see how that is going to happen when I'm sitting in the kiosk or following uninterested people down the hallways of a mall like a barely legal stalker. As you can see, my forty hour work weeks are pretty full of never ending excitement."

The impudent nature of the boy caused a chuckle to escape his lips. Madelyn would absolutely love him.

"I think you misunderstand my intentions here, Kevin. As I said in the beginning, this is not a job interview. This is an opportunity for both of us to make photographic history. And we're going to do it with this." Balaam reached under the table and brought a leather case to the surface.

Opening the case with a flourish, Kevin looked inside, and was honestly quite disappointed.

The inside held a sole item. Kevin possessed a remarkable depth of knowledge when it came to cameras, and this was instantly recognizable as a Canon T-80 circa 1985. He stifled a chuckle out of respect, but if this old man thought they could change the world with this antique, he was sadly mistaken.

"I know what you're thinking, Mr. Collins. You're thinking that this whole thing has been a gag and we've just reached the punchline, am I right?"

Kevin nodded his head.

"One piece of advice my mother gave me was never judge a book by its cover. I can assure you that the camera in front of you is capable of things you can not imagine. Shall I continue?"

The look of dumbstruck awe remained plastered across his face, as Kevin found himself nodding his head once again."

"In the early 90s our economist had already foreseen the economic downturn that would change the face of retail in the future. It was decided by the board that the time had come to expand our reach. And expand we did. By the mid 90s, we had branched out into markets that could take advantage of our quick turnarounds. We began shooting class and team photos for schools. Local events, parades, things of that nature. You could hire us with a booth or just roaming photographers. Like the ones you see at fairs and carnivals. You'd be surprised how much money is in that."

Kevin pondered that for a moment. He had certainly run into the type of photo set ups. At $5 a piece, even if you only reach a twenty percent sell through, when you factor the hundreds if not thousands of people who would pass through a local fair over the course of a weekend. You take one of the kids from the kiosk division, give him an SLR, and pay him eight dollars an hour. Easy enough to clear a few thousand dollars on a good weekend.

"In the early 2000s, we broke into the world of fashion modeling when one of our other divisions came into possession of a sizable agency. I won't name names, but you'd know it if you heard it. Nowadays, if there is a group of photographers gathered for a news story, we have a man on the ground. Sometimes we get lucky and the news happens around us. The point of all this, my boy, is to impress on you that beauty shots in a mall are not part of your future."

Kevin looked back and forth between Balaam's face and the antique camera sitting on the table. This morning when he pulled into the parking structure, there was nothing anyone could have told him that would have led him to believe he would be where he was right now. The air went cold and silence overtook the space as the server returned with the entrée.

After the room returned to normal, the two men sat enjoying their meal. There was still an unspoken curiosity hanging in the air. Balaam brought his napkin to his lips, dabbed them gently, and the napkin disappeared back under the table.

"So, shall we get down to business, Mr. Collins?"

"What did you have in mind Mr. Balaam?"

Over the course of the next hour, Balaam laid out a career path for his newest prodigy. Collins was to be moved out of the kiosk immediately. He would be assigned to a special project directly under the supervision of the Technology Acquisition team. Balaam would oversee the project from afar, checking in from time to time. He would be under contract with Above the Skin for two years. According to the terms of the contract, an initial payment of one million dollars would be made, along with Kevin taking possession of the Canon T-80. Following the final signatures on the contract, he would be responsible for capturing one thousand unique photographs over the length of the contract. Each photo would need to be accompanied by a signed release. Once the task was complete, regardless of remaining time left on the contract, Above the Skin would pay out the balance due in the amount of two million dollars. The only caveat was that all pictures must be taken by June 17th 2023 by 11:59:59 p.m. Failure to complete the contract on time would lead to forfeiture.

There was something sinister in his usage of the word forfeiture.

"And you want me to accomplish all of this with that thing?" nodding towards the Canon.

"I certainly do, Mr. Collins. Now allow me to explain to you exactly how you are going to accomplish that." he removed the Canon from its custom foam fitted holder and handed it across the table. It felt solid but oddly light. An examination of the machine raised a variety of questions. The camera lacked the traditional features of a standard mid 80s thirty-five millimeter. There was no flash or battery compartment to support one. There was no focus or aperture ring. No film advance lever or rewind knob. The shutter release was in its standard location. It was the counter that didn't belong. The standard exposure counter on this model camera was a circular dial that featured a countdown mechanism. The standard counter normally stopped at thirty six. This one however had been modified to display four digits. Other than the counter, the device was as faithful a replica as he had ever seen. On the back of the camera, there was the standard door for a film compartment, although there was no option to open it. Kevin placed the camera on the table in front of him.

"As you can see, this isn't exactly a run-of-the-mill Canon T80. Believe it or not, it was one of the most reliable cameras ever publicly released. Over the last thirty-five years, our research team has yet to find a model to be more compatible with their testing. This model, for example, has been sitting on the shelf for five years. We've been waiting for just the right person to operate it. Mr. Collins, we believe you are that person." Balaam pulled a folded contract from the inside of his coat. "Everything is explained here in black and white. Feel free to take your time and give it a read. I think you'll see that everything I have offered is contained within."

Kevin took the pages and began to peruse them. Except for some legalese, it was as Balaam said it would be. Two years was a long time. The promises sounded great, but he would be locked down with no resort if promises didn't come to pass. Of course, three million dollars was a lot of money. It was a life changing amount of money. A two-year deal, where he would be working as a photographer, and not trying to lure uninterested people with BOGO coupons. Amongst the time tested idioms he was raised with, one was "Don't look a gift horse in the mouth" and while he was still only twenty-two years old, it was unlikely he would ever be lucky enough to see a gift like this again. He thought about that pile of bills on his desk and the seventeen cents in his pocket. "Mr. Balaam, do you have a pen?"

8

Kevin woke up with a start. Sitting up in his bed, he blindly grasped at the nightstand in search of his cell phone. His eyes widened when he saw the digital display read 9:45 a.m. He leapt from the bed and began to dash around the apartment, looking for something clean enough to wear to work. He was halfway dressed when his phone rang.

"David, I am so sorry. I must have overslept or something. I'm leaving in five minutes and will be there in ten."

"I told you Mr. Collins, the activities of the Above the Skin kiosk are no longer of any concern of yours." Offered the familiar voice of Mr. Balaam.

Kevin certainly remembered having that conversation, he was just surprised that when the man said immediately, he actually meant it.

"Good morning, Mr. Balaam. Sorry for the confusion there."

"Not a problem, Mr. Collins, not a problem at all. So tell me, are you ready for your first day's assignment?"

Kevin informed his new boss that he was raring to go. Balaam provided him with an address and told Kevin to meet him there at exactly 11:00 a.m.

"Oh, and Kevin, don't forget the camera." The other end of the line turned to silence.

Punching the address into his phone, he saw the location was ten minutes away, barring traffic. Walter Reck Elementary School was maybe three blocks away. On the days he was working out of the house, which prior to his most recent employment, had been a few more than he would have preferred, he could hear the

3:15 release bell when the windows were open. He wandered into the kitchen and started the coffee pot. He now had some time to kill. Kevin wondered what his business at the school might be.

It was 10:56 when Kevin strolled up to the front gates of the school. Across the street was the dark red StingRay that belonged to his new boss. He cut across to the other side of the road.

"Ah, Mr. Collins, good to see that punctuality is a part of your skill set. I see you've brought the Canon."

"If I may inquire, what are we doing at an elementary school at 11:00 a.m. on a Thursday?"

"I do so enjoy your inquisitive nature, Mr. Collins. Allow me to explain exactly what we're doing here. Last week, one of our competitors was brought in to take all the annual school pictures of the students, classes, and staff. Unfortunately for them, a fire broke out in their van. From what I hear, it was the damndest thing." Balaam offered with a devious smirk on his face.

"So we're here to retake all the school pictures? You, me, and one camera? Um, I'm good, but I can't make you any promises." Kevin's mind began racing, searching for a solution to what seemed to be an insurmountable problem.

"Relax, Mr. Collins. If reshooting the whole school was our task, I can assure you there would be a lot more people standing here with us. No, they saved the children's photos as they had been shot on digital. They were all backed up to both the internal memory and the Cloud. However, the fire did break out before the staff pictures had been started. Our job today is simple, get each of the thirty-two members of the staff to sign the waiver, and we do the session. Easy Peasey."

"Well, this is certainly easier than that bullshit at the mall." Kevin thought to himself.

"It certainly is, Mr. Collins. It certainly is." replied Balaam, as if he had read the young man's mind.

The process was pretty streamlined. Since the appointment had been made a week earlier, Above the Skin was able to prep the school administrators and offer them advice on the easiest ways to streamline the process with a minimum of disruption to the classes. One by one the teachers came down to the office, signed a standard ATS release form and headed into an office that had been prepared for the purpose. Once again, Kevin was impressed by the expertise and flawless execution the company had perfected over the years.

Over the course of the next hour, starting with Jason Ayiers, the school's head custodian and ending with Diane Ziering, fifth grade math teacher, each member of the staff sat in front of the Walter Reck Elementary School flag, and had their picture added to whatever mysterious storage medium the Canon was using. Kevin packed up their gear, handling the Canon with great care, while Balaam followed the Principal into her private office. The two emerged minutes later, shook hands, and went their separate ways.

"Come on kid, we don't have all day." he snapped at Kevin, who picked up the gear bag and hurried to catch up to his boss.

"What the hell was that about?" Kevin asked in a voice that almost sounded courageous.

Balaam spun on his heel and stared into the boy's eyes. It was a cold, hard stare. The kind of stare that makes it feel as if your heart was going to stop. Kevin dropped his eyes to the ground.

"I'm sorry, Mr. Collins, did you have something you wanted to say to me? Especially keeping in my mind that you could be back chasing soccer moms with coupons at the mall tomorrow."

Kevin raised his head back up and met Balaam's gaze.

"Yeah, as a matter of fact, I do have something to say. First, you came to me. Sure, I wasn't happy working in the mall, but I was making do with what I had. You are the one who called me. You are the one who made a lot of promises in that contract you had me sign. I'm no lawyer and I'm sure there were things in there that I would have rejected if I was, but that's neither here nor there. For whatever reason, I was your choice, so let's not pretend I would be so easy to replace. Secondly, I'm a grown ass man. When you speak to me, just as when I speak to you, it will be with respect. Thirdly, and perhaps most beneficial to me, we do have a written contract, sir. So you can go ahead and threaten to send me back to the mall, but I can assure you of one thing, I will be the best paid employee in the mall's history. Now with all that being said, do we still have a problem or do you want to tell me what happened during that little pow-wow with the Principal?"

At some point during Kevin's diatribe, a look of disbelief had overtaken Balaam's face. In all of his years in this business, he had never been spoken to that way as an employee. If he was being honest, he was impressed. The older man took a deep breath.

"There were supposed to be thirty three."

"Thirty three what?" Kevin stared quizzically at his boss.

"Thirty three staff. There are thirty three employees on staff here. One of the teachers called out sick today." Balaam stood, shaking his head.

"So they don't end up with their picture in the yearbook. Big deal. Who the hell has even ever heard of an Elementary school yearbook?"

" This is my fault," Ballam thought to himself. He took the boy out before explaining the whole process to him. Granted that today's excursion, while not unexpected, was not the best way to break the kid in. They needed to have a sit down so he could put all the cards on the table.

"It's a lot more complicated than that. Throw the gear in the back seat, we're going to lunch." Balaam stated, sliding into the driver's seat and keyed the ignition.

Today's lunch, while in no way comparable to yesterday's experience, was pleasant. Balaam had driven from the school to the RestWay Diner as if he had done it a thousand times. The car rolled to a halt in a conveniently placed empty spot. He hopped out and grabbed the Canon case from the back seat. The two men climbed the three concrete stairs and headed inside.

Kevin had been living in California since moving out for the start of school five years ago. Originally, he was from a small, exclusive community in Mid-Western Connecticut. And even though there were less than three hundred people living in the gated community and another three to four hundred in the immediate area, there were at least three traditional diners in a five-mile radius. Kevin found it cute whenever he saw a diner in California. It was the same with pizza. He appreciated the attempt, but it would never be the real thing.

A somewhat disinterested server came over and took their order. Within a minute, she was back with coffee. Kevin did have to admit it was a damn fine cup of coffee.

"It occurs to me, Mr. Collins, that I have not been completely honest with you. There is much more involved here than simply taking pictures. The Canon doesn't actually take pictures. I'm sure you've noticed there is no film or place to load it."

Kevin nodded his head. It was, in fact, the first thing he noticed after being handed the machine.

"You see, Mr. Collins, this particular camera works more like an x-ray machine than a standard camera."

Kevin cocked an eyebrow and looked even more confused.

"I was going to wait to break you into all of this, but it looks like it was sooner than later. Above the Skin is not really a business. I mean it is, you worked there, so you know the public face. What we actually do is far more interesting than just taking pictures. Since the advent of photography, many cultures have shared the belief that what they saw was magic. They viewed these machines as soul eaters. They believed that having their image captured on film was a trap. Of course, none of this was true. That was, until we entered the picture."

"And if I may ask, with no jeopardy.."

"You want to know how long we've been in business. Feel free to ask any questions you may have, there will be no jeopardy. If I can answer them I will, if not we'll move on to another topic. Sounds reasonable, my boy?"

Kevin nodded his head to signify agreement.

"Our original business charter was signed in 1820. We were registered as Au-dessus de la peau as we were in France at that time. There had been some interesting early experiments being done with photography, so we helped move things along. And that is exactly what we did. Over the next one hundred and fifty years, the business led to advances in technology, which led to advances in the business."

"So all this time, you've been working on ways to what, capture souls on film?" Kevin could feel his heart beginning to race.

"Not in the beginning. At the start, it was simply curiosity. The medium was new and exciting, and if there is one thing my boss loves it's technological advances. They've been known to make his job easier on occasion."

"Who is your boss?"

"As exciting as this new science was, our research and development teams saw the future and from that point on began pushing the limits of what we could do. The only real detriment to our experiments was time and the limits of the technology. We had the best minds working either with or for us. Edison's creation of the motion picture camera was a happy accident that originated from this project. In a lot of ways, we've changed the world."

Kevin propped his elbows up on the table and buried his face in his hands. From his first meeting with Balaam, Kevin had suspicions about the nature of the project he had signed on for. After the history lesson, he found himself wondering if harassing people in a mall had really been that bad.

"I know that was a lot of information to absorb at once, but it made more sense to do it this way. Now you know who we are and what we do. So now that we've gotten that out of the way, let me tell you about the Canon." Kevin leaned across the table as Balaam unpacked the camera.

"This particular Canon, for the most part, functions like any other T-80. We've installed an auto focus feature and sealed the film compartment door. When you look through the viewfinder, you will see one of two images. The display will either show the image as it appears to the naked eye, or in some cases individuals will appear in black and white."

Kevin turned the Canon in his hands. The resemblance to the original was remarkable.

"So what causes the black and white display?" He asked. Simultaneously wanting and not wanting to know for certain.

Balaam threw his head back and released a laugh that sent a chill down Kevin's spine.

"An individual who appears in black and white has corrupted their soul. In order to morally corrupt a soul, one must knowingly and repeatedly violate any of the Seven. That camera you hold in your hand has the uncanny ability to capture those souls."

Kevin sat, a gob smacked look on his face, trying to rationalize the concept. Prior to any of this, he was pretty comfortable being an Atheist. Now he was being asked to render unto Caesar the souls of his fellow human beings. How did he end up being the one to determine their fate using a modified Canon T-80? If he had thought to ask more questions at the start of this whole thing, he wouldn't be in the mess that he was in now.

"I'm sure a lot of this is very confusing, but I assure you once you get the hang of things it will become second nature."

"I'd like to think that I won't ever become that callous when it comes to making these decisions. These are human beings, you know. They have family and friends and lives. Who am I to send them to…"

"Hell, young man. I believe the word you're looking for is Hell. Don't worry though, you'll be surprised how quickly you can get used to something when you don't have a choice." a dark smile came across Balaam's face.

Kevin felt a jolt of electricity that caused goose pimples to rise on his arms, and the hair on the back of his neck to stand at attention. Balaam was right though, he had no choice. He still wasn't exactly sure what the elder man had meant when he said Kevin would be in forfeiture and he wasn't in any hurry to find out.

"Now, if you will excuse me for just a moment." Balaam rose from the table and headed in the direction of the men's room.

So far, Kevin understood what his role was to be. How he was supposed to get such things organized had not yet been explained to him. This was not anything he had expected. What business did he have capturing souls? He motioned towards the server, indicating a refill on his coffee was badly needed.

Several minutes passed before Balaam returned to the table.

"I have just been informed that your studio is ready for business. Would you like to go see it?"

Kevin's jaw dropped. Balaam pulled a roll of bills from his pants pocket, left several twenties on the table, took his awestruck recruit by the arm, and walked out the door. The next thing Kevin knew, he awoke in the front seat of Balaam's car.

10

From his vantage point through the passenger side window, Kevin was able to see directly into the front window of a high end photo studio and gallery. Balaam was standing outside the door, pulling it open.

"Mr. Collins, allow me to be the first one to welcome you to the new home of Kevin Collins Photography: An Above the Skin company. I told you before, nobody is going to open that car door for you."

The space on the inside was magnificent. While attending CalArts, Kevin had been lucky enough to work in some of the most technologically advanced shooting workspaces in the world. This place put them all to shame. The lighting itself must have cost a fortune. Traditional studio lamps had been replaced with fully programmable smart lights. They had quickly become a must have for all hot shot photographers. The lights did not cast shadows and were fully programmable with over three thousand colors. In many studios, that feature alone was worth the asking price. Looking around, Kevin saw at least a dozen sets built above, under, and into the space. This was the type of place that art could be made.

"I hope everything is to your liking, Mr. Collins." Balaam stated as the front door closed itself behind him.

"This is a truly excellent space, and I don't want to appear ungrateful, but are you sure you want me to run it?"

"Listen, Kevin, your CityScapes project last year was outstanding. The promise we saw in your work told us we would be foolish not to work with you. You have a real gift, son, and as the high end photography house in the world, it only makes sense to bring you into the fold. You very well could be the future of this company. I can promise you this, when you complete the contract for us, I'll give you the option to stay or go. It will be entirely up to you, no repercussions, you keep everything you were promised and we go our separate ways."

He had nothing more to lose than anything he had already signed up for. He did, however, have one last question for his mysterious benefactor.

"Back at the diner, you said the camera has the ability to capture souls. How exactly does that work? What happens to the people in black and white?"

"Why death, my dear boy. Anyone whose capture comes back black and white won't see another seventy-two hours. These souls are, without a doubt, ours. They have zero redeeming qualities. They are dangerous. Sometimes to themselves, more often than not, they are a threat to others. The primary goal of this project is to find such people, get them in front of the camera and delete them."

Kevin sat down in one of the lobby chairs and closed his eyes. There seemed to be an awful lot involved in what he had foolishly believed was just a run-of-the-mill photographer gig. Now he was being asked to pass judgment on people based on the revelations of a magic camera. Technically, he wasn't judging anyone, that was the camera's doing. These people had made their own choices and damned themselves. No one ever led them to temptation, and it was his job to deliver them to evil. He was there to capture one of their final moments in time.

"So tell me, Mr. Collins, are we ready to open for business?"

Kevin had to admit that they were. He introduced himself to Lucie, she apparently had been hired to answer the phone and keep customers happy in case of delays. She was an affable enough older woman who seems to have been doing this type of work for a while. The electric chime to indicate the opening of the door went off just as the phone began to ring. Lucie scooped up the receiver while Kevin headed to the door to greet who might be his first customer.

As it turned out, his first arrivals were a young couple who had come in to inquire about an engagement photo for her local paper back in Wichita. After some brainstorming, they developed a plan. Kevin slipped an ATS release form in front of each of them, gathering them up once signed and passing them to Lucie for filing. After that, he flipped a switch and took Stephanie Miller and Andrew Wilkins into the workshop. It would be the last picture of Andrew Wilkins anyone would ever take. One week later, local police discovered the body of a man who may be a match for a recent missing person report. He was slumped over in the doorway of a red-light district hotel room with a needle hanging out of his arm. As it turned out, old Andrew wasn't actually Andrew at all. His name was actually Hal Jensen. He was thirty-two years old, originally from Dearborn, MI. Jensen fled Michigan once local police began looking at him for a series of rapes. The pattern continued in Boulder, Phoenix, and Reno. Three months earlier he had settled down in L.A. where he met Stephanie Miller, as she was literally getting off the bus. After learning all of this, any remaining hesitation Kevin had about the job drifted away once he realized he saved that young girl's life. The four digit counter on the Canon changed from zero to one.

12

As the weeks went by, Kevin became fully immersed in his new role. He met all kinds of people who, unlike the ones in the mall, actually wanted to be together. They wanted to capture these moments, and they were willing to pay big bucks to do so. In the first three weeks, Kevin had made more money than he had ever seen in his life. It allowed him to pay his bills and move out of the rat trap that he had called home since graduating. As far as he could tell, everything was going well. The counter on the Canon had gone from one to forty two in just the first month. What initially sounded like an impossible task, one thousand pictures meeting the criteria set forth in the contract, was starting to seem more and more feasible. Lucie was worth her weight in gold, Kevin was convinced he couldn't run the place without her, and she made sure he knew it. Business was on the rise and he hadn't seen or heard from Balaam since the day he moved into the space.

Business had been booming, and as the only shooter in the shop, he was starting to run out of gas. This was something he was going to have to talk with Balaam about if he ever saw him again. It would be another six months before his boss popped in for a visit. Kevin was happy to see him, despite the surprise nature of his visit.

"There's my boy. How's it going, young man?" Balaam offered, stepping forward to offer his hand in greeting.

"Things couldn't be going any better. We're booked from open to closing every day. I don't want to open on Sundays, but I might have to. Some weeks I just can't handle the influx."

"We have been monitoring your progress and you are exceeding all of our expectations. What's the counter up to now?"

"As of last night, it was up to 312. Like I said, I've been really busy."

"What can I do to help you? Do you need a break, that can be arranged. It doesn't stop the clock, but you are on track to meet your goal, so now may not be a bad time for that." Balaam offered. Kevin shook his head.

"What I really need is another photographer. I've got all that space and it's just me and Lucie. Surely I can afford to bring in some more help."

Balaam paused for a moment, stroking a goatee that Kevin couldn't remember having seen before.

"I am a fan of that idea, however, given the nature of what we do here, it's just not as simple as collecting resumes."

"I understand that. Is there maybe someone in the organization that we can bring in? Somebody who already has a signed NDA. What about David or Lyndsey from the kiosk?"

"Ah yes, the kiosk. Sincerest apologies, my boy, we closed that location a couple of months ago. Actually, we closed twenty locations a couple of months ago. It's just as we discussed over that first lunch. All the numbers that we were presented ended up being off by less than one half of a percent. At this point, all the mall operations will be closed down in the next eight months. As soon as the last Christmas appointment is scheduled, that's all she wrote. As far as I'm aware, Lyndsey moved on to another job. Although I can't recall having heard anything about her recently."

"What about David? He's a pretty good photographer."

"He was. Sadly, he was found hanging from a support beam in his garage two days after we closed that location. It was very sad."

"The company could have done a better job of letting that word get around. I only worked with him for a couple of months, but he seemed like a good guy whose work should have been acknowledged much more. Especially by the company. I would have at least liked to have paid my respects."

"It was very sudden. His family pushed the whole thing through pretty quickly. I believe he was buried two days after they found him. No wake, no memorial service, just claimed the body and laid it to rest."

Kevin shook his head. From the sounds of things, he was going to be here alone for a while.

"Well, thanks for the heads up. I guess. I don't mean to be rude, but I've got three shoots set up for the next hour, so if you don't mind I'm going to go sleep for five minutes in my office." Kevin turned towards the door marked employees only.

Balaam took one last look around, gave a nod and a wink to Lucie, and walked out the door. He wasn't worried. The kid was holding up and doing a great job. He was on schedule, and according to the print labs, all of his work had been categorized properly. Balaam continued to be confident in his decision with the hiring of Kevin. And whether or not he knew it, Kevin had made the right decision by accepting the offer.

13

The five minute nap ended up being a ten minute nap, not that it put him in any better of a mood. At least his day was winding down. Three shoots left and based on the intake forms, they all seemed to be run of the mill. A family picture, a new baby, and an actor's headshot. All things being equal, all three sittings went pretty well. The family and the baby came back fine. Families were, at times, a tricky proposition. From time to time, a sole member of a family would come back black and white. To his initial surprise, children would be revealed as frequently as any of the adults. In a situation like that, there wasn't much to do. Any contract signed by someone under the age of eighteen was non binding. The best that Kevin could hope for is that someone will keep an eye on the kid and lead them down a different road. At least that's what he hoped would happen. Of course, if a child had already committed enough sin to morally corrupt their soul at such a young age, Kevin was unsure how effective a change would need to be to save him. The actor's headshot, on the other hand, came back a crisp black and white. He had no way of knowing what this guy did, but he clearly did something. With the day's work completed, Kevin sent Lucie home and went about cleaning up.

14

It was the end of a very long day as Kevin turned the key to lock up. He had but one thing on his mind as he pulled down the security shutter, and that one thing was sleep. His first appointment wasn't until eleven tomorrow, so he planned to take advantage of every extra moment he could. At least that had been his plan until he heard a familiar voice from behind.

"Sure beats that shit hole in the mall."

Across the street stood one of the few people Kevin considered to be a friend since he moved out west. They had only worked together for a couple of months before Kevin got dragged into his current situation, but Lyndsey Davis had been a person he could actually talk to as opposed to the general platitudes he offered his potential customers.

"I could be working out of an actual shit hole and I would be happier than I was there." Kevin crossed to the other side of the road and was quickly embraced by the girl.

"Do you have any idea how much you suck, Kevin? Any idea at all? We closed up together one night and then I didn't see or hear from you for seven months. What the fuck dude? Seriously."

"I know, I know, I'm a terrible friend. I am so sorry. You would not believe what has happened in the last few months."

"What are you doing right now?" Lyndsey asked.

He didn't want to tell her that his entire plan involved going home and falling asleep on the first piece of furniture he came across.

"I just closed up for the night, and I don't have to be back until eleven tomorrow morning. What's on your mind?"

"We need drinks! Follow me!" Lyndsey proclaimed, as she began to skip down the street in the direction of the nearest bar, which happened to be Cutty's Tavern on the corner. He did his best to put some hitch in his giddy up and followed his enthusiastic friend into the bar.

15

The music of the Rolling Stones echoed off the walls as they made their way to a dirty booth in the back corner of the room. Lyndsey waved in the direction of the waitress.

"What are you drinking, Kevin old buddy?"

"Beer will be fine."

The waitress, who introduced herself as either Meg or Peg, it was a little hard to make out over the guitar wizardry of Keith Richards. Lyndsey shouted over the noise and ordered a pitcher of whatever they had on tap.

"So spill it man, what the hell happened to you?"

The first pitcher had arrived as Kevin began to fill Lyndsey in on the events of the last seven months. He told her about Balaam and the Canon. He told her about them giving him the studio. For a moment, he almost lost his place, and told her the rest of the story, but decided against it. It had been quite some time since they had seen each other, and he didn't think tales of capturing souls with a magic camera were really the way he wanted to reconnect with her. By the time he finished talking, there were three empty pitchers on the table and a fourth had been well worked on.

"Well, Kev, that is a hell of a story right there. It does look like you're doing better for yourself. I too am living a charmed life. Great job, great place, great friends. You know how it is."

The clock on the wall said 11:56. At least that's what he thought it said. Truth be told, the whole room had gotten a bit blurry about a half hour ago. It was time to go home.

"Well, my dear, it has been an absolute delight seeing you again. I did regret the way things went down with the mall, but like I said, it all happened quickly. I was actually going to ask you out the last time I saw you."

Lyndsey began to blush after hearing this declaration. Kevin saw a devious grin cross her face.

"What do you say we get out of here?" She didn't need to ask twice.

16

Despite having moved into his new place six months ago, he hadn't actually spent enough time here to unpack. He had set up his basic kitchen needs and his bedroom. The rest was still a work in progress. He rolled over to see that the previous night had not been a dream and that the girl of his dreams was still lying in bed next to him. The only downside to this otherwise perfect morning was that the bedside clock read 9:45 a.m. He did his best not to disturb her as he slipped from the bed. He may not have gotten as much sleep as he planned to, but given the circumstance, he wasn't complaining.

It was an hour later when Kevin pulled into his spot behind the shop. He came in through the back door and dropped his jacket and bag in his office. He made his way up front to find Lucie engaged in conversation with Balaam.

"Mr. Balaam, always a delight when you drop by. Especially when those visits come so close together. What can I do for you, boss?"

"We need to talk about you and Lyndsey."

The two men made their way back to Kevin's office. Balaam sat behind Kevin's desk, a power move if he had ever seen one.

"Okay, so my first question is how do you know about me and Lyndsey?"

"Dear boy, you work for me. I'm pretty much aware of what you're doing during every waking hour. Don't ever forget that. With that being said, what exactly is your plan there?"

"I don't really have a plan. We just hung out last night for the first time. It's not like I'm planning a wedding or anything. As far as I can tell, we're just friends."

"Let's keep it that way shall we. Remember that you have a contract to fulfill, and even though you're doing great so far, that doesn't mean you can rest on your laurels. We still need six hundred plus photos from you. When you complete your contract, I won't care what you do, but until that happens, I'll expect you to find better ways to spend your time. Do we understand each other, Mr. Collins?"

"You're the boss." Kevin was taken aback by his demeanor. Something had put a spur under Balaam's saddle.

Kevin watched Balaam turn and walk out the door of the studio. He held it open as Kevin's eleven o'clock passed through. The day had begun. For better or worse, nine of the eleven adult clients he had came up black and white. The rest had been beautiful pictures of happy families and newborn babies. It was a busy day, but it ended in a considerably better way than it had started.

17

He had begun to grow concerned that he hadn't seen or heard from Lyndsey since leaving for work this morning. As a matter of course, he didn't leave anyone alone in his apartment. It wasn't as if he thought someone was going to rob him or commit some other variety of mischief. It had more to do with his neighbors when he lived downtown. They were always in everyone's business, and although it was never proven, at least prior to him moving out, it was commonly assumed that they were porch pirates. This, however, was a much classier neighborhood. After closing up for the night, he took the two block stroll back to his building. An amazing aroma filled the hall as he exited the elevator, and it only improved as he approached his apartment door.

Kevin's head was quickly filled with confusion as he looked around his apartment. Things had been cleaned. Boxes emptied and removed. And yes, that enticing aroma from the hall was being generated from his apartment. Looking around the corner, he was slightly surprised to see that Lyndsey was still there.

"Oh good, you're home. Dinner will be ready in just a couple of minutes. You want a beer?"

Kevin nodded, still trying to figure out what the hell was going on in his house.

Moments later, the best home cooked meal he could remember having in years was laid out on the table.

"So this looks and smells wonderful. When did you find the time?"

"Oh, I was in and out of the apartment all day. I went to the market to pick up some supplies for dinner. I did some laundry at the place down the block. I saw there was a room here in the building, but it must need a key card or some such thing, because I could not get in there. While I was out, I grabbed a few things from my place and came back to start dinner."

"Lyndsey, and I mean no disrespect here, but why are you still here?" Kevin inquired.

Kevin saw the look on her face change. It went from scary excitable to deep and brooding in a flash.

"That's what you have to say to me? Not thanks for getting the laundry done, Lyndsey. Not thanks for making this delicious dinner, Lyndsey. Not thanks for unpacking all my shit, Betty. No, nothing like that. Nothing positive. Just hey crazy Betty what are you still doing in my house?" She grabbed the edge of the dining room table and upended it, causing a barrage of dishes and food to splatter throughout the apartment.

Kevin, having been raised in a volatile household, knew the best way to react to this situation was to stay low to the ground. One too many close calls with an airborne dish. What he needed to do at the moment was get this crazy bitch out of his apartment. Based on his observation of the situation, that was going to be a task much easier said than done. Then the apartment was filled with an eerie silence. Kevin carefully stuck his head up to get an idea of what was going on. He was taken aback by the sight of Lyndey passed out cold on the floor in the living room. Right now, there was only one thing he needed to know. It may be wrong, but after what just happened he wasn't too concerned with right or wrong at the moment. He was more concerned with good and evil. Grabbing his camera bag from his office, Kevin carefully made his way through the broken glass and remnants of food that were decorating the dining room and into his office. Opening his camera bag, he pulled out the Canon and made his way back into the living room. He stood there for what felt like forever, and stared down at this broken creature, passed out from too much rage on his living room floor. The woman who had shared his bed just the night before had now stepped outside of her mind and trashed his house. He needed to know what to expect, because next time, if there was going to be one, he might not be as lucky. He lifted the Canon and framed the girl. The view finder immediately showed him the black and white girl lying on a full color carpet. As if it had become second nature to him, he snapped a picture of the dark. In a few days, a week at the most, something terrible was going to happen to this girl. Balaam must have known. That certainly would explain his mood the last time they met.

18

Approximately a half an hour had passed before the sounds of stirring started to come from the living room. He looked around the corner from the kitchen and into the living room. From his vantage point, he could see the girl trying to get up from the floor. It occurred to Kevin that shit had gone sideways.

"Ah man, what the fuck!" Lyndsey's voice came drifting in from the remnants of what used to be his dining room.

Kevin scanned the room for anything that could be used as a weapon. He wasn't sure if she was still crazy, but he sure as hell was going to take that chance unarmed.

"Kevin?" The disembodied voice sounded closer now.

He stood behind the support beam, waiting to see what her next move was going to be.

"Kevin? Kevin, what happened here?" a true tone of confusion rising in her voice. He stepped out from his hiding space.

She looked around at the disaster surrounding them. She had no recollection of anything that happened after putting dinner on the table.

She looked over at Kevin, whose skin was beet red and buckets of sweat were pouring down his face.

"Oh man, I think it happened again." she offered remorsefully.

"What happened again?"

"When I saw you the other day, I wasn't exactly honest with you."

His breath had begun to return to normal, his heart was no longer throbbing, and his skin had returned to its normal color. He looked at the girl directly in the eye and said…

"Start talking."

And start talking she did. The truth was that she had been out of work since the kiosk in the mall was shut down. After missing rent for the second month, she came home one day to find her stuff on the sidewalk. She grabbed all she could fit in the Ford Taurus. It was less than half her stuff, and she doubted there would be much left if she went back for the rest.

"For the first couple of days, things were okay. I had found a couple shelters I could float between, so I wasn't sleeping in my car. That's supposed to be really dangerous, especially for women. Truth, though, is that there are just as many handsy fuckers in those places. Especially if you're a young woman. So after that, it was back in the car. I never parked in the same place twice. No point in giving the cops or the creeps easy pickings. Anyway, I was driving down the street, headed to see a friend for some dinner, and low and behold, Kevin Collins Photography. Big as all get out, and I think to myself.."

"Oh, that must be what happened to my good buddy, Kevin. So I left the car in a vacant lot and hung around the park, waiting for you to close up for the day. And here we are."

Kevin stared at the girl in disbelief. Her story was tragic, and he might be the only friend she had. It still didn't explain the freakout at dinner, but it was a start.

"There was no one out there for you? No family, no friends?"

She looked up at him, tears running down her cheeks, which had now taken on a red color similar to the one most recently displayed by Kevin.

"My parents died in an apartment fire. The police said that the cause was faulty wiring." She had been lucky the fire escape was directly outside her window. She climbed down the three story ladder and dropped into the arms of a waiting firefighter.

"Good lord, how old were you?" Kevin asked, a look of shock across his face.

"I was nine then. From that night' til the day I turned eighteen, I was passed around a series of foster homes. Which takes a strong second place for places to go if you want to get molested. Not long after getting out of that situation, I got the job in the mall. I thought I was in the process of making new friends, and then I found out that one of them had killed himself and the other had just moved on without a word. It's been a rough couple of months."

Kevin couldn't come to grips with what he was being told. This poor girl, whose life was shattered by the death of her parents, was then forced to live with perverts before finally being free a year ago. The system had failed her. He slowly rose from his chair and sat next to her on the couch, wrapping a blanket around her shoulders. She leaned into him and before long was fast asleep.

In the morning, Keven walked from his room, his bathrobe cinched at the waste. He quietly stepped into the living room, expecting to see an empty room. He found her curled up on the couch, half covered in the blanket he gave her last night. From the corner of his eye, he saw the Canon sitting on the pass thru. He grabbed the camera and once again aimed it at Lyndsey. Kevin looked up from the camera and through the viewfinder again. The picture was in full color.

Over the course of the last year, Kevin had shot four hundred and sixty two black and white photos. He had shot hundreds more in full color, but never had he seen one person photograph both ways. He thought that Balaam probably knew what it meant, but the last time the two had met, tempers started to flare over his involvement with Lyndsey. This was certainly not going to go over with the boss, but maybe there was somebody else he could talk to.

19

He left the apartment that morning around 8:30 AM. His first shoot wasn't until ten, but he wanted to have a chat with Lucie, and preferred to do it when they wouldn't be interrupted. He had always felt that Lucie knew a lot more than she let on. Like the day the studio was open, she was there. Her desk was set up, she even had a personalized placard. He pulled into his spot behind the studio and came in through the back door. He hung his jacket from the hook attached to the outside of his office door and made his way to the front of the house.

"Good morning Mr. Collins. How is your day going so far?"

"Lucie, would you mind if I asked you a personal question?"

"Sure, but if it's something disgusting or sexual, I won't answer it."

Kevin chuckled at the thought of having a sex talk with his elderly receptionist. He was pretty sure that such discussions would have violated a couple of laws.

"No, no, nothing like that. I was just wondering about how long you've been working for ATS."

Lucie looked over at her "boss", wondering why after all this time he finally got around to asking the question.

"Young man, that is almost as rude as asking a woman her age. I'll say this: in my time with the company I have seen a lot of things and watched people come and go, but I'm still here."

Kevin paused for a moment, trying to figure out exactly what that meant.

"You don't really work for me do you?"

"I am an employee of ATS and my first loyalty will always be to ATS, and more specifically, SVP of Special Technology William Balaam. I "work" for you in whatever capacity Mr. Balaam requires me to."

"So when Balaam talks about knowing everything that goes on around here...."

"Most of that information is coming directly from me." Lucie offered without hesitation.

So for eight to twelve hours a day he was here with only one other person, and now it turns out that person can't be trusted. The little holes that kept popping up in his contract made him really start to question if the whole thing was even worth it. Three million dollars. That's what was on the line. He would be out of debt, and would have made enough of a name for himself that the idea of opening his own studio was beginning to look like a reality. A place of his own where he could run things his way, and he was fairly confident that his clientele would follow.

From a week before Christmas until the middle of January, there was always a lull in business. The Christmas card orders have been submitted and were being processed. He had been hired to shoot a wedding on New Year's Day. It had been a long time since Kevin had shot couples tying the knot, and he was really in no mood to go back to that line of work, so when he provided his estimate, which was twice his normal fee, he found himself painted into a corner when the bride and groom agreed to the price. He marked the date on his calendar. They wrote up the contract; he received a twenty-five percent retainer.

"And the very best part of working with me is that I'll show you what your pictures can look like. If you would just step into room two and we'll take a couple of shots for fun." The couple beamed and headed into room two.

"You're starting to get really good at this." he heard coming from his receptionist.

Kevin rolled his eyes. After the Christmas holidays, the counter on the camera had jumped up to 590 signed and delivered. He knew he was coming up on less than six months before this complete clusterfuck was finally over. The name Kevin Collins had become synonymous with high end photography. After a year and a half, he had taken in almost as much money as was tied up in his contract. The studio had been a success since day one. As if by magic, the entire building, sign, equipment, everything they needed to get up and running just appeared. And even though Kevin had been willing to accept that such a task could be accomplished with enough bodies and know how. What he had never wrapped his head around was the immediate success. Usually, all new businesses have a rough patch in the beginning. Word of mouth, digitally or orally, can take time to spread, but not for Kevin. From day one forward, he continued to grow his success. His social media presence, whoever was in charge of that, continued to be on point and had begun to end up in the hands of the influencers. This led to appointment requests from all over the state. And through it all Lucie was there to dutifully keep track of every minute. Despite his occasional uneasiness towards the elder woman, the two of them did make a fantastic team.

20

While he still wasn't making the type of art he wanted to, once he got this monkey off his back he would have the means to do what he wanted. Meanwhile, he had begun to live as frugally as possible. After the first major meltdown, things with Lyndsey were being handled slowly. The more he found out about her life, the more he felt like he should try to fix her. Her time on the street had brought back her demons. He had moved her in with him, not long after that first night. The agreement was made that they were to be friends and roommates. They were not a couple, nor were they going to be. He laid it out that there would be no drug use outside of prescriptions. Kevin, having no knowledge of psychiatry or such things, wasn't sure what exactly was wrong with her, but he knew that sleeping in her car certainly wasn't a positive step in any direction. During the first few weeks, it had become quite clear to Kevin that there was something seriously wrong with Lyndsey. Something that he wasn't going to be able to fix. They were going to need a professional. Lyndsey, who depending on the day of the week could be in any condition depending on what she had been able to beg, borrow, or steal to get the next hit. While he knew he could keep her from getting high in the apartment, he couldn't keep an eye on her twenty-four hours a day.

According to Dr. Jennifer Kale, a very helpful Psychiatrist at a local clinic,

" It's very difficult to actually make a diagnosis without seeing the patient in person, but based on what you've told me, it sounds like Lyndsey is displaying classic signs of behavior commonly referred to as self medication. The behavior is most common amongst people with diseases such as Bi-Polar 1, and Schizophrenia. These diseases, and others like them, can be difficult to treat successfully and continuously. The problem with psych drugs is that if they do what they are supposed to, the patient feels "normal" again, decides they must be cured, and that they no longer need to take the meds. Of course, we know that's not how these things work. The medication provides balance to an askew brain. Thing is, no two cases of mental illness, especially ones involving severe chemical imbalances are the same. That is why it takes so long to find a proper balance of medications and why it is very dangerous for patients to just stop cold turkey. The sudden imbalance can cause a variety of antisocial behavior up to and including violent outburst."

"Well, that is certainly something I will have to look out for." Kevin offered, somewhat distraught.

"Mr. Collins, this is no joke. If your friend is displaying any of these behaviors, the very best thing you can do for her is to get her help. My schedule here is pretty packed, but I am quite concerned about your situation." She reached into the pocket of her white lab coat and pulled out a business card. "I'm going to put my pager and cell number on the back. I want you to discuss what we talked about with your friend. Explain to them they don't have to live that way anymore and that there are people who want to help her. Call me to let me know what she said."

"Thank you so much for all your help Dr. Kale. I will definitely be in touch with you soon." He shook the woman's hand and headed back to the parking structure. His blood pressure began to rise upon arriving at the vehicle and finding the word "rapist" haphazardly painted on both sides of the car. Attached to the windshield wiper was a small folded sheet of yellow paper. Kevin looked around and saw no evidence of anyone else on this level. He unfolded the note and was shocked by its contents..

"You may have forgotten about me, but I sure as fuck haven't forgotten what you did to me. Just know this, I know where you live, where you work, I can come for you anytime I want to. Betty,"

Kevin had been raised in a generation that was taught to believe women who claim they have been sexually assaulted. Of course, he never thought that such a belief should include the immediate public crucifixion of the accused. This left him with a quandary. He could call the cops and report the incident. It should be a simple process, taking into account he had no idea who the hell Betty was. He wasn't sure how hard that might be to explain to the local authorities. On the other hand, he certainly couldn't be seen driving around in the car in its current condition. He reached into his coat pocket, pulled out his cell, and dialed 911.

The interaction with the police had gone easier than expected. Kevin insisted that not only hadn't he raped anyone, he didn't even know anybody named Betty. He asked the officer if this type of thing was common? The cop proposed that perhaps the perpetrator had picked the wrong car. Or, he quickly added, and this is one is far less common, it is someone you know who, for some reason, has decided to fuck around with you. Neither one of those options sounded like anything Kevin wanted to be involved with. He was far more comforted, which seemed strange, by the idea that some crazy stalker picked the wrong car. It wasn't like his Canyonero was all that uncommon. There were two other models on this parking level alone. He complied with the officer's request to leave the vehicle for further investigation. The two men exchanged business cards in case either had any further queries or recollections. Opening the Going Your Way app, he ordered a ride and headed to the elevator.

21

The ride home, for the most part, was delightfully quiet. Most of the time, he could muster up enough interest to engage in an ultimately pointless conversation. He had never stepped out of a hired car, feeling as if he had taken another step towards the eternal bliss of Nirvana. Tonight was not one of those nights. As they approached his apartment, the car's windshield was filled with the red and blue flashing lights usually associated with emergency services. The driver got as close as he could without risking an encounter with the police. Having already spent more time than he preferred in the company of law enforcement, Kevin slipped out of the passenger side rear door and onto the corner one block down from the building. He worked his way down to the corner, explaining to anyone who asked or even looked in his direction that he lived in the building and was more than happy to show everyone on sight his driver's license. A large officer directly in front of the door grabbed the license from the much smaller Kevin's hand. The hulking peacekeeper scanned his UV flashlight, verifying that all identifying watermarks were present. The officer handed the card back to Kevin and waved him through the front door.

Concern was the immediate emotion that filled Kevin's mind upon stepping off the elevator. For every cop downstairs, there were two up here. As he approached the gathering, he began to see broken, but familiar pieces of furniture outside in the hall. He was stopped by an older black gentleman in what is commonly described as a "cop suit" He stuck out his hand…

"You wouldn't by any chance be Kevin Collins would you?" the man asked. Kevin looked at the hand suspiciously. It was removed.

"Yes, I am Kevin Collins. Yes, this is my apartment. I've lived here for almost two years. This is my second encounter with law enforcement today, and frankly it's getting a little tiring. Now I have two questions for you. The first is who are you and the second is why are you in my place?"

"Mr. Collins, my name is Detective Jason Watershed. I am a homicide detective for the Westdale Police Department. I am here responding to a 911 call."

"911? What the hell happened?"

"Well, I was kind of hoping you'd help me out there. Your neighbor from downstairs called us after she heard screaming and yelling followed by at least one gunshot. She said it might have been two, but wasn't sure."

Kevin slid down the wall until he found himself sitting on the floor, looking up at Detective Watershed.

"Is she dead?" he croaked

"Who exactly are we talking about?"

"Lyndsey of course. Who else would there be?"

"Well, see that's an interesting question Mr. Collins. For starters, Lyndsey is alive. We took her by ambulance to Greendale Community Hospital. She was in pretty bad shape."

Kevin made a move to head back to the elevator when Watershed grabbed his arm.

"Mr. Collins, you running off to the hospital is not the best thing for anybody right now. There are a number of very curious aspects to what happened here today, and I'm going to need as much of your help as you can give me. By then, we should have an update on Lyndsey, and I promise you I will drive you to the hospital myself."

Kevin had to admit that this cop wasn't so bad and genuinely seemed to care about this situation. Kevin extended his hand to Watershed in a sign of respect and cooperation. The two men took the elevator downstairs and grabbed a table at the cafe on the first floor.

Over the course of the next several hours, Kevin laid out the exact circumstances under which he and Lyndsey met. He told him about the freak out on her first night at the apartment, the suspected drug use, and his conversation with Dr. Kale about some of her stranger behavior. That topic was exactly what he had planned to discuss with her upon arriving home that night.

"Here's the thing that's got us all stumped here. Your building has a rather impressive security system. I guess you get what you pay for. So after discovering the scene upstairs and locking everything down, my next course of action was to get a look at those video tapes. Fortunately, the company that provides the security for the building has an open book policy when it comes to dealing with police requests. In less than a half an hour, I was sitting in an air conditioned room, staring at a wall full of monitors that offered coverage of 98% of the public areas."

Kevin's patience was beginning to wear thin. He didn't give a shit about how many security cameras there were in the building or how much coverage they provided. All he wanted to do was get the fuck out of here and go to the hospital to see his friend. Watershed could see the frustration building in Kevin's face.

"My point, Mr Collins, is that nobody gets in or out of this building or any individual apartment without the building being aware of it. Now what I'd like you to do for me is sit here and watch this footage with me, and then we can go to the hospital."

What followed was eight hours of footage from three cameras that recorded the comings and goings of the floor. One static camera across from the elevator doors and motion sensors, one at each end of the hall provided a constant view of any activity. Thanks to the wonder of time lapse video, they would only need to be here for minutes as opposed to hours. The first section of the video was of Kevin leaving for the studio around 9:15 AM that morning. There was no activity anywhere on the floor from the time he left until the timestamp read 3:44 PM. At that exact moment, the door to his apartment opened, and Lyndsey was suddenly tossed into the hallway. A moment later, she began to flail her arms and throw herself against the steel door. She then returns to the inside of the residence and appears to be arguing with someone out of the shot. This was followed by his front door flying open and objects began being hurled at the wall across the hall. The door was closed and the next time jump was approximately twenty minutes later when the first of the officers arrived to answer the noise complaint.

"You see the problem I have here Mr. Collins. After you leave for work, no one enters the floor. When your door was opened, Lyndsey was clearly seen arguing with someone. No one comes in or out of the apartment until our officers arrive, yet when they get here, they discover Lyndsey who has been savagely attacked and the apartment ransacked. Nailed to the back of the door was this note." Watershed handed the yellow paper to Kevin, who didn't even need to open it, to know who it was from.

"Kevin, I told you I can get to you and yours anytime I want. I look forward to seeing you this holiday season. XOXOXO. Betty."

"I spoke with one of the officers in auto theft. He told me about what happened to your car today. He also mentioned that there was a note at that scene as well. Let me guess, this Betty person?"

"I don't think I've ever even met someone named Betty. This whole thing seems to be escalating quickly. First my car, then she tries to kill Lyndsey, I dislike the direction this thing is going in. Can we go to the hospital now?" Watershed grabbed his coat from the back of the chair and pressed the down call button for the elevator.

22

The last of his scheduled appointments was in mid-December, with pick ups happening until December 21st. After that the shop was going to be closed from the twenty second through the middle of January. He had the wedding scheduled for New Year's Day, but aside from that, his time was his own. He had originally planned to use that time working on his own projects, but this new circumstance had thrown a spanner into the works. There was no sign of Lucie or Balaam once he arrived at the ER. That was good, he really wasn't in the mood for a lecture right now. He ran up to the information desk and breathlessly inquired about the status of Lyndsey. The nurse began her search, all the while doing her best to calm him down. As the search proceeded, an alarm suddenly went off, and a speaker came over the speaker system announcing a code black.

"Are you the one who called 911?" a nurse stood up with a clipboard filled with papers.

"Um, no I just got here. What the hell is a code black?"

"And your relationship with the patient?"

"No, seriously, what is a code black?"

If Sheryl hadn't been on her thirty-seventh continuous hour of work, she may have been a little more protective of the meaning of this particular medical code.

"It's a psych code. It means a patient has committed or threatened to commit self harm. Somebody should be down to deal with it soon."

Kevin walked away from the desk, scanning the room, looking for a way past the desk and further into the hospital. His wait for an opportunity was short lived, as a doctor wearing a key card with a red stripe across the top. Assuming this was the psychiatrist he had been waiting for, he stood, making as if to head towards a vending machine, all the while keeping an eye on the small bespectacled man, waiting for his one chance to present itself. The moment finally came as the doctor removed a small plastic card from his coat pocket and pressed it to the plate. A door marked 'Medical Personnel Only After This Point' swung open and Kevin was able to slip through.

The room beyond the door crackled with the chaotic energy that Kevin assumed existed in all Emergency Rooms. While the men and women of the hospital staff did their very best to keep things at least an organized chaos, Kevin had to believe that things moved at a rate he couldn't comprehend. He quietly made his way across the room, doing his best not to disturb any of the patients. Finally he peeked through a slightly askew curtain, and there she was. The doctor that he had followed in was standing over her, scanning the information on her chart. As if he had super hearing or eyes in the back of his head, the doctor, still not looking away from the chart, spoke to Kevin.

"Husband?"

"Pardon?"

"Are you here husband? Boyfriend maybe? How do you know this young woman?"

"Um, she's my roommate?"

"Roommate? I don't think that's covered under our direct family only policy for patients admitted into psychiatric wards, and that only begins after the initial seventy-two hour observation."

"So the plan is to isolate her further than she's already been feeling? I'm not a doctor or anything, but having spent the last six months with this girl, I think it's safe to say I know her a little better than you. She's sick in the head. I'm not here to tell you how to do your job, I'm just saying you may not want to start there."

"Thank you for your advice. Mr.."

"Collins. Kevin Collins. What do you think happened here doctor?"

"Well, Kevin, there is very little psychiatric history here. You say you've been roommates for the last six months, is that correct?"

"Yeah, maybe closer to seven months, but that's about right."

"So during that time, what kind of behavior have you seen from our girl here?"

Kevin stopped and pondered for a moment. He didn't want to say anything that might put Lyndsey farther in the hole here, but he knew that omitting things from the professionals never proved to be helpful. This was certainly one of those situations where speaking up was the right thing. Over the next hour, Kevin filled Dr. Wallace in on the strangeness that was living with Lyndsey.

Wallace agreed with the initial diagnosis by Dr. Kale. This girl clearly suffered from a severe mental disorder. It could be Bi-Polar or Dissociative Identity Disorder. The only way they would be able to tell for certain was to run tests. Of course, that would have to wait until her wounds had begun to heal.

Kevin shook the doctor's hand and headed towards the exit, as he saw security headed in his direction.

"Mr. Collins. One more thing. Who's Betty?"

"I wish I knew Doc. I wish I knew." Kevin answered, shaking his head.

Kevin took the escalator down to the lobby level, where he ordered a car to bring him home. All he wanted was eight to ten hours of uninterrupted sleep. He should have known better.

23

It was a stream of light pouring into his room that jarred him from what was the best sleep he'd had in weeks. But curtains don't open themselves. He rolled over to see the neutral face of his boss William Balaam, sitting in a kitchen chair staring at him, presumably while he was sleeping. Kevin wasn't sure if it was six feet, but he definitely sprung straight up. Balaam began to laugh with that disturbing chuckle of his.

"Good morning, Mr. Collins, it's so good to see you again." Balaam's face twisted in a sneer.

"Not that I don't cherish the time we spend together, but what are you doing in my house again?"

"Just checking in with you my boy, How are the numbers looking these days?"

It always gave Kevin a pause when Balaam would ask a question like that. Kevin assumed that he would have that information. Maybe he just enjoyed talking about it.

"As of last night, we're currently at 680 distinct photos." Kevin offered.

"You do know you are down to your last six months, right?"

"Oh, I am well aware, sir. The studio is booked solid from February through May, there are three weddings scheduled in April, and since it worked out so well the last time, I'm also shooting the Mills County High School Prom. So, between all of that, I don't think we'll have a problem hitting the numbers on time. Probably a day or two early at this rate."

"And you've been giving all your paperwork to Lucie for filing?"

"Yes sir, we've got the routine down pretty good. It took us a little too warm up to each other, but everything was running smoothly. I really don't know if I could run that place without her."

"So whose genius idea was it to shoot a prom? You know we don't sign contracts with minors."

"I know, but I also know that there will be a good handful of teachers, chaperones, etc. there as well as any seniors who have already turned 18. I'm guessing there may be a few bites there. So the more important question is why are you here?"

"Just a routine visit, my friend, Just want to make sure everything is running smoothly. What's your calendar looking like right now?"

Nothing had been on Kevin's calendar in weeks. Winter weather did little to encourage people to schlep through the snow and ice just to get photos taken.

"I am wide open, sir. Lead the way." He grabbed his jacket and followed Balaam out the doors. Surprisingly, there was no car waiting.

"No need for a car today, I don't know if you know this or not, but that restaurant across the street has the best cheesesteaks outside of Philadelphia. People have come from far and wide to put their meat and cheese where their mouths are. It wasn't even a competition. Like all great neighborhood gems, Jack's had a simple name and a simple goal. And I assure my boy, they achieve that goal with stunning accuracy."

The two men crossed the slush covered street. Kevin did his best not to fall on his ass, while Balaam moved with the surefootedness of a mountain goat. It turned out luck was with him today and Kevin made it across in one piece.

Kevin was entranced from the moment the door to Jack's Steaks swung open.

The aromas of a thousand cheesesteaks hung in the air like some kind of carnivorous pot-pourri. A mustachioed gentleman in a shirt and bolo tie approached them as they entered.

"Ah Mr. Balaam, a pleasure to see you again, it's been far too long." the man said, extending a hand in Balaam's direction.

"That is true, Jack. Sadly, us management types just don't have the free time we used to." Balaam smiled as he shook the man's hand.

"Jack, I'd like to introduce you to my new find and your new neighbor. Kevin Collins, meet Jack Evans. Founder, owner, and culinary mastermind behind the fine establishment we are now sitting in."

Kevin shook the man's hand and complimented him, stating that if the food tasted half as good as it smelled, he would eat until he burst.

Jack snapped his fingers and perhaps the most stunning redhead he had ever seen entered the space. In her hand was a serving tray. Placing the tray down, she quickly emptied its contents which consisted of two beers, which must have been some kind of Microbrew based on the mysterious label, and a basket of the most delightful smelling bread and rolls.

"Gentlemen, this is Alice. She's going to take care of you. Anything you need, don't hesitate to ask. Mr. Balaam, could I have a moment of your time in my office?" Balaam rose from the table and followed Jack towards the back of the restaurant.

Kevin couldn't help but notice a pale of sadness fall over the girl's face after what her boss had implied before leaving. He stopped her as she went to leave.

"Hey, hold on a second okay? I want to take your picture."

She looked at him suspiciously.

"Oh, no, no, I'm not a creep or anything like that. I'm a professional photographer. If you look outside the window right here, you can see my studio across the street."

She slid into the booth as he lifted the blinds and pointed out the green awning on the other side of the road.

"Kevin Collins, nice to meet you, Alice."

"Alice Wilson. Pleasure to meet you, Kevin."

"So I meant what I said. I really would like to take your picture."

The girl's cheeks began to turn rosy as she covered her face with her hands.

"I'm serious. I think you have a classic beauty and want to capture it on film. Nothing weird. I just think that it would be something that could bring some light into this world."

Alice looked up from her hands and met Kevin eye to eye. She could tell he meant what he was saying. Most of the fast talking slobs that came in here every night were trying out whatever new line they had heard on dipshit radio that morning. She might think he was crazy, but that was far from the truth.

"You don't want to do it here in the restaurant do you? I'm not exactly looking my best in a grease and cheese covered apron." She smiled at him.

He found her smile to be infectious.

"You may be onto something there. What time do you get off work?"

"I'll be closing tonight, so probably around 9:30. Kind of late." she replied.

"That's okay." Kevin replied. "I can keep the shop open late. It's the nice thing about being the boss." He smiled at her. "So why don't we say you meet me there around 10:00? That way, you can get yourself situated and I'll make sure the studio is ready."

From the corner of her eye, she saw her boss closing the door to his office. The two gentlemen returned to the table and Alice took orders from Kevin and Balaam.

The lunch was amazing, and while there were no major revelations, they confirmed everything was in order. He was on track to reach his contractual obligations ahead of schedule. Both Balaam and Sinclair were happy with the progression of the project, and there had been some rumblings about future work. After all was said and done, Balaam left several twenty-dollar bills on the table. Kevin reached into his pocket and pulled a fifty from the bills, sticking it under one of the empty water glasses.

'That good of a waitress?' Balaam offered jokingly.

"She really was. Maybe the best ever."

The men walked out on the sidewalk of Main St. The day had begun to warm up and significant parts of the sidewalk were now covered in half frozen puddles. A little less hazardous than what had been there. Balaam and Kevin concluded their business with a handshake and went their separate ways.

25

To his dismay, although not to his surprise, the shop was empty except for the always present Lucie.

"Anything I need to know about Lucie?"

"Nope, looks like the only thing on the calendar is your little rendezvous tonight with the waitress."

Kevin opened his mouth to ask how she knew about that, but realized such an inquiry would be fruitless. Lucie just knew shit.

"Well, if that's the case, why don't you pack it in early tonight old girl? You must have something better to do on a Friday night?"

"Well, I do like to go out and hurt people who call me old girl." she grinned at him. A shiver ran down his spine.

"Oh, there was one thing. Somebody named Betty called. Said you would know what it was about. Her number is on my desk if you want to call her back." Lucie grabbed her purse and coat from under her desk, bundled up, and headed out the back door to the parking lot. She paused for a moment, turning back to her boss.

"Kevin, I know you see me as an old nag who reports your every movement to our boss, and while all of that is true, let this old girl give you a smidge of advice. Be careful with that one. There's something really wrong there." He looked up to see her walking out, the door swinging shut behind her.

Kevin walked over to Lucie's desk and plopped down in the well worn desk chair. He'd have to remember to ask her if she would like a new one. It wasn't like they weren't doing well. He found a yellow sticky note attached to the monitor. The number didn't look the slightest familiar, and even if it did, it still didn't change the fact that he didn't know anyone named Betty. Using the desk phone, the shop's number was a matter of public record whereas his cell phone was not, he dialed the number on the note. The phone rang six times before going to voicemail. It was a generic message, doing nothing to help him identify this mystery caller. He hung up the phone, pocketed the yellow square, and made sure the shoot room was ready for his next appointment.

26

It was just before ten when there came a rapping on the front gate of the shop. Kevin stepped out of his office and unlocked the front door and security gate. Alice slipped underneath the partially raised gate and into the waiting room. Kevin re-locked the front entrance and turned to face his guest. The two shared a brief embrace.

"So I figured we'd start with the nickel tour if that's okay with you."

"That sounds great. Lead the way, good sir." Alice replied, doing her best to stifle a laugh.

When Kevin said it was a nickel tour, even that may have been a bit of an exaggeration. The reception area, the studio, and the lab only took up twenty-five percent of the total space. Balaam had never mentioned any type of expansion to him. Most of the space was actually behind a locked door to which Kevin had never seen the key.

"And that brings us to the end of our tour. I hope it was as exciting for you as it was for me." he offered in his best tour guide voice. This brought a smile to her face. She stepped forward and kissed him.

His initial reaction was to jump back in surprise, but at that moment, he wanted nothing more than to stay where he was. That was when someone started rattling the security gate out front. Separating himself from the moment, Kevin walked towards the front of the store and was in shock to see that it was Lyndsey. He unlocked the door and threw open the gates.

"Lyndsey, what the hell are you doing here? You're supposed to be in the hospital."

"Oh, so it was you that put us in there. Well, Mr. Collins, I have to thank you for that. Lyndsey had been slipping in and out over the last couple of years. Since she's known you, she has been doing her best to make sure you and I never met."

Kevin couldn't wrap his mind around what was happening in front of him. If this wasn't Lyndsey who the hell…

"Let me guess, you must be Betty." He offered confidently.

"Very good Mr. Collins. And who, may I ask, are you?" she set her glare on Alice.

"She's no one. Just a customer with a late night appointment. She has nothing to do with any of this." Kevin spoke in a tenor designed to bring Betty's attention back to him.

"Let's just let her go, and you and I can figure out what we're going to do next. How does that sound?"

From the corner of his eye, Kevin could see Alice making her way towards the fire exit in the rear of the building.

"Why don't you start by telling me what's bothering you today?" He offered in a calm and empathetic tone.

"Listen picture boy, that shit didn't work when the professionals tried it, I'm pretty sure you're not going to have any better luck."

Kevin slowly backed away from the intruder. He found himself behind Lucie's desk. His hand started fumbling around, looking for something to protect himself.

"Everything was going just fine before you showed up. We had worked out a deal to share space equally. That all changed after that first night you brought us back to your place. She felt safe with you. I, on the other hand, was not completely sold. That's why I trashed your place."

"You destroyed my apartment to test what my reaction would be? Seems like a bit of an overreaction, if you ask me. All I wanted to do was get to know this sweet girl who I hadn't seen in months. There was nothing sinister in my intentions, I assure you." Kevin continued to slide his hand around Lucie's desk until finally he came up with a letter opener. He hid it in his hand.

"So what happens next, Betty? Are you here to kill me? How exactly did you see this playing out in your head? Did you have a plan, because I do."

At that moment, Alice had reached the fire door and flung it open, setting off the store's alarm system. Betty turned her head to find the source of the noise, and in that second Kevin plunged the letter opener into the back of her skull. Her body hit the floor with a thud. In the distance, Kevin could already hear the approach of the sirens. He confirmed with Alice everything they had seen that night. There was a dead woman on the floor of his studio, and that was the least of his problems.

27

As expected, the police arrived within minutes. They were quickly followed by William Balaam and a massive companion. Kevin could not recall if he had ever seen a man that big in his life. That assumed that it was, in fact, a man. Knowing Balaam, anything was possible. The police spoke with both Alice and Kevin before being pulled aside by Balaam. Fifteen minutes later the police had heard all they needed. They thanked Alice and Kevin for their time and walked out the front door. This still did not solve the problem of the dead woman on the floor.

"What did I tell you?" The glare from Balaam's eyes was enough to freeze his insides.

Kevin opened his mouth to respond..

"No! You do not get to talk right now. How long ago was that? I want to say it was like two years ago. So that means either you've been seeing her behind my back, or you really pissed her off two years ago, and she's just terrible at carrying out a revenge plot. Now, of those two options, which one sounds more realistic?"

"I know what you said and in retrospect you were right, but in the beginning she was just a lost soul that needed someone to be nice to her. We were never a thing after that first night. She just needed a place to crash, and I had the room. Obviously, I did not know it was going to go sideways so badly. All I can say is that you were right, and I am sorry for disregarding your orders."

Balaam nodded towards the monstrosity who had been standing in silence near the back of the room. The beast took two massive steps forward and scooped up the dead body in the center of the room.

"Mr. Collins, I am a man of my word, and I will honor every word of the contract we signed, but I will tell you right now, if and when the work is complete, that will be the end of our relationship. You've got six months to go. Get to it.' Balaam and his muscle left out the back door.

Alice, much to Kevin's surprise, was still in the building.

"I don't know if this was supposed to be a date or something, but if it was, I can assure you it's still not the strangest I've ever had." She said, smiling.

"Why don't you tell me what kind of mess you're in, and maybe I can help you out of it. I do, however, need to ask that we get the hell out of here?"

Kevin let a chuckle slip through his lips as they walked out the front door and locked up behind them.

28

Despite the time of night, they were happy to see that the Frontier Diner was still open. They grabbed a table for two near the back, away from the loose handful of diners occupying the front section. They placed their order, and Kevin spent the next half an hour explaining exactly how he got himself into this trouble.

Taking a moment to process what she had just been told, Kevin sat nervously on the other side of the booth, waiting for her to take off running. Another moment passed, and she raised her head.

"So over the last year and a half, you've been taking these pictures, some of which show you the nature of the soul of your subject. And you do this because you signed a contract with Mr. Balaam, who you think may or may not be the Devil. Was that what you were planning on doing to me? Were you going to capture my soul in your magic camera so you might add another number to your counter?"

"Alice, you need to understand, I was at rock bottom when Balaam showed up. He offered me three million dollars to take one thousand pictures for him. It sure was a lot better than working in that crap shack of a mall. I graduated from CalArts for fuck's sake. What was I doing chasing down moms with strollers? I had given up. That's when Balaam showed up."

Looking her in the eye, he could see her face was turning the same shade as her hair.

"So boo fucking who. Your life didn't work out the way you wanted it to. I got news for you buddy, neither did mine. Did you know I have a five octave vocal range and graduated from Julliard? I was considered one of the best young vocalists in the world when I was nineteen. Now I'm days away from being twenty one and I work in a fucking greasy pit to help my Uncle out after my Aunt died. I love him dearly and am happy to help, but there are certainly other things I'd rather be doing with my life."

Kevin stared, jaws agape, in reaction to the verbal beating he just took.

"Sorry about that, but based on the information you gave me we really don't have time for pity parties. How many pictures are left?"

Kevin thought for a minute. Since the last time he had seen Balaam, there had only been five sittings. Of the eighteen people combined, seven of them appeared in black and white. The counter of the Cannon read 881.

"We need one hundred and nineteen. Let's take a look at the calendar."

For the next several hours, Kevin and Alice went through the booked sittings and scheduled events. Based on sitting numbers and estimated headcount for the events, if they had even a thirty-five percent turn around, they should acquire the last of the pictures three days before the agreed upon date of June 17th 2024. There was no more time for games. Now the real work would begin.

29

The next five and a half months were some of the busiest and happiest he had ever spent. Every day at work ended with a sigh of relief, knowing that this was one day closer to being rid of Balaam. Knowing that the infernal counter on the Cannon was one click closer to the end. The work would have killed him if it hadn't been for Alice. Knowing what he was going through would make it easier for her to react to him when he came home. The first thing she would do was have him show her the counter. Every picture was a cause for celebration.

As May came to an end, the graduation day ceremonies had added some additional opportunities. There were plenty of graduate's families that wanted studio shots to celebrate.

After finishing up, he was glad he didn't have kids. He was also quite pleased that the counter on the Canon now read nine hundred and ninety. Ten to go. Ten more and he was free. He tossed the camera bag in the back seat and headed home.

As usual, Alice was waiting for him when he walked in the door, although this time she was sitting at the dining room table. He could tell something was wrong.

"What's up baby?" he asked while hanging his coat in the hallway.

"I was just thinking what we should do when this is all over. I mean you need ten more pictures, there's seven days before the contract is up and you've got a wedding tomorrow night. By the time we get home, Balaam should be here to collect. After we're done with him, what should we do?"

Kevin had to admit he hadn't given the matter very much thought. When he started down this path two years ago, his life was completely different. He was poor and living in a crappy apartment. He was wasting his quarter of a million dollar education taking head shots in a dead mall. But now, well, now he had Alice. In less than a week, he'd have three million dollars. He supposed they could do what they wanted.

"Well, I think the first thing we should do is get out of the city. Once this is over, we're going to have plenty of money to do whatever we want, and the first thing I want is to put all of this behind me and get the hell out of the city."

"That does sound wonderful. Maybe we can find or build a cabin somewhere in the woods. Maybe something off the grid. You could take nature photos and publish books. I could go back to singing. Maybe teach classes."

Kevin had to admit that sounded like a pretty good life to him. After everything that life had dealt him, that sounded like things would finally even out. Just one more show to go, and then they could begin their life together.

As it turned out, the wedding was much smaller than had been discussed when he was booked, and as a result he walked away with two new photos as opposed to the ten he was hoping for. He wasn't overly concerned just yet. He still had six days until the contract expired. In that time he had three championship little league team shoots, three sittings, and another high school prom. He called it a night, grabbed a piece of cake for Alice, and headed home.

Much to his disturbance, between the three little league teams, four of the coaches showed up in black and white. Kevin rarely got involved in such things, but in this case an anonymous call to the local police was only going to turn out to be a good thing for those kids. With the day's new tally, that brought him up to nine hundred and ninety four. Six photos to go and five days to make it happen.

The next day's sittings were run of the mill. Suburban families who rarely traffic in the kind of sin that would put them on his list. One of the dad's, although Kevin wasn't sure if he was a dad or a step-dad, but there was definitely evil in him. Nine hundred and ninety five. Four days to go.

Even more disturbing than the little league thing were the results of the second prom shoot. He wasn't sure if location had anything to do with it, but he came up with a lot more black and white at this school. Some of these kids were really fucked up, and surprisingly many were over the age of eighteen, which meant that the contract they signed for pictures was legally binding. The camera's counter reached one thousand. It was over.

30

June 17th, 2024. 11:45 PM.

Three days had passed since Kevin had fulfilled the terms of his contract with Balaam. He had expected him to show up the night of the prom or the morning after to collect the camera. As far as he knew, and Lucie certainly would have loved to have mentioned it to him, there had been no sign of his elusive boss. Here it was, fifteen minutes to midnight, the deadline on his contract, he had a camera with one thousand souls captured in it, and thanks to Lucie and her OCD, one thousand signed and dated contracts to accompany every single one.

11:50 PM

"This should have been taken care of days ago. That horrible prom brought him to one thousand pictures." Alice said to no one in particular as she paced back and forth through the apartment's hallway. Something was very wrong. She grabbed her purse from the hall, her keys from the hook, and headed down to the car. She keyed the ignition and headed to the studio.

11:55 PM

Kevin heard keys jingling at the back door. When he turned around, he found himself face to face with Balaam.

"Where in the hell have you been? I finished up your little task three days ago. I've just been hanging around waiting for you."

"Over the course of our time together, I have to constantly remind myself that you're a little on the sensitive side. Otherwise, I would have had your head removed years ago. Now then, Mr.Collins, the reason you have not seen me is that you have not completed your assigned task."

Kevin let loose a frightful laugh in Balaam's face. His voice reached a fever pitch..

"Oh, you are so wrong, old man. Look at the counter of your precious little camera. What does it say? Well, if you look here, it says that a thousand pictures have been taken. Since the camera doesn't store standard pictures, that means there are one thousand consented souls trapped in that camera. I believe we are done here."

A smile painfully stretched itself across Balaam's face. It was nightmare fuel.

"See once again you've gotten ahead of yourself dear boy. You are absolutely correct that there are one thousand trapped souls in that camera, but only nine hundred and ninety-nine signed up."

Kevin's mind began to race. Nine hundred and ninety nine. What had he missed? Who didn't sign the form? In the confusion, neither man noticed that Alice had slipped in the back door.

"If I may," said Balaam, grabbing the Canon from Kevin's desk. He pulled out a small bronze key and opened up the previously sealed film holster. Balaam counted to himself, so quickly Kevin couldn't make it out. Suddenly, he stopped and removed what appeared to be a plastic slide.

Kevin felt his heart sink when he lifted the slide to his eye. He had nothing to say.

"Looks familiar, doesn't she? The night you were "introduced" to Betty, what was the first thing you did?"

It struck him then. Like a bullet in the head. He had used the Canon to determine what he was dealing with.

"It took up a slot, but you never had her permission to take the picture, so that leaves you one short my friend, and unless you can find someone who has violated a cardinal sin and is willing to have their picture taken, I think you and I will be taking a trip together. Of course, there is one other option available."

Kevin frantically searched for an out. What he was being asked to do was going to be impossible.

"What do you have up your sleeve old man?"

Balaam gestured towards the back of the room.

"Alice, you can come out now, honey. I know you're here."

Alice stood up from her hiding space with her hands in the air.

"You can go ahead and put your hands down. I'm not here to arrest you. I'm here to make our good friend Kevin here the deal of a lifetime."

Kevin cast a concerned look in Alice's direction. The look on her face said she knew something he didn't.

"You see my boy, my business interest runs deep. Photography is great, but it's not the only thing I have my hands in. For instance, did you know I own eighty percent of Jack's Steaks? I doubt you would. I mean why would you need to know something like that? Well, maybe you would need to know because of that eighty percent, twenty-five percent is your little girlfriend over there. Jack is a very rich man. Much richer than one man with one sandwich shop should have any business being."

"Don't do this." Alice said pleadingly to Balaam.

"Oh, do shut up. We're past all of this at this point. As I was saying before being so rudely interrupted, this girl's soul belongs to me. It is mine to do with what I please."

Kevin could see tears streaming down Alice's face. It felt like Balaam was stalling for time.

"Get to it already, old man. What is it you are offering this time?"

"I will miss your impetuous behavior when this is all over. This is my proposal. I will give you this girl's soul to satisfy the terms of our agreement. Since she already belongs to me, no paperwork will be necessary. All you will need to do is snap a picture to fill the empty slot. In exchange, you walk away. Keep what you have made and leave the key under the mat. Our business is concluded and we shan't meet again. I really don't see how you have a choice here. It's either this or you spend an eternity in hell. Do we have an accord?"

The look on Alice's face was one of acceptance as she looked back at Kevin. Then it occurred to him..

"What is the length of her contract?" Kevin pressed Balaam.

"That is no concern of yours. Now I will ask again, do we have an accord?"

"It's fifty years my love. I'm bound to that place for the next forty-eight years of my life. No singing, no joy, all so my Uncle could be a success."

This was Kevin's doing. He was the one who started them down this path, and it was up to him to save her. And that was when it hit him.

He grabbed the camera from the table where Balaam had left it. With the slide removed, the camera now had room for one more picture. He closed the door and ran towards a mirror in the beauty room. He lined the shot up and snapped, what in his opinion may have been the best picture he'd ever taken. He handed the shot over to Balaam so he could observe the picture was taken at 11:59:49 PM. The clock on the wall read 12:01 AM.

"Well, I'm sure you thought you were being clever, and I applaud the effort, we may have the photo time stamped, but there is no signed contract stating your image can be used as ATS and its affiliates see fit. So you lose Mr. Collins, and now we own you and everything you have."

When Kevin grinned slightly, Balaam was puzzled, to say the least. This kid was going to serve an eternity in hell, and all of his work would have been for nothing.

"Thank you for raising that very important point Mr. Balaam. I don't have a signed contract here to accompany the photo, but I'm pretty sure I know where I could find one." He allowed the grin to stretch wider.

It finally occurred to Balaam what had just occurred. When Kevin joined the Above the Skin retail business, he had signed an employment contract, which among other things signed away his image rights to the company. When he was selected by Balaam for this project, the company didn't need a newly signed contract because he never technically left their employment.

"Well, well, are you a clever little son of a bitch? Of course, you know what this means, right?"

"It means that I both win and lose. It's quite the predicament we find ourselves in, because technically I fulfilled my part of the contract, so I believe I am owed some money, but I also understand that I lost, so what I propose is simple. You keep your part of the payment and I, well someone, will keep my part. If you can agree to that, we can take that walk right now."

Balaam looked at Kevin with something that he thought might be pride. A kid like this could go a long way down below.

Suddenly finding herself alone, Alice slumped down against a pile of empty cardboard boxes. She knew what had just happened. A man she barely knew went to Hell for her. It hardly seemed fair. To bring someone into her life for such a brief period, only to take them away before they were able to make a bigger impact. That impact was felt the next morning when a text message from her bank arrived, notifying her of an incoming transfer of one and a half million dollars. For the first time in a long time, she allowed herself to believe everything was going to be alright.

What It Takes

Howard stood on the taped X behind the curtain as the music swelled. The applause of the audience soon followed, its volume level quickly rising to drown out the music. The crowd noise increased even further as the announcer introduced the host of the show Wilfred Hall. Howard took a deep breath knowing that in mere seconds he would hear his name and the production assistant standing next to him would usher him out onto the stage. In these precious few seconds, he began to recall the events that led to his being here.

It was six months ago that he had received the call from his mother. Living fifteen hundred miles away, Howard did not get to see her outside of holidays, but they had a long standing tradition to be sure that they spoke once a week. Those calls usually took place on Wednesday, so it struck him as odd that she would be calling on a Saturday afternoon. Casting a suspicious eye towards his phone, he answered with a cheerful tone doing his best to mask any concerns he might have.

"Hey Mom, how are you doing?"

"Hello Howie, do you have a minute or two to talk?"

"I'll always have time to talk with you." He assured the older woman.

"My doctor's office just called," she began.

Howard's mind began to race, running through a number of worst case scenarios. Despite his mother's advancing age, she was seventy two years old, her health had always been excellent.

"What's going on mom?" Howard had just spoken with her three days earlier and she had said nothing about any appointments, which in and of itself was unusual as she regularly made him aware of financial or health related issues.

"Well I have been having some trouble catching my breath lately, so I went to see Doctor Cooper on Thursday afternoon."

Howard could hear the emotion building in her voice. He suddenly had a sinking feeling in the pit of his stomach.

"He ran some tests and the results came back late last night."

Howard plopped down in the recliner that sat next to his landline.

"Howie, I have lung cancer."

The world suddenly went gray and he found himself glad that he was sitting down.

"Howie, are you there?"

The sound of his mother's voice suddenly quickly brought the color back to the world.

"I'm here mom." He wasn't sure if she could hear the shaky quality of his voice, but he did his best to steady himself.

"What did Dr. Cooper say?" he inquired of her.

"He said that it's not too late and that we caught it early. He wants to begin a series of treatments as soon as possible. He thinks if we act aggressively that we might have a chance of beating it."

Again Howard found his mind racing in a thousand different directions. His entire family had been blessed with good health and the sudden shock of his mother's announcement was overwhelming.

"OK, what do we do next? How do we begin the process?"

"Well he wants to start preparing me for chemo-therapy on Monday. Can you make it out here?"

Not that there was a good time for a cancer diagnosis, but Howard did find himself grateful that it was July. As a school teacher, he wasn't scheduled to report back to school until the last week of August.

"Of course I can. Let me get started on making the arrangements and I'll call you back in just a bit."

"Do you need any money? I can pay for your flight if you need."

Howard moved to his computer and brought up his bank balance. He winced when he saw that there was only $482 in his checking account and an additional $200 in his savings.

"I'm OK mom. I've got it covered. Let me get everything taken care of.

We'll talk in a bit."

"You're a good boy Howie and I love you."

"I love you too mom."

The next few hours went by quickly but not without frustration. Given the last minute travel plans the cost of a flight out of Hartford down to St. Petersburg was going to cost him in excess of $1,500. As much as he hated to use it, Howard found himself glad that he had decided to keep the one credit card he had acquired for emergency purposes. Before long the arrangements had been made and Howard informed his mother that he would be catching an early morning flight and would be there by tomorrow afternoon.

His attention snapped back to the present as he heard Wilfred Hall offer a little personal information about him. Howard knew that it was time to go and once he heard his name announced he was shoved through the curtain and out to the stage.

Striding across the stage, Howard's attention was drawn to a patch of impenetrable blackness that despite its void, was where the uproarious applause he had heard just seconds before had come from. The bleachers were poorly lit and the stage lights made it all but impossible to see through the dark. There was no applause or reaction to his name being called or to his first appearance on the stage. Despite the uncertainty, he offered a quick wave in the direction of the bleachers as he made his way to the contestant's podium.

"Howard, welcome to What It Takes. I know that the rules have been explained to you in the back but let's just do a quick recap for our audience both in the studio and those watching at home. The rules are simple; you will be asked a series of increasingly difficult questions pertaining to a variety of subjects. For each answer you get right, you'll win $50,000. Answer all twenty questions correctly and you'll win $1,000,000. However if you get an answer wrong you'll have to make a choice. You will be presented with two boxes, inside one is a gold coin that will allow you to keep the money you have won and continue. If, however, you choose the wrong box you will lose any money won so far, but you will be given an option that will allow you to continue. If you choose the action listed inside the box you get to keep going and still have a chance to go home with some money. So are you ready to play?"

"Let's get started Wil." Howard offered while nodding his head.

"Excellent! Let's play What It Takes." Howard heard a smattering of applause coming from the dark hole that was the studio audience.

"OK Howard I see our first two categories are the Academy Awards and Medical History. Go ahead and choose."

Howard's eyes darted back and forth between the two titles on the screen. While his knowledge of medical history was almost non-existent, he did know a thing or two about the movies and that made the decision a bit easier.

"I'll go with the Academy Awards, Wil."

"Very good. Your first question is as follows. Since the creation of the Academy Awards in 1929 only three films have won the "Big Five," that is, Best Picture, Best Director, Best Actor, Best Actress, and Best Screenplay. For $50,000, name two of these three films. You'll have 45 seconds. Let's start the clock."

Howard breathed a sigh of relief as he pressed the button in his hand.

"Well that was quick. What's your answer?"

"One Flew Over the Cuckoo's Nest and Silence of the Lambs."

"You are correct! Congratulations Howard you've just won $50,000. Of course the third film to accomplish that task was It Happened One Night starring Clark Gable. Well done."

With the pressure of the first question out of the way, Howard was feeling more confident about his chances.

"Alright, let's take a look at the next two categories. They are Opera and Literature. You have thirty seconds to make your choice."

His choice between the two came easier than the first round. He had minored in literature in college.

"Let's take a look at the literature question Wil."

"Very good! For $50,000 dollars your question is which literary genre features coming of age stories?"

Howard responded even quicker than the first time, fully confident in his answer.

"That would be Juvenilia."

"Correct again. You're up to $100,000, are you ready for the next question?"

Howard could feel his confidence building and he enthusiastically nodded his head.

"Ready when you are Wil."

"Very good. The next two categories are the World Series and Business and Industry. You have thirty seconds."

This one was a bit tougher. Howard wasn't much of a sports guy, but the other category was pretty vague.

"I'll go with the World Series Wil."

"Outstanding Howard! Although the World Series is known as the October Classic, what was the first year that the series ended in November? We'll be right back with Howard's answer after these ads from our sponsors."

Once again Howard heard but did not see the studio audience as the show went to commercial. Despite struggling to find the answer, he found his mind going back to his mother.

The first month of her treatments had taken a tremendous toll on both of them. The chemo caused her to lose her hair and had caused substantial weight loss. For every session he was right there by her side. The sickness was even worse. The poor woman often woke during the night and needed to be helped to the bathroom. Howard suffered in silence as he watched the woman who had raised him quickly waste away. On top of the sickness, the medical bills were quickly adding up. In just the first month she had reached the limits of what her health insurance was willing to cover. Her only income had been social security and a small monthly stipend from her twenty-five years working in the public school system. To make matters worse the summer was coming to an end, and if nothing else Howard had to return home to Connecticut. He has spoken with his union and bosses and explained the situation. They were more than willing to work with him, but they needed him to come in to finalize the arrangements. With a deep sense of regret, Howard left St. Petersburg at the end of August, promising his mother that he would be back shortly.

Howard's attention was snapped back upon hearing the show's theme song.

"And welcome back to What It Takes. Before we left for the break Howard had chosen the World Series category. His question was what was the first year that the World Series ended in November? Howard, we're going to need your answer."

He could feel a bead of sweat drip down his forehead. He had no answer but figured that taking a guess would be better than standing there like a deer in the headlights.

"I'm going to go with 1997 Wil."

"Oh I'm sorry that is incorrect. The right answer was 2001. The baseball season suffered a small delay after the events of 9/11 which pushed the series back. So now it's time to make a choice."

From behind the curtain Howard saw a shapely model make her way out pushing a small cart. The cart contained two black boxes, each featuring a large white number on the front.

"All right Howard, which box is it going to be? You've got fifteen seconds to decide."

While the rules of the game had been very clearly explained to him, Howard was not given the slightest clue as to what the boxes may contain. He let a deep breath leave his body and answered the waiting host.

"I'm going to choose box #2 Wil."

"Alright, Sabrina will you please open box #2."
In one smooth and clearly practiced motion the model moved from the side of the cart to the rear. She slowly lifted the lid from the box. The camera zoomed in to reveal the contents of the box. Inside was a gold coin.

"Congrats Howard you chose well. The gold coin will allow you to keep the money you have already won and continue on to the next question."

A wave of relief washed over him as he saw the coin. He only had a moment to revel in his good luck as the host was ready to move on to the next question.

"If we could have the next two categories please." Wil said to someone off stage.

The two screens to the host's right suddenly revealed Howard's next two choices.

"Right so it looks like your choices are Superstitions or Billboard Achievements. And to clarify we're talking about Billboard magazine and it's music charts. You have fifteen seconds."

"I'll take Billboard Achievements."

"Excellent. Which musical artist or act holds the Billboard record for the most number one albums? "

Howard was certain that he knew the answer, but after the misstep on the last question, he took a bit more of his allotted thirty seconds before answering.

"That would be the Beatles Wil."

"And that would be correct. That brings your total so far up to $150,000. You're doing great Howard. Let's have a look at the new categories."

Again the screen flickered before displaying the new categories. Howard was slightly concerned when he saw his options were Newspaper Comic Strips or Philosophers. Neither of which was Howard's strongest suit. The exuberant voice of the host brought him back to attention.

"Howard, we need your selection."

"Umm, let's go with Newspaper Comic Strips."

"First printed in 1924, this long running American comic strip is the only one to inspire a radio show, a Broadway show, and five feature films."

A smile came across his face when he heard the question. He knew right away that the answer was Little Orphan Annie. It was his mother's favorite musical.

"I'm going to go with Little Orphan Annie, Wil."

"And right you are. That's $200,000. How much more money will Howard win? We'll be right back after this commercial break."

After the first month of treatment, Howard returned home to finalize the arrangement with both the school and his landlord. He was granted an indefinite leave of absence from his teaching position. Both his union head Erik Moreno and his boss and longtime friend Carol Barker wished him luck and told him to call if he needed anything at all. The school board however was a bit more difficult to deal with. They had no issue with providing him with the time, but they were not so willing to pay him while he was gone. He was told he would receive six week's pay and after that he could choose to use his personal and sick days to supplement his income. While it was not the ideal situation, he could see their point. Fortunately, his landlord was also very understanding. After explaining his situation, his landlord told him that as long as the rent was in his hand no later than the tenth of each month that everything would be fine. He told Howard that he would check the apartment periodically to make sure everything was ok. With his affairs in order, he headed back down to Florida to be by his mother's side.

The music signaling the show's return blasted from the studio speakers. Wil was back at the podium and ready to proceed. Again, Howard noticed a muted response from the audience section.

"Okay Howard, so far you've won $200,000 and got lucky with the first two boxes. Let's move forward and get ready to play What It Takes."

The two screens came to life and two new categories appeared larger than life. A smile came over Howard's face as he saw his new choices, one of which was The War of 1812.

"I'll take The War of 1812 Wil."

"Between December 24th and January 8th, 1814 the United States defeated the British in the Battle of New Orleans. This battle was one of the few victories gained by the United States during the War of 1812. What is significant about this battle?"

"The battle took place after the war was over."

"It sounds like you know a thing or two about American history, Howard. Congratulations you've won a quarter of a million dollars. Now this is the part of the show where I like to take a moment to get to know a little about our contestant. So who is Howard Taylor?"

"Well Wil, I graduated from University of Connecticut with a Master's degree in American History in 2004 and have been teaching at Central High School back in Bridgeport, CT, where I live."

"Well that certainly explains your quick answer to our last question." The host interrupted with a slight grin on his face. "So what brings you to What It Takes today?"

"Well Wil, six months ago my mother was diagnosed with lung cancer. She's currently in remission, but the medical costs had caused her to lose her home and she is currently living in an assisted living facility. I'm here today to win enough money to pay off all her bills and get her house back."

"Well that is certainly a noble reason. Let's get back to the game and see if you can't make that dream come true. What are the next two categories?"

The screen revealed Labor Law and World Currency. Howard winced at the choices.

"Well Howard what's your next pick? You have fifteen seconds."

Sometimes fifteen seconds seems to take forever, this time however it seemed like no time at all. Before he knew it the timer buzzed and the host was looking at him.

"I'll take World Currency."

"During its first eighty years in existence the coin that today is known as a nickel was officially called what? Can we have thirty seconds on the clock?"

Howard could feel the sweat returning to his forehead. He had chosen the lesser of two evils this round and now was drawing a complete blank. Despite its digital existence, he could swear he heard the sound of a clock counting down. His heart sank when he heard the buzzer.

"Howard, we're going to need your answer."

"Is it five pence Wil?"

"Oh Howard, I'm so sorry. The correct answer is the half dime. Sabrina, can you bring out the next two boxes please."

Again Sabrina, the silent model, rolled her cart out to the stage. The boxes were identical to the first two with the exception being they were now numbered three and four.

"All right Howard you have fifteen seconds to choose a box. Audience please refrain from offering any help."

Once again Howard found himself making an uninformed decision. The first time he was lucky and drew the gold coin. Would his luck continue? He closed his eyes, took a deep breath, and chose box number four. His breath stuck in his throat as the box was opened.

"Howard, I'm afraid you've chosen wrong. Now you have to make a choice. You can walk away now and give up all the money you have won so far, or you can choose the envelope inside the box. Now keep in mind that if you choose the envelope you will have to partake in the activity listed inside."

Howard's head fell in defeat. He needed this money more than anything. While he had no idea what the envelope may have contained, he knew that he could not let his mother waste away in that horrible place.

"Wil," he began. "I'll take the envelope."

There was a muffled noise from the audience as Sabrina brought the envelope up to the host podium.

"Let's have a look at what's inside shall we?"

Howard watched as the smiling host slowly tore the top off of the envelope. Once he removed the contents, Howard saw the smile turn into a twisted grin.

"Howard, you've chosen the envelope. Are you ready to take part in your choice?"

He knew that he was as ready as he was going to be and slowly nodded his head in the host's direction.

"All right! You've drawn bamboo shoots under the fingernails. Melonie, can you bring out the shoots please?"

Howard could hardly believe what he was hearing. Bamboo was often used to torture prisoners during World War II and had been described by some as one of the most painful experiences a human being could endure. Surely they couldn't be serious. He could hear the host begin to chuckle and an increasing rumble from the crowd void.

"Are you out of your mind? You can't really expect me to allow you to do that to me."

"Well Howard, the rules of the game were explained to you in detail before you agreed to come on the show, were they not?"

"Well yes, but nobody said anything about torture. There is no way that is going to happen."

"I'm sorry to hear you say that. You see you had your choice to walk away, but you choose to continue the game. These are the rules. We've played fair and square with you and now we expect you to honor your commitments."

"Well you can go to Hell, Wil. I'm leaving."

"I'm afraid it's not that easy anymore, Howard. Mr. Todd, would you be so kind as to come out on stage please?"

Howard turned his head in the direction of the curtain he himself had exited through to see Mr. Todd making his way out. To say the man was massive would be an understatement. Howard was a man who stood 6' 4" and even from his place across the stage he could tell that this man was much larger. Again a muffled noise rose from the dark.

"Howard, I would like you to say hello to Mr. Todd. Mr. Todd serves as our enforcer here on What It Takes. His job is to make sure that our contestants follow through with their promises. Trust me when I tell you that bamboo shoots under your fingernails will be a sweet dream compared to the things that Mr. Todd will do to you if you try to renege."

Howard had no trouble believing what he was being told. Mr. Todd seemed like the type of man who took great pleasure in bringing pain and suffering to people.

"Look, Howard, it's simple. We slip the bamboo under two of your fingernails for five seconds, and then we can move on with the show. You've lost the money you've won so far, but you'll still have a chance to win more. Think about your mother and what you need this money for."

Howard knew he was stuck between a rock and a hard place. He didn't know how bad the bamboo would hurt, but he knew that he would be in for a lot worse with Mr. Todd. He also knew that he couldn't leave here empty handed.

"OK, Wil. What choice do I have?"

"Melonie if you would be so kind."

Howard let loose a sigh of relief to hear that it wasn't going to be Mr. Todd that was doing the insertion. He watched as the model drew two six inch lengths of bamboo and headed over towards him. Up close he could see an apologetic look on her face. Bracing himself, he held his breath as she inserted the first shoot.

The pain eased its way through his finger, up to his hand and then, like a shot, tore up his arm. He let out a howl that seemed to get a rise out of the crowd.

"Very good Howard, just one more to go and then we'll take a commercial break."

Knowing that he was familiar with the pain, Howard assumed that he would be able to handle the second shoot with a bit more control. He quickly found out how wrong he was. As he unleashed a string of profanities that would make a sailor blush, the show went to commercial.

Despite the agonizing pain in his arm, Howard did his best to center his thoughts and get back to the reason why he was there in the first place.

The four months that followed his mother's initial diagnosis were the most difficult either of them had to endure. The constant sickness coupled with an ongoing doctor's schedule had left the poor woman exhausted, and Howard with growing concerns about where the money was going to come from. His pay from the school board had run out and he had quickly burned through his vacation and sick days. While he was able to make his rent in the beginning, he found that to be an impossible task. Despite his current situation, his landlord had informed him that if he had missed more than two month's rent, he would have no choice but to begin eviction proceedings. Howard said he understood, and after hanging up placed a call to a few of his friends back home. Carol had a key and he arranged some people to meet her at the apartment and start moving his stuff into a storage place. Carol told him not to worry about the monthly charge for the space. She would take care of it and they could work it out later.

Soon the studio lights flashed to indicate the show was coming back from break. The pain in his hand had begun to subside a little and he thought he was ready to continue.

"Welcome back to What It Takes. Just before the break Howard missed his question, and was unfortunate enough to draw an envelope. Despite some initial resistance he was willing to man up and continue forward. He's back to zero but he's still in the game. Let's play What It Takes."

Howard got very lucky over the course of the next four questions. Three were ones that he was able to answer without hesitation. The fourth was a little more difficult as his knowledge of the Law was limited, but at the last moment he was able to come up with the correct answer. Once again the show went to commercial break and he was able to catch his breath.

It was during the fifth month of his mother's sickness that things began to get really bad. All her savings had been exhausted and her pension was not enough to cover her monthly expenses. After exhausting all efforts, the only choice they had was to sell the house. After retiring from teaching at the age of 65, Howard's mother had moved from the harsh winters of the North East to the sunnier climates of St. Petersburg. That had been in 2008. The house wasn't close to being paid for, but if they could sell before the next payment was due, they could at least break even. So while his mother was undergoing her third cycle of chemo-therapy, Howard sold the house and walked away with nothing. He moved her into Babbling Creek Nursing Home in nearby Gulfport. Her insurance was willing to cover 80% of the cost and Howard took a part-time job to help cover the difference. It certainly wasn't the nicest of places, and not someplace he wanted his mother to die in, but at this point it was their only option.

Once again that familiar music came over the speakers informing Howard that they were back. He saw the host come from the back and take his place.

"And we're back. Howard, you're doing pretty well. You're back up to $200,000 and we're ready to move on to question 12. Are you ready?"

"Let's do it, Wil."

The screens flashed and Howard was presented with his next two categories. He winced as they revealed themselves to be World Religions and African Mammals. Neither category instilled any confidence in him. He knew the clock was running out, so he chose African Mammals.

"What is the average size of a group of gorillas and of that number how many are male?"

Howard's mind went blank. He knew very little about African Mammals and that knowledge contained no information about gorillas. Again he could feel the clock ticking down and the sweat pouring down his body.

"Howard, we're going to need your answer."

"I'm going to say twelve with two males Wil."

The moment the words came out of his mouth he could tell they were wrong. The look on the host face only confirmed what he already knew.

"That is incorrect. The average group of gorillas, also known as a band, is nine with one male. Sabrina, roll out the boxes."

Once again the model appeared from the side curtain with her cart. Boxes five and six sat menacingly on top.

"Howard, you know the deal by this point. Please pick a box."

After choosing wrong the last time around, and now knowing what may be inside, terror began to creep into his mind. He wondered if as the questions got harder, if the punishment increased accordingly. He was a man with everything to lose and this time he saw no need to hesitate.

"I'll take box number 5." He croaked.

As it turned out luck was on his side this time. The model raised the box top to reveal another golden coin. He was safe for the moment.

"Well done, Howard. Are you ready for the next question?"

He nodded his head and turned his eyes to the screens. His elation at picking the gold coin was short lived, however, as the two next categories were revealed to be Charities and Human Sexuality. Howard knew this did not bode well.

"So, what's it going to be, Howard?"

"I'm going to go with Human Sexuality, Wil."

"Excellent. Your question is: on what scale does a zero mean a person is exclusively heterosexual and a six is a person who is exclusively homosexual?"

Howard's mind raced looking for the answer. He had in fact heard of this scale and knew that somewhere in the back of his head he knew the answer.

"The Kinney Scale." He offered confidently.

"So close. The correct answer is the Kinsey Scale named after scientist Alfred Kinsey in 1948. Let's bring out the boxes."

Howard felt as if he had been kicked in the chest. He was so certain that was the correct answer that he was shocked he was wrong. On top of it all he found himself forced to pick another box.

"So Howard, is it going to be box seven or eight this time?"

He scanned the faces of his host, the model, and the intimidating Mr. Todd but learned nothing. It was possible that they didn't even know what was inside.

"I guess I'll go with number seven, Wil."

Time seemed to stop as Sabrina the model lifted the lid from the chosen box. Howard could tell right away that it wasn't good. His fears were confirmed in mere seconds as the young woman lifted an envelope from the interior of the box.

"Looks like bad news Howard. Sabrina, would you please open the envelope and show us what's inside?"

Instead of words this card contained two pictures that assured no words were needed. One was of a human thumb and the other was of a cleaver.

"I'm not going to lie to you, Howard, this is going to hurt a lot. Melonie, please bring out the cleaver."

This time, Melonie came out with a cart of her own. It contained only a wooden chopping block and a stainless steel cleaver. Howard felt as if he was about to faint, but bit the inside of his cheek to keep him on his feet. He was terrified to think what they might do to him if he passed out. He felt the woman take his arm and strap his wrist and four fingers to the cutting board. His thumb was left to hang over the side. In an instant the blade came down. At first Howard thought perhaps she had missed as there was no pain. In the next second he knew he was wrong.

"Let's hear a few words from our sponsors while we clean Howard up. We'll be back with more ``What It Takes.''"

After the sale of the house, Howard found himself with no place to stay in St. Petersburg. He certainly couldn't stay with his mother at the home, so he bounced around between two or three shelters, spending two or three nights before moving on to the next. He didn't want to outstay his welcome at any one place and after explaining his circumstances to the supervisors, he wasn't hassled when he came through. In the day he split his time between a few different sub jobs and the nursing home. He was glad for the work despite the fact that as soon as the money came in it went right back out. There were so many expenses that he couldn't keep up. He spoke with his landlord back in Connecticut and informed him that he had already moved his things from the apartment and that he was now officially vacating the place. He promised to send the keys back by the end of the week. While he was sad to see him go, the landlord thanked him for his honesty and promised to send him a check to refund his security deposit.

The excruciating pain in his hand had become a dull throb by the time the show returned from commercial break. Despite the show's barbaric measures, they were not without compassion, or they knew that if they didn't provide their guest with any pain killers the show would be over much quicker. The medical crew backstage had patched him up, shot him up with a cocktail of drugs, and less than two minutes later he was back on stage.

"Howard, you're back at zero but the game isn't over yet. Are you ready for your next two categories?"

The whole thing seemed like a waking dream now. His head was filled with a fuzzy feeling and while he could make out what the host was saying, he found that he was rather indifferent to the whole thing.

"Do your worst, Wil."

The new categories appeared on the screens and Howard broke out into a small, sickly, smile.

"I'll take Gems and Minerals."

"Very good. What mineral has a hardness of nine on the Mohs Scale?"

Howard did his best to clear his mind from the drugs and think back to his science classes. He knew that the hardest mineral was diamond. As the buzzer sounded he opened his mouth to speak.

"Is it corundum, Wil?"

"It is in fact corundum. Congratulations Howard. Shall we proceed?"

"It doesn't seem like I have a choice, does it?"

He heard the man chuckle as he called for the next two categories to be revealed. Again Howard got lucky and questions fifteen and sixteen were both easily answered. He got into a bit of trouble again with seventeen, but at the last moment he came up with the answer.

"Howard, you're doing great. You've come back now and once again are up to $200,000. I'd say if things keep going your way you're going to be able to help your mom out of her troubles. Are you ready for question eighteen?"

Howard could see the end in sight. Just three more questions and he could walk away with enough money to buy back his mother's house and get back to his life in Connecticut.

"Let's do it to it, Wil."

"Your choices are Phobias or Games. What's it going to be?"

"Let's go with games."

"The Curse of Scotland is a nickname used for which playing card?"

Fear settled in as Howard realized that he had no answer for this question. He didn't even have an inkling of an idea. He knew there were fifty two cards in a standard deck of cards. He knew that aces and eights were called a "Dead Man's Hand" in poker, but beyond that his mind was blank.

"We'll need your answer Howard."

"The king of hearts?" he offered without a trace of confidence in his voice.

"That is incorrect. The correct answer is the nine of diamonds. Sabrina, the boxes please."

Howard felt a sinking feeling in the pit of his stomach. His last choice had cost him his thumb and he couldn't imagine what may lay in store for him.

As he stared out into the dark space that was the studio audience, he knew that he had to continue, no matter what.

"I'll take box number ten this time Wil."

The lid on the box was raised and on the inside was a golden coin. Howard almost fainted from the reveal.

"Outstanding. How are you holding up Howard?"

"Let's just get on with it, shall we?"

"We will Howard, right after this last commercial break."

It was during the middle of the sixth month that two remarkable things happened. The first, and the most important was that after all of the chemo and treatments, his mother's cancer had gone into remission. As a matter of fact she had actually begun to put on some weight, and the color had returned to her cheeks for the first time in a long time. While this was great news, it in itself created a new problem. The nursing home she was staying in was a care facility. Due to its small size, there was always a demand for beds, and it was common practice for residents to be moved out after their recovery. With his mother on the mend, Howard was now stuck with finding her a place to live outside of the home. It was during this time that the second remarkable thing happened. Or at least, it seemed that way at the time.

One of the residents in the home was a man named Gary Ingram. He had always carried himself as a gentleman despite the cancer that was eating away at his stomach. He always had a smile on his face and during her stay there, his mother had struck up quite a friendship with the man. Howard had also taken a shine to him and would often spend an hour or so shooting the breeze. It was during one of these conversations that Howard had explained his situation, hoping that the man could offer some advice. As it turned out, Gary Ingram had spent forty years working in the television business. Game shows were his specialty. He was involved in all of the big shows in the seventies and eighties and still maintained some connections. When he heard of Howard's money woes he offered to help him out. He explained that there was one show that some former associates were involved with that could give Howard the chance to make the kind of money he so desperately needed. The old man explained to him that there were certain risks involved in participating, but if he was truly willing to do whatever it took to help his mother, then he would be more than happy to set it up. With only two weeks left before his mother was going to have to leave the home, he said he would take the chance.

And now he knew what those risks were. As he stood on the stage of What It Takes, minus one thumb, he understood what the man had meant.

"Welcome back. So we're down to just two questions. Are you ready to move forward, Howard?"

"The end is in sight, Will. Let's finish this thing."

"Very well. Let's see the choices for question nineteen then. And they are Film Festivals and American First Ladies. What's it going to be Howard?"

"I'll take American First Ladies."

"Which First Lady, of a one term president, suffered from Epilepsy?"

"That would be Ida McKinley."

"You are correct. So here's where we stand, you currently have $300,000 built up. There will not be any categories for the last question. If you get it right you walk away with all of the money. If you get it wrong, however, you'll have to pick a box and you may walk away with nothing. Are you ready for the last question?"

"I've come this far, there is no turning back now. Let's have that last question, Wil."

"For $300,000, who established Daylight Savings Time and what year did it first take place."

It was over. He didn't have the answer to the final question and this had all been for nothing. He slowly turned his head towards his host for what most likely was the last time.

"William Hurst." He answered, knowing that he was wrong.

"I'm so sorry Howard that is incorrect. Sabrina, please bring out the last two boxes."

For the last time the model worked her way onto the stage with the cart. Boxes numbered 11 and 12 displayed to the audience.

"Alright Howard, which box is it going to be?"

He knew what the odds were. He knew how this could end. He took a deep breath and let it go.

"I'll take box 12 Wil. Let's end this."

"Number 12 it is. Sabrina, please open the box."

He knew it was an envelope before he even saw it. He knew that he had failed. He had resigned himself to his fate, when he heard the voice of Wilfred Hall for what he assumed was the last time.

"Howard, your story has touched the heart of my producers and they are willing to make you an offer. This is unprecedented. They are willing to let you walk away right now. You'll take nothing home with you, but you will avoid whatever surprises the envelope might hold for you. Or you can choose to complete the task inside, no matter what it is, and regardless of the outcome we will deposit $100,000 in your mother's account. I'll give you a few seconds to weigh your options."

Admittedly, Howard was taken aback. After the things he had endured on the show, the last thing he expected was for the people behind the scenes to have a heart. For Christ's sake, they had cut off his thumb. He knew that whatever was in that envelope was going to be worse than that. He also knew that $100,000 would help in finding his mother a new place to live. It would help him start a new life in St. Petersburg. He knew he really only had one choice.

"I'll take the envelope, Wil. No matter what happens, at least I'll be able to take care of my mother."

"All right, Melonie, let's bring out the last box."

Howard watched as the model made her way over to his podium. She placed the box in front of him and walked away.

"This is it Howard. For $100,000, open the box.

Howard placed his good hand on the lid and raised it. He saw what was inside and he knew what he had to do. He did what it took.

Story Notes

For all intents and purposes, you have reached the end. The stories have been told and I'm getting ready to close down for the night. All that's left is a little behind the scenes info on the creation of the stories within. If you aren't interested, then I thank you for stopping by and hopefully we see each other again soon. For those of you who are curious about where some of these ideas came from, then I hope this shines a little light on things.

Three O'Clock.

I hate bullies. I had minor issues with them when I was in school, and I had major issues with them when my kids were in school. While I would never advocate any type of revenge in real life, as a writer this is how I see it going down.

Aviophobia.

From birth until I was in my late twenties, I had only ever been on a plane once, and that was when I was six months old. Between the ages of 33 and 40, I flew over 20,000 miles. I learned a lot about air travel and what life on an airplane, especially when you're sitting next to a stranger, was like. This one definitely falls into a trip to a certain dimension.

Ward C

There used to be a lot more to this story. The original draft was more than twice the length of the version included here. The idea was the same, but there were several dead serial killers in the ward. It was fun, but ultimately it rambled on way too long.

An All New Yesterday

This one is definitely outside of my regular wheelhouse. The one thing that I truly do fear is losing who I am. To have my mind slip away one day at a time. To look at the people I love and not know who they are. There is little to no actual science, (at least as far as I am aware) in this story. Fresh Start is a key element in the slowly evolving world I am creating.

Going Down

Elevators are strange to me. I know how they work. I've seen them designed and built. I understand there is nothing out of the ordinary about them. But when you step into an elevator and find yourself inside with a stranger, a cone of silence is created as if it was the most normal thing in the world, quickly becomes an anxiety riddled ride of unknown length and uncertain destination. Be careful of friendly strangers in an elevator, you'll never know who you might meet and what they might be offering.

A Turn of Events

This may be the most accurate title of any story I've ever written. Turn actually started life as two different stories. The first part was about the abduction of a stranded driver along a stretch of dark road. The second was strictly a lycanthrope story. Individually they were created during the period the stories in my first book were written. When I was putting the book together, I felt that both stories were not strong enough to stand on their own, so they got tossed in the "writer's bin." After some time had passed I picked them both up again and found that with some minor changes the two stories came together and became a stronger tale.

Crunch

What can I say? It was a lot of fun comparing various garbage disposals and figuring out just how much horsepower would be needed to dispose of human bones.

Fine Tuning

Another story definitely inspired by the Twilight Zone. The unusual item, the mysterious stranger, the trip back in time. All ideas that Rod Serling and company laid down the groundwork for.

Resurrection of the Worm

I've only drank tequila once in my life. Drank way too much and made some bad decisions. It occurred to me that alcohol could serve as the perfect delivery device for a number of microorganisms. The revenge story came together after that. This is one of those times that I would love to see this one come to life, if for no other reason than to see the boot scene.

Central Monitoring

For a long time, I did not have live TV. I streamed pretty much everything from various services. When I decided to add live TV, I was reminded of why I prefer streaming. So many commercials, and thanks to the way ad time is sold, you get to see the same ads over and over again. Aside from pharmaceuticals, one of the more common spots I saw were for home security systems. After a while it came to me that we as a society have become awfully trusting when it comes to the people we allow into our home in the name of offering us the illusion of security. The person who sells you the system and the person who installs said system are often two different people, and I'm relatively certain that neither one of them is asking for proof of residence beyond a driver's license.

Car Note

We've all found something on the windshield of our cars at some point. A flier, a menu, a note from some jackass who backed into your car. Sometimes something creepier like notes from a stranger or flowers. In this day and age a Poloroid picture is about as likely as a one hundred bill. And in case you're wondering, there's not always a reason.

Eight Hours

The basic idea for this story is easily the oldest of all the tales in this book. The very first version was written when I was in my twenties. The general feel was the same, but it took place on a mountain with the main character being an experienced climber who takes a nasty fall. Like pretty much everything I wrote back then, it had a certain charm, but overall was pretty weak and parts of it felt like a straight rip off of a Tales from the Crypt story. It hung around in the back of my head for twenty years, and finally worked its way out into this story. I also think that the opening of this one might be the best thing I've ever written.

Worth a Thousand Souls

For about a year I worked as a photographer in the photo studio of one of the larger department stores. It was actually a pretty good gig. Sure you had the occasional screaming child or bickering families, but when you got it right, you were helping a family create memories that would last a lifetime. I never had to chase people down in a mall to get customers, but I did work in a cell phone kiosk for about 6 months and jumping through hoops was certainly part of the job. Again it's one of those unusual item stories partially inspired by the Twilight Zone, and delves a little bit deeper into the mysterious William Baalam.

What it Takes

It is a very rare occasion that an idea comes to me almost complete. While waiting for a bus one day, I was reading The Moving Finger by Stephen King. There is a part in the story where the protagonist is watching Jeopardy. Now, I've read this story a dozen times in my life, but that day something was different. An idea popped into my head. Eight hours and 7200 words later, the first draft was finished. It's been tweaked a little and corrected for accuracy and grammar, but it's more or less exactly how it came to me on that bus ride home.

Christopher Pelton
Bridgeport, CT
2/17/2022

Made in the USA
Columbia, SC
26 March 2023

4c34be63-dd26-40df-acb2-0d9064fe76acR02